THE FIRST WHITE MAN.

ARRIVAL

WRITTEN BY T. J. CORBETT

ISBN # 978-1-0695543-1-4

For my dad who taught me the love of stories, and my mom who laughed as I lived mine.

Also, for my wife Jennifer, my best friend, my confidence, my muse, my love. The one that has stood beside me, and who has walked every step of this journey with me.

To the magic that is reading that transports us to those places we have never been but have always wanted to go.

Acknowledgement

A big thank you to Rachel for using her many years of teaching to Proofread and Edit sections of this book. Her help was greatly appreciated.

Book One

Most people spend their lives trying to escape the past. Ryan never thought he would literally be dragged into it.

Ryan Woodman grew up in Arizona, working cattle in the summer and hitting the books for the rest of the year. It wasn't easy juggling hard labor and school, but he had dreams bigger than barbed wire fences. He wanted something wild, something different. So, when he got the chance to be a stuntman in Hollywood, he saddled up and never looked back.

Turns out, the leap from the ranch to movie sets wasn't that big. He could fall off a horse, get thrown from a car, and take a punch like it was second nature. Life was fast, dangerous, and for the first time his.

Then came the stunt that changed everything.

One moment he was climbing down a high waterfall for a scene. The next, lightning cracked the sky exploded and he landed in a world that wasn't his. With no people, real danger. And no director yelling, "Cut."

Now, Ryan must survive in a time that has no business being in and find a way home before history buries him for good.

Chapter 1

Gerry stood on the observation deck at the bottom part of the falls looking out over the pool, straining his eyes to see if he could see anything in the pool. He could see nothing but the churning water of the pond and the cascading waterfall flowing into it.

He turned to Diane standing next to him and asked, "Did you see him hit the water?"

Diane shook her head, answering, "No, I saw him kick off from the rock face, then cut the rope and start to fall. Then there was that big flash which blinded me for a few seconds, so I didn't see anything after that."

"I know it's the same with me. He was falling, then there was a big flash. It was so bright that when my sight came back to me, all I saw was spots."

"That flash was almost like lightning, but did you notice there was no noise, no big boom or crack?" She said.

"No, I didn't." He said continuing to scan the water. He looked at the group of people standing in the upper observation deck and yelled up, "Can you see anything?"

Johnny and Carl just shook their heads and yelled back, "The water is too choppy. We can't see into it."

Diane and Jerry continued to scan the water when Jerry noticed the bubbles coming to the surface, and then he saw a shape starting to come up from underneath.

Then the person broke the surface of the water and waved his hand and shook his head. It was Tony the safety diver.

"Can you see him?" Jerry shouted at the man.

Tony took the regulator out of his mouth and shook his head and yelled back. "He's not down there."

Jerry was surprised and yelled back, "What do you mean He's not fucking down there?"

Tony yelled to be heard over the falling water, "I've been all throughout the pond, twice. The water is clear there's no big stone that he could get snagged under. I found his knife, but I'm telling you he's not down here. I thought he might've been pinned by the falling water of the falls, but he's not under there. I don't know where he is. I'll make one more pass, but like I told you he's not in this pond." With that, Tony slipped the regulator back in his mouth and disappeared under the water.

Jerry looked at Diane and asked, "How is it possible that he is not in there?"

"He may have gone over the lip and into the main river." she said to him.

"It's only a foot high. We would have seen that happen." Jerry said, still looking over the pond.

"Not if he went over right away when we were blinded by the flash." she commented.

They both looked at the ledge, the pond went deep in the middle up to shallow area about a foot before the water cascaded down into the river and continued all the way out to the Bow.

"I can't see that. I'm sure we would have noticed." Jerry said to her. not wanting to believe it was a possibility.

Carl came walking up to Gerry on the lower deck and said, "We just checked the playback on the cameras and it's weird. You could see him coming down then suddenly it looks like he noticed something. He kicks off, cuts the rope, and starts to fall. Once the flash happens. We have nothing for at least sixty seconds before it start up again."

"Really?" said Jerry in disbelief.

"That must have been a major electrostatic charge. That's the only thing that could have caused that. It is almost like something erased part of it. I have never seen anything like this before." Carl said, shaking his head.

"Not what I wanted to hear." Jerry said, rubbing his forehead.

"What do we do now?" Carl asked Jerry.

"I don't know." Jerry answered, still scanning the pond and down the river looking for his friend.

Diane turned to the man and said "I'm going to have to head back to the beginning of the trail and call in a team."

"A team?" Jerry asked.

Diane just looked Jerry in the eyes and said, "Yes Jerry, it will start as a search team, but I have a bad feeling that it is going to turn into a recovery."

Jerry just lowered his head and leaned back on the rail. "This can't be happening." he said.

Carl walked up to Jerry and put his arm on his shoulder, "Not your fault." He said trying to console his friend.

"My responsibility." Jerry said looking down.

"It may be your responsibility." said Carl, "But we will never know why Ryan broke protocol and cut the line.

That is something that only he would know, and he's not here to tell us."

Jerry just nodded his head, knowing that Carl was right but not making the possible loss of his good friend any less painful.

Tony finally climbed out of the pond when his oxygen tank was almost empty. He looked at Jerry and said, "Jerry, I am so sorry, but I can honestly tell you there is nothing in that pool at all. I have no idea where he is. He must have gone over the edge."

Jerry was slowly starting to accept that his friend of all those years now gone. Fighting back his emotions and not wanting them to show in front of all the crew. When Jerry looked around, there were not a lot of dry eyes from the people standing around him.

He then looked at Diane and said, "OK Diane, I think it might be time that we call in that team you were talking about."

Diane just nodded her head turned and started walking back so that she could make a call with Tina walking up to join her.

Don and Carl came up to Jerry and asked, "What do we do now?"

Jerry just took his head and answered," I don't know. I guess we should pack up and get ready to hike out. I don't want to leave but I do not know what else to do."

Once all the gear was stowed away on the carts again, the crew started to head out.

Carl looked back at Jerry who was just standing in the lower observation deck looking into the water and asked, "Are you coming?"

"I'll catch up with you shortly." he answered, so Carl turned to catch up to the rest of the crew.

Jerry stood there staring in the pool, then down into the river hoping that his friend would just pop up out of the water with his smile on his face saying, "I got you good. I can't believe you fell for it."

But he knew that was not going to happen. Tears slowly started falling down his face as he realized his friend was gone for good. He knew he was going to miss him and that a small piece of him died as well today. A wave of nausea came over him as he realized the phone calls he was going to have to make. It was not too sure whether he would be able to do it or not. He smiled himself a little bit as he thought of what Ryan would be telling him right now, and could hear Ryans voice in his head saying, "Quit being such a pussy. It's done, now. Do what you got to do." Jerry smiled a little at that.

Then taking one last look into the pond, he turned and started to walk up the trail to catch up with the crew.

Chapter 2

Ryan woke the next morning to what he thought was a baby crying. As he sat up quickly and started looking around, he noticed a fox about ten feet away from him, screeching at him.

"Well, good morning to you, little fella." Ryan said to the fox.

The fox went quiet, sat down and just looked at him.

Ryan still looking at the fox said, "Aren't you going to say anything to me? After all the strange shit that happened to me yesterday. It wouldn't surprise me if you asked me to tea."

The fox decided this thing in front of him was neither animal nor food, so it just turned around and walked away.

"Nice." Ryan said to the fox, "Just leave me here."

The fox didn't answer back. It just continued to walk on. Ryan's stomach growled and he thought, "Got it, I'm not going to get food sitting here, so let's start walking Ryan." With that he got up and continued to follow the river. By midday, Ryan had covered a lot of ground but was still unsure how far he had to go. Ryan stopped a few times on his trek to get water, and the last few times, Ryan drank a lot, hoping that it might quench his hunger a little bit. It did not work, he was still hungry as he kept on walking late into the afternoon, passing herds of deer and elk as they were walking down to the river for water.

It was quite fortunate that there were not a lot of trees close to the edge of the riverbank, and Ryan was walking quite quickly, even in bare feet. He did wish that the river was a little straighter, as it twisted and turned its way down the valley, adding to the distance he had to travel.

A few hours later, Ryan came to a grove of trees on the riverbank, and rather than walk around It, decided to cut through it. These trees went all the way down almost to the river, as Ryan was picking his way through and nearing the end of the grove of trees. He noticed a movement in the water up ahead. Ryan stopped and was very still, he moved quietly along with leaves, and branches obstructing his view. He didn't want to step out and find himself face to face with a bear, so he slowly worked his way through the bushes and the trees. When he got a clear view of the river he stopped, not believing what he was seeing. In front of him standing up to her waist in the water was a beautiful woman washing herself. Ryan couldn't believe his eyes, he wanted to shout out to her, but decided he didn't want to scare her. She was beautiful. She was tall, with a dark complexion, long black shiny hair down to her waist, and as Ryan looked down, he noticed her firm looking breasts.

Ryan thought, "She is absolutely beautiful. No, beautiful is not the word…. Stunning, that's the word." She was still a distance away from him, and Ryan just stood there and stared at her.

After a few minutes, Ryan caught himself and then thought, "Come on Ryan. How creepy is this? You're hiding in the bushes, watching a naked woman take a bath. Wow, you are a sick puppy."

Ryan decided that he did not want to sneak up on her, so he backed up a little way and then started to make a longer loop around the trees making a lot of noise, while singing out loud so that she would know he was coming and could cover herself up. When Ryan came out of the trees, and then turned back towards the river, he was surprised to see that she was still standing there, but this time staring at him. Suddenly, her eyes opened wide, and she backed up a little. She said something to him which Ryan didn't understand, but Ryan smiled broadly, waved, and then started walking towards her. She casually walked out of the water showing no signs of modesty whatsoever, but not taking her gaze from Ryan.

Ryan walked towards her and said in his friendliest voice, "Hi there. My name is Ryan. What's yours?" The girl was bending over to pick up her clothing. She lifted her head, just stared with a quizzical look on her face. She then put her head down, picked up her clothing, and put a wrap around her waist. She stood there staring at Ryan and then put on her top. As Ryan looked at her more closely, his first assessment was correct.

"She is absolutely stunning." He thought.

As she stood there Ryan noticed that she was a little shorter than him and had beautifully long black shiny hair and her body was well toned, and lean. He also saw that her eyes were as black as Obsidian.

Ryan could not help himself. He just looked at her and said, "You are absolutely the most beautiful woman I have ever seen in my life."

The girl looked at him, shook her head, and then said something again in a language that he didn't understand.

Ryan said, "I'm sorry I don't understand you. Do you speak English?"

She started to talk to him, but he couldn't understand what she was saying. Ryan asked where she was from, and again got the same type of reply.

"This is stupid, obviously she doesn't understand a word that I'm saying." Ryan said out loud.

They both stood there staring at each other for a while, and Ryan thought, "The only reason she wasn't running away in terror, was because I am standing here with a stupid grin on my face, and she must think that I'm just an idiot."

After a while with neither of them talking, she bent down and gathered up a bundle of what looked like bull rushes, and then started to walk away.

Ryan watched her go for a while and then thought, "This is stupid. I need to follow her. I have no idea where I am, or where I am going."

So, Ryan started to follow her, he kept well back because he didn't want to scare her. She would turn around occasionally, to look back to see if he was still coming. They kept walking for about forty minutes when Ryan was starting to wish that he hadn't drank so much water earlier, because it was becoming uncomfortable, and he was going to have to stop and relieve himself. When Ryan had gone as far as he could go without embarrassing himself by having an accident, he waited till he got close to some trees, and he stepped in behind them. The girl looked back when she saw the movement, and smiled to herself, because she knew what he was doing, but she kept on walking.

Ryan stood there for quite a time thinking to himself. "Why is this the time I need to get rid of everything? Come on Ryan, hurry up let's get going. You have to catch up to her."

When Ryan was finished, he came out behind the trees and noticed that he could no longer see her. So, he just continued in the direction in which she was going. He noticed that she was heading a little way away from the river, so he then headed in that general direction. When he looked up, he saw a grove of trees that he was going to have to enter. Ryan quickened his pace to try to catch up with her. As he started into the forest, Ryan noticed that there was a bit of a path that he could follow, which he thought was great, because he had not seen any trails this whole journey. As he was looking down following the path, he started to go around a couple of trees, and when he looked up, he came to a complete stop. About fifty feet in front of him were five men standing and talking animatedly with the young woman that he had just met. All the men turned and looked at Ryan as he came around the corner. Ryan noticed that they were all extremely fit, had long black hair and were wearing what looked like short leather wraps around their waist and two of the men were wearing what looked like leather shirts. But the one thing he really noticed was that all five of them started walking towards him carrying spears and talking to each other.

As they got closer Ryan heard them talking, but like the pretty girl, he could not understand them. He then noticed that the spears the men were holding were tipped with stone of some sort. Once the group of men got within fifteen feet they stopped and looked at Ryan. Two of the men were talking to the other three and pointing in Ryans direction.

"Kanti was right." said one of the men to the group, "I have never seen anyone with hair that white, he is also very pale."

Another man spoke up and said, "Do you think he is a spirit?"

The largest of the men just shook his head and said, "I do not think so, he tried to talk with Kanti, and was very friendly, and made no angry moves towards her. Let us see if we can find out more about this man." He motioned to the group to follow him.

Ryan could not understand what they were saying but concluded that they were talking about him. Suddenly the largest of the men, made a loud comment and slapped his hand on his chest, then looked at the other four. The other men just nodded their heads.

Ryan figured that he couldn't just stand there not doing anything, so he raised his hands and said "Hello." Then pointing to himself he said, "I am Ryan."

The men walked a little closer and stopped again. The man that slapped his chest pointed at himself and said something that again Ryan did not understand. Ryan copied his jester and said slowly, "Ryan."

The man thought about it for a moment, and then repeated, "Ryan." As he pointed at him.

Ryan smiled and nodded his head, and answered, "Yes, Ryan."

The man seemed pleased, and then pointed to himself and said, "Latona."

Ryan pointed at himself and then said. "Ryan." Then looking at the man standing in front of him, he pointed at him and said "Latona."

The man standing in front of him, smiled, nodded his head, tapped himself on the chest and said "Latona."

Quite excited, as now he knew the stranger's name. Latona turned and looked at the other men and stated. "We can not just leave him out here. Let us take him back to our camp."

"Do you think that is wise?" asked one of the men.

Latona answered, "I do not see it being a problem. This man Ryan seems friendly. We need to get our kills back to the camp as well, so we may as well bring him along with us."

Latona looked at the other four men, and they nodded back at him in agreement.

Ryan was standing there listening to the men talk, frustrated that he could not understand what they were saying. He did notice his name in there at one point, but that was the only thing he could understand from the entire conversation.

Latona turned around and looked at Ryan, smiled and waved his hand in a beckoning motion to come with them, then all the men turned around and started walking.

Ryan thought to himself, "Why the hell not, I'm not going to stay out here by myself."

So, he started to follow the five men. As they got down the path a little way, they came upon two deer that were obviously killed earlier by these men. The deer had their legs tied together, with a poll between them so that they could be carried by two men. Without saying anything, two men grabbed each end and lifted it up, with two of the other men lifting the other one. The six men started walking down the trail with the men carrying the deer in the lead.

They had walked a little way, and Ryan's stomach started to growl. Latona looked over at Ryan and smiled at him.

Ryan looked a little sheepish and rubbed his stomach. Latona smiled, nodded his head, and reached into a small pouch, attached to his belt, and pulled out a piece of dried meat, and handed it to Ryan. Ryan smiled back at him and took the proffered meat, nodded his head, and started chewing. It tasted like a T-bone steak to him, he was so hungry. As they walked further down the trail, Latona tapped one of the men on the shoulder, and took the poll from him, giving him a break. Seeing this, Ryan tapped the other man on the shoulder and pointed to the poll. The man got the idea and handed the poll over to Ryan.

The man then looked at the rest of the group smiling and said to them, "Well, at least he is not afraid to help out."

The group continued to walk for another hour, following the river and taking turns carrying the loads. At one point when Ryan looked up, he noticed he was coming into a clearing with tents and what looked like large grassy mounds. As they continued, he could tell this was a camp of some sort, with a fair number of people in it, going about their daily routine. As they got closer Ryan noticed that the people were stopping whatever it was, they were doing and staring at him. Ryan watched as people from around the camp started to form groups, and we're talking amongst themselves, glancing over towards the hunting party.

Ryan then noticed a group of men walking towards them with spears in their hands. He saw that they weren't being threatening, as they were just letting the spears hang at their side while they walked towards the group. Latona looked up and saw this, and he held his hand to stop the hunters, and then started moving forward on his own.

Ryan started to follow him, but then noticed that the other hunters were staying back and thought it might be a good idea to stay with them as well.

Latona walked towards the group of men, and when he got close enough, he heard one of the men from the group say to him, "So I see your hunt has been successful, and that you bring back two nice size deer. We see you also bring something else back as well."

Latona looked at the men and asked, "Did Kanti not tell you we were coming, and that we were bringing this man with us?"

The man answered, "Yes, she did. We thought she was teasing us when she described what the man looked like. I can see now that she was telling the truth." He then asked, "What do you know of this man Latona?"

Latona looked at the man, turned to look at Ryan, and then back at the man. Then answered, "This man's name is Ryan. I cannot tell you where he is from because he does not speak our language, nor does he speak the language of the people from the north, west, or the east. I think he may come from the far North and that's why we cannot understand him. Kanti said he was nothing but kind to her, and he had no hesitation in helping us with our burden from the hunt and getting it back to camp. He seems to be a good man, who may have come up on hard times."

"Why do you say that Latona?" Asked another man in the group.

Latona addressed the man, "He has no travelling companion, he has no provisions, and if you look carefully, he also has no footwear. This is a mystery that I would like to solve."

"Maybe he was cast out from somewhere." said the man that spoke first, and now seemed to be speaking for the group.

Latona nodded his head and said, "I cannot see that, but it is possible, we will need to find out more about this man Ryan, but for now we should make him welcome. Do you not agree?" He asked.

"Yes, you are right Latona. We are known for showing hospitality to all the travellers that cross through this territory, and just because someone is....," The man hesitated for a moment then continued, "Strange looking, we should not change that."

The man then looked past Latona and stared directly at Ryan. Ryan could feel the man's eyes piercing into his soul, but decided this was not a time to be weak willed. Ryan stared back, looking directly into his eyes, and focused on projecting his biggest and brightest smile. The man stared back at Ryan and started to crack a slight smile, then said to the men around him, "I have never seen anybody with eyes bluer than the sky, or darker than glacier ice."

The men around him all nodded their heads in agreement. Ryan had no idea what they were talking about but had a pretty good idea, they were talking about him, as he had heard his name mentioned a couple of times. The group of men that were talking to Latona turned and started walking back to camp, Latona turned and waved the hunters forward. As he walked into the camp, Ryan noticed people were looking, but not getting too close to him.

The men carrying the deer went in one direction, and Latona went in another direction, Ryan was unsure what to do so he decided to follow Latona.

As he caught up to Latona, the man turned and smiled, the two kept walking for a short distance, when Ryan looked over and noticed a woman walking towards them. She was an older woman with long black hair with some greying on the tips and along the front.

She looked about the same age as Latona and held herself with an air of grace as she walked towards them. Ryan noticed that she had a leather wrap around her waist and a shirt that also looked like it was made from some type of leather. She wore a necklace which looked to him as if it was made of animal teeth, and a broad smile on her face, as she walked up to Latona, put her arms around his neck and gave him a kiss.

"It is good to see you woman. I missed you, and that smile." Latona said to the attractive lady.

"You say that every time you go away for a day and then come back." She said with her arms still around his neck.

"That's because it is true. Should I stop?" Lakota asked with a teasing smile.

"No, never." she said quickly, then added, "I see you brought a guest with you.?

"Yes, Kanti found him while she was bathing in the river and collecting bull rushes. We do not know much about him, or where he is from, but so far, he has not done anything to make us regret bringing him back to the camp.

"He looks so strange." said the woman, "I have never seen anyone with light skin as well as that colour hair." and then Nila noticed his eyes for the first time and she said in surprise, "They are a dark blue!"

"Yes, it does take a while to get used to it. I had to force myself not to stare and appear rude." Replied Latona.

He turned, looked at Ryan, then looked back at his mate and smiled, pointing at Ryan, he then said Ryans name out loud. He then pointed at the woman standing next to him and said, "Nila."

Ryan got the gist, nodded his head at the woman and repeated the name, "Nila."

Nila smiled, nodded her head, and just said, "Ryan."

A big smile spread across Ryans face, because now, he knew the name of two of the people around him and it was a start.

Latona continued speaking to his mate and said, "I have a feeling that this young man is hungry, as his stomach has been talking for the entire trip back. I had a piece of dry meat which I gave to him, and he ate it faster than a wolverine devouring a kill."

"Well, I'm sure we can fix him up with something." She said, "I have some soup and some deer meat that I've just finished cooking. Bring him to the lodge and we will get you both fed."

Latona looked at Ryan and extended his hand and started walking, hoping that he would understand that he wanted him to follow. The three started walking towards one of the large mounds that Ryan had noticed when they first entered the camp. Suddenly there was a little yip, and Ryan looked down to see a white puppy at his feet, sitting down on his haunches and wagging his tail.

"Well, aren't you a cute little one?" Ryan said as he leaned down and scratched the little dog behind the ears. When he stopped and stood up, and started to follow Latona and Nila, the little dog fell in beside him.

Ryan looked at the little thing and said "I'm pretty sure you can't follow me. You should go back to your owner." The little pup stood there looking up at him wagging its tail.

Ryan started walking again and the little pup started following him. "Well, you are just way too adorable." He said to the little pup as it came bounding up to him again.

Ryan picked him up, gave him a good scratch, and then put him down again.

The little pup watched Ryan start to walk away and started following Ryan right up until he caught up with Latona and Nila.

Latona looked at Ryan, then down at the little pup and said, "The spirit wolf seems to have taken a liking to Ryan."

Nila looked at Ryan and the pup and said, "Well that is strange. Usually, he follows whoever is feeding him, he just seems to like this man."

They smiled as Ryan tried to shoo the little pup away, but to no avail. Ryan just looked at the couple and shrugged his shoulders, hoping for some suggestions. Nila and Latona just continued walking, so Ryan and the little pup followed them.

As the three reached the top of the mound, Ryan noticed a log at an angle sticking out of a hole about three feet in diameter at the top, he then saw that the log had notches cut into it, making it look like stairs. Nila walked up to the log, stepped on it, and facing the log climbed down using the notches as stairs, Ryan then watched Latona do the same thing. Ryan stood there looking down and noticed that it was about ten or twelve feet to the ground, he took hold of the log, and then climbed down backwards like he saw Latona, and Nila do. As Ryan stepped off the log at the bottom, he looked around and was surprised by what he saw. There were four main posts forming a square in the centre of what looks like a dome roof.

He then noticed that at the top of each four of these logs, was another log going across making it look like a T, to which three other logs were attached from the ground going upwards in a triangle shape.

As he looked closer, he saw several other logs were laid out from on top of each other, almost giving a log cabin effect from the ground all the way up to the roof.

He noted that the dirt floor was packed hard and had some woven mats laying on the ground. Ryan then observed that around the outside there were ledges cut into the Earth, which seem to make benches going all around the outside of the circle. He also noticed there were what looked like drapes hanging down, they seemed to be made from the same material as the mats on the ground were made of.

"This must be how they partition it off to make rooms." Ryan thought.

The centre portion was quite roomy, and had a small fire going in the centre, with the smoke going out the hole that they had just climbed down. Ryan was still looking around when he heard the little pup yipping and whining above him. As he looked up, he saw the little white pup walking back and forth around the opening, staring down and whining.

Ryan called up to it and said, "You should be going home now."

With that the little pup looked at him, tilted his head, and stopped whining. When Ryan started to walk towards Latona and Nila, the dog started up again, whining, and crying.

Nila looked at Latona and said, "I've never seen the little wolf act like that before, have you?"

Latona shook his head and answered, "No I've never seen it do that either, but it looks like it wants to come down and be with Ryan."

Nila just smiled and said, "Maybe you should go up and get him then. He won't cause any damage down here. He's too little."

Latona was going to come up with an objection, but then decided not to bother and climbed back up the center log, wondering if the pup would even come to him, so he could bring him down. When he reached the top. The little pup came running over to him as if he knew he was going to take him down, Latona picked up the little pup and tucked him under one arm and carried him back down. When he got to the bottom, he put the little pup down, and it went running up to Ryan, sat down, and let out one quick little puppy bark. Ryan smiled, reached down, and rubbed the top of his head. The little pup fell over on its side, then rolled over on his back.

"Oh, so you want tummy rubs, do you?" Ryan asked and knelt to scratch the little pup's tummy.

When he finished and stood up, he noticed that Nila was over by a basket container next to the fire. Ryan watched her stick her finger into the basket, which had some sort of liquid in it, nod her head and then reach into the basket with a branch that had two ends on either side like tongs, and she pulled out a stone. Ryan thought this was rather strange, but he watched her put the stone on the fire and then reached into the fire with the tongs and pick out another smooth round stone, hold it up, take a bit of evergreen bow that she had, brush the ash off, and then she dropped that into the liquid. Ryan could hear it sizzle as it went in and then looked on as Nila reached into the fire and took out a second stone, brushed off the ash, and put it into the basket as well.

She let it sit for a few moments and then stuck her finger in again and smiled, Latona came over and put his hand on Ryan's shoulder and beckoned him to come and sit down on one of the mats. Ryan sat down with Latona, wishing that he could talk to him because he had a ton of questions that he needed to have answered.

The pup followed Ryan over and when he sat down the pup laid down beside him. When Ryan looked over at Nila, she had what looked like a wooden cup on a stick, and she was dipping it into the basket. Latona looked at Ryan and rubbed his stomach and nodded his head. Ryan just smiled and nodded his head, rubbing his stomach as well. Nila walked over with two wooden bowls and handed one to her mate and the other one to Ryan. Ryan looked at the bowl and noticed it was some form of soup as it had greens in it, and it looked like it had some meat, and it smelled wonderful. Ryan was waiting to see if he was going to get a spoon, and then noticed Latona holding the bowl to his mouth and drinking from it like a cup. Ryan followed his lead and did the same. Ryan thought it tasted great as he was so hungry. He was about to turn to Nila to try to relay how much he was enjoying it, when she appeared holding a platter that looked like it was made from a moose antler, with slices of cooked meat on it. She looked at Ryan, smiled, and then held out the platter for him to take a piece.

Ryan thought, "Well you don't have to ask me twice." and took a piece of meat.

He held the meat in his hand and waited until he saw what Latona was going to do. Latona picked up a piece of meat, took a bite of it, and then folded it, and put it in the bowl with the soup in it. Ryan nodded his head and did the same thing. Ryan wasn't sure what type of meat it was, but like the soup, it tasted delicious.

Once Ryan had drunk the liquid from the soup. and was eating the meat, he wondered how he was supposed to eat what was left in the bottom of his bowl such as greens and pieces of meat. Ryan was wondering if he would need to pull them out with his fingers or tip the bowl back. He looked over at Latona who had put his bowl down and looked over at him.

Ryan was just about to do the same, but then Latona reached into a sheath on his side and pulled out a knife of some sort. Ryan couldn't see it very well, but he watched Latona use the knife to spear the vegetables and the meat from the bottom of the bowl.

Latona looked up and noticed that Ryan was watching him. He smiled to himself and then said, "Nila, could you please grab one of our home knives and give it to Ryan. I don't think he has a knife for eating."

 Nila grabbed a knife and brought it over and handed it to Ryan. Ryan smiled, and nodded his head in thanks, and took the knife. When Ryan looked at the knife, he noticed that it was made of stone. He felt the edge of it as well as a tip and discovered that it was very sharp. He had to be careful not to cut himself, and found the handle was wrapped in leather. Ryan started using it the same way that he saw Latona using his. While he was eating, he looked a little closer at the knife Latona was using and noticed the blade seemed to be made from the same material but his handle was made of some other material other than leather, and it had some carvings on it. When Ryan had finished, Nila came over and pointed to his bowl and then pointed back to the basket a few times. It took a couple of times for Ryan to figure out that she was asking if he would like more. Ryan nodded his head "Yes," Nila took the bowl and went over to the basket and refilled it again.

Ryan also helped himself to another piece of meat off the platter, this time ripping a piece off and giving it to the pup.

Nila walked over smiling at both Ryan and the pup, watching the pup happily devouring the meat he was given, and handed the bowl to Ryan. Ryan found he wasn't as hungry as he was before, so this time he started paying more attention to the bowl he held in his hands. It was carved out of wood and was sanded smooth.

On further inspection he saw that it was smooth on the outside, as well as smooth on the inside, like it had been sanded for a very long time.

"This bowl is really well made." Ryan thought, "I would love to know how they got it so smooth."

They sat in silence eating, and Ryan shared some more of his meat with his new little friend, who only lifted his head and took the meat Ryan offered.

Nila looked over at her husband and said, "I have never known that little one to be so well-behaved."

"I know, he has really attached himself to Ryan. Maybe that's not such a bad thing as he won't be wandering around the camp getting into trouble." Latona said with a smile.

"He has certainly taken a liking to Ryan." Nila said to her mate, and then continued, "How could he make his way through the mountains with no footwear, food, or any tools?"

"I don't know." said Lakota watching Ryan scratch the pup behind its ear. "It is a mystery we are going to need to solve, I hope he stays with us long enough that we can find out the answers to some of these questions."

"I'm sure he will." Nila said, "but we are going to have to try to learn his language."

"Or he will have to try to learn ours." Latona said. With that, he bent down and picked up an empty bowl from the ground and held it in front of him. Ryan saw Latona pick up the bowl and was watching him. Latona pointed to himself and then said, "Latona."

Ryan, nodded his head, pointed to himself, and said, "Ryan."

Latona smiled, nodded, and then pointed at the bowl and said, "Bowl."

Ryan thought he understood, and pointed at the bowl and repeated, "Bowl." In Latona's language.

Latona smiled, nodded his head, then reached down and picked up a cup and held it up. The cup was made of wood like the bowl, but taller and smaller in circumference, but still as Ryan noticed, well made, and sanded smooth. Latona pointed to the cup, looked at Ryan and said slowly, "Cup."

Ryan thought about it for a few moments, then once he thought he had the pronunciation right, he repeated, "Cup."

Nila smiled, nodded her head, and said, "Good."

Ryan looked around and made a motion with both of his hands to encompass where they were sitting and then looked back at Latona.

Latona thought about it for a moment, then smiled and said, "Ground lodge." He made the same gesture that Ryan had made with both of his hands and repeated, "Ground Lodge."

Ryan smiled, and trying to get the pronunciation right, said. "Ground Lodge."

Latona smiled and nodded his head again.

"Well, this is good." thought Ryan, "I can now say three words in their language. At least it's a start." Ryan had thought about how he was going to communicate with these people and thought that maybe he could teach Latona and Nila how to speak English, but Ryan quickly ruled that out because he was the only one here that knew how to speak English, so it would be a lot more practical for him to learn their language.

Nila looked at her mate and said, "He learns fast. Hopefully he can remember things as well, and it might not take him long to learn our language or at least enough to communicate with us. I was thinking Latona, do you not have a set of old foot coverings that we could possibly give to him so that he is not walking around barefoot?"

"I do have an old pair that I keep as extras. I also have a fair knife and belt that I no longer use that he may have." With that Latona got up and walked to the far end of the lodge.

Nila thought that she would carry on teaching, so she looked at Ryan, pointed to the fire and said to Ryan, "Fire."

Ryan looked at her with a big smile on his face and repeated the word back to her.

Nila smiled at Ryan, then pointing to the fire, waved her fingers and then moved it up and down in the air and said, "Smoke."

Ryan got the idea right away, did the same hand motions and repeated the word, "Smoke."

A big smile crossed Nila's face, and she nodded her head at Ryan. As they looked up, Ryan noticed Latona coming back to where they were sitting. Latona sat in front of Ryan and his mate and handed him a pile of items.

The first thing that Ryan picked up, looked like they were a pair of shoes or moccasins. Ryan put them on his feet and tied the lace around his ankle to hold them in place and stood up. He walked around the lodge, and when he came back to Latona and Nila, he had a big smile on his face. Ryan looked at Latona and said, "Thank you."

Latona did not understand the words, but thought it was some form of gratitude, so he nodded and smiled back at Ryan.

Ryan bent down and picked up a belt that was made of woven strips of leather, as well as a knife like the one Latona was using during dinner and a sheath to put it in. He held them for a moment not quite sure how to put them on. Nila smiled at her mate, who then stood up, walked over to where Ryan was, and took the belt from him. He put the belt around Ryan's waist and showed him how to tie it, then taking the knife he tied the sheath to the belt. He then put his right hand on Ryan's shoulder, nodded his head and smiled.

Ryan smiled back and again said, "Thank you."

Ryan was starting to feel a little better because now he at least had some shoes and a belt to hold up his pants, which were starting to tend to slide down a little bit.

Nila looked at Latona and said, "Maybe we should take him and show him where the traveler's tent is, do you not think?"

Latona looked at his mate and said, "Yes, you are right. He could stay here in the lodge with us, but I think we should put him in the traveller's tent for the first little while. Just until we know a little bit more about him."

With that Latona started walking to the centre of the lodge where the log was going up through the hole, he motioned to Ryan for him to follow. Nila had gotten up and passed her mate and was now heading up the poll. Latona turned and followed her, and again motioned back for Ryan to follow. Ryan started up the log and when he was almost to the top, he heard whining, and when he turned around, the little pup had tried to follow him up but had made it up three notches and was now stuck and whining for Ryan to come back to help. Ryan climbed back down the log, scooped the little pup up, tucked him under his arm, and then headed back up the log.

When he got to the top, he put the little pup on the ground and then climbed out himself. Latona and Nila were waiting for him at the bottom. As Ryan started to walk down the mound towards the open area, he started to look around and really take things in for the first time. They were in a beautiful valley with mountains on either side and if he had his bearings right, the mountains were to the south and to the north. As he was looking at the mountain to the north, he couldn't help but think it looked familiar to him. The more he stared at it, the more familiar it became. Then suddenly out of nowhere a name came to his mind, "Cascade." thought Ryan. "But that can't be right, the Cascade Mountain can be seen from downtown Banff, and you shouldn't really be able to see this view from anywhere else."

That's when the realization hit him. He was in Banff, but there was no Banff, no buildings, no roads, nothing. Ryan felt his knees go a little weak as the full reality of the situation slammed into him.

Nila and Latona were staring at Ryan, when Nila turned and said to her mate, "What is wrong with him, he looks like he has seen a bad spirit."

Latona shook his head and answered, "I don't know." He then called out to him, "Ryan!" and then waved for him to follow.

Ryan, hearing his name, noticed that Latona and Nila were staring at him and wanted him to follow them.

"I've got to try to figure this out, somehow." he thought to himself, "But right now, let's see where we're going."

Ryan headed down the outside of the lodge towards Latona and Nila with the little wolf padding along behind him.

As he headed towards his new friends he looked up and noticed that the sun had gone down behind the mountains and the valley was getting darker. As well the temperature was getting a little cooler but not uncomfortable. Once the pair had caught up to Nila and Latona, they headed off across the field towards several conical tents spaced widely apart. As they were getting closer, Ryan observed a group of people sitting around a fire, talking.

Ryan noticed that they were not sitting around a circular campfire, instead they were sitting around a pit that was about eight or nine feet long and three feet across with logs on either side for the people to sit on. Ryan considered this for a second and thought, "What a great idea. You can get a lot more people sitting around the fire if it's long, rather than being circular."

As he got closer, Ryan noticed that the people stopped talking, looked up, and watched them approach. As they drew closer one man waved and called out "Latona, how is our new friend settling in?"

Latona smiled, waved back, and answered, "Ryan is settling in well. He seems eager to learn our language.

Crona smiled and asked, "Really, how are you accomplishing that?"

"Well, we started out with our names, then we moved on to important things, like cup, bowl, then went on to fire and smoke." Latona stopped, then smiling, looked at the people sitting around the fire and continued, "That's all we've done so far. But hopefully the rest of you could join in and help as well."

The people were now looking at Ryan and smiling. Ryan did not understand a word Latona, or the other man said, but strangely he did get the words like cup, bowl, fire, smoke, and was quite pleased with himself that he remembered those words. As he looked around, he saw the people smiling and looking at him. Crona motioned for Nila and Latona to join them at the fire. Latona sat on one side of the pit while Nila sat on the other. She patted the log for Ryan to sit beside her. Ryan sat down and looked at the people gathered around the fire, and he noticed at the end of the log across from him was the young lady that he saw bathing in the river earlier today. He smiled at her and waved feeling a little foolish. She briefly looked at him, smiled, then looked away.

"How can she be shy now, when she was not earlier today." Ryan thought to himself.

The man that was talking to Latona looked at Ryan, pointed to his chest and then said, "Crona,"

Ryan understood, pointed to himself, and said, "Ryan." Then pointed back at the man, concentrated for a moment, and then said, "Crona."

The man smiled and nodded his head.

"Well, this is good." Ryan's thought, "Now I know three people.

Ryan felt a tap on his shoulder and when he turned around, he saw a young girl around five years old standing there holding a rock. She looked at him, smiled, then pointed to the rock and said, "Rock."

Ryan wasn't too sure what was going on, but when she repeated the motion and the word, he smiled and nodded his head, looked at the pretty little girl and said "Rock."

A big smile came across her face and she nodded and repeated the word. Suddenly there was a young boy maybe around ten years old holding a knife like the one that he and Latona used during dinner. The boy held it in the palm of his hands, looked at Ryan and said, "Knife."

Ryan smiled at the young lad and repeated the word back to him. The young man smiled and nodded his head. Ryan could see that this is going to probably turn into a game of some sort with the children, but he didn't seem to really mind that much, if he could retain the words and their proper meaning.

As Ryan sat there, the little pup climbed up beside him, then onto his lap. Ryan reached down, scratched him behind the ears, as it curled up on his lap and started to go to sleep.

Crona continued, "Well Latona, so I guess we will have to wait until his understanding of our language gets better before we can find out where he is from."

Latona nodded his head in agreement and answered, "Nila and I have been discussing this. We feel it will be worthwhile because we are sure that he has a great story to tell."

"Agreed." Said Crona.

One of the people on the log turned to look at Kanti sitting at the end of the log and asked, "Were you scared when you saw him today at the river?"

Kanti looked up, smiled, but did not look at Ryan, and addressed the person who spoke, "No Cita, I was not scared, he seemed to come out of nowhere. He was standing there watching me and talking to me. He made no moves that I thought to be dangerous.

To be perfectly honest, he looked a little silly standing there, not too sure what to do. I tried to talk to him, but when we did not understand each other, I thought oh well, I had to get back to the camp, and if he decided to follow me, that would be fine. Then I ran across father with the hunting party, told them about him, so they went back to talk to him."

Once Ryan heard Kanti speak, he looked up and was watching. While she was talking, he couldn't understand a word she was saying, but it just reaffirmed his thoughts of earlier in the day, that she was breathtaking. He couldn't put an age on her, but with the fire light hitting her hair it shone, and she still looked as attractive with her clothes on, as she did with them off. As Kanti was telling her friends about the day's events, she saw out of the corner of her eye that Ryan was watching her, and for some reason she started to blush.

Cita, the woman the Kanti was talking to noticed this, and said, "My, Kanti I see that your face is red. Maybe you are getting too close to the fire."

Kanti shot Cita a look, and just said, "Yes, that must be it."

Cita smiled at her friend and then decided not to push the issue anymore.

Nila asked, "Kanti, have you seen your grandmother?"

Kanti looked at her mother and answered, "Yes, she is with one of the other healers from down the valley. Why?"

Nila replied, "I don't think she knows Ryan yet. Could you please go get her so that we can introduce them."

Kanti was still aware that Ryan was staring at her, and she thought this would be a great excuse for her to get up and get away. "Yes mother, that sounds like a good idea. I'll go do that now."

With that, she got up and headed off towards the tents. Ryan watched her leave with a smile on his face wondering if he would ever get to know her. He then realized that she had not introduced herself to him. Ryan continued to stroke the young pup laying on his lap, gently, rubbing his fingers through its fur and listening to everybody talk.

Ryan could not understand what they were saying but was comforted just being around people. He kept looking in the direction in which that pretty girl had left and was wondering to himself when she would be coming back. Cita noticed Ryan continuously glancing in the direction that Kanti had walked away in and smiled to herself.

"There definitely seems to be some interest there." Cita thought to herself.

"Well, are you going to put him up in one of the traveller's tents?" Crona asked.

Before Latona could respond Nila answered the question for her mate, "Yes, we are. We were just on our way over there before we stopped to visit. Hopefully he stays around for a while, and we can get to know him better, and find out more about him."

"I have never seen anyone that looks like him in my entire life." said someone in the group.

There was a murmuring and a lot of nodding in agreement.

Latona nodded his head as well and said, "He does look different, and I wonder if there are more of his people that look like him, and where he comes from."

"Good questions. It will be interesting to find out the answers." Crona added.

Nila stood up, looked at Latona and said, "Do you think we should show Ryan to the traveler's tent now?"

Latona stood up and said, "That is a good idea." Then reached out to help his mate up. Ryan noticed Latona and Nila standing, put the pup down from his lap and stood up to join them.

He didn't know what to do so he looked at everybody and gave them a smile as well as a small wave of his hand. A few of the people sitting around the fire returned the wave. Latona, Nila, and Ryan started walking away from the group of people. The pup sat there for a little while watching the people walk away, then set out running after Ryan. As they were getting close to the tents, Ryan felt his stomach starting to churn and realized that he had to find a toilet but was pretty sure there were none around. Ryan tried to figure out a way to communicate his needs to Latona, then an idea came to him. He walked up to Latona, tapped him on the shoulder and beckoned for him to follow him a little way away. When the two men stopped, Ryan looked at him, scrunched up his face as if he were straining, and then reached around and touched his butt.

Latona nodded his understanding and turned to look back at his mate. "Ryan needs to go to the trench and doesn't know where they are."

"That's understandable." said Nila, "Why don't you show him where they are, and I will meet you both at the tent."

Latona turned, looked at Ryan, and started walking towards the forest. Ryan fell in step with Latona as they walked up towards a path that led into the forest for about three hundred yards and opened into a small clearing where Ryan noticed a twenty foot trench was dug. Latona pointed towards the trench, then turned and headed back in the direction they came.

Ryan could smell the trench as he approached it and tried to figure out how this was going to work.

He noticed that the trench was only about two feet wide, and quite deep, with mounds of dirt on either end and what looked like a moose antler cut down and resembled a scoop or shovel. Ryan thought about it for a moment and figured the best way for him to do this was to put one foot on either side of the trench and squat down that way. He also realized that it would probably be better if he took his pants completely off. Once this was done, he managed to squat over the trench and complete his business. When he was finished, he looked around and then caught himself "Ryan you're an idiot, of course there's not going to be any toilet paper around." He thought, but he did notice several piles of what looked like a dry green moss. He picked up the moss in his hands and concluded. this must be what they use. He was surprised that it wasn't as rough as he thought it was going to be and did quite a good job of getting him clean. Once he stood up and put his pants back on, he investigated the pit and noticed that everything was covered so he reached over, grabbed one of the antlers, scooped up some dirt and spread it over his excrement. Ryan looked around and found the trail which he and Lakota had come up and started walking back through the forest towards the field.

When he came to the edge of the forest and stepped out onto the clearing, he found Latona waiting for him. The two men started walking towards the cluster of tents. Latona walked up to one tent, pulling the flap back, and tying it as they walked inside. Nila was there laying out a mat on the ground as well as a fur on top of it. She had a leather sheet folded on the end of the fur, Ryan looked at it and assumed that this was going to be his bed, and this would be his home temporarily.

He noticed that there was a small fire pit in the center, but no wood or ashes, it looked like it hadn't been used for a while which makes sense because the temperature was not cold. The young pup walked over to the bed, sniffed at it, climbed into the middle and curled up and proceeded to go to sleep.

Ryan looked at the little thing with a big smile on his face and thought to himself, "Looks like I'm going to have a little friend for the night. I hope your owner is not going to miss you."

Nila reached into a bag that she had slung over her shoulder and pulled out a package wrapped in what looked like woven leaves and handed it to Ryan. She pointed to the package and then brought her fingers up to her mouth and said, "Food."

Ryan thought about it for a moment and wondered if the package she had given him was called food, or what was inside was called food. He opened the package on one corner and looked inside and saw that it was some of the meat that he had had at their lodge.

Ryan looked at Nila, smiled and said, "Thank you."

She just smiled and turned to step outside. Ryan was looking around the dwelling and was surprised at how spacious it was and then concluded that you could sleep five or six people in here with no problem.

Ryan looked at Latona then around at his surroundings and pointed at the walls and shrugged his shoulders.

Latona looked at him, went over and touched the walls and said, "Tent."

Ryan nodded his head and then repeated the word tent. Latona also nodded his head and thought to himself, "How long it was going to take before he would be able to have a decent conversation with this man."

Ryan heard voices outside and heard Nila talking to someone. as he stepped out of the tent, he noticed Kanti had come back and was talking to Nila.

Latona and Ryan approached the two women and Latona asked, "Did you find your grandmother?"

"Yes, I did." Answered Kanti. "She will be here shortly, she is very interested in meeting the man, Ryan. She did not want to come at first, but once I explained what happened today and what he looked like, she became very interested and is finishing up her business with the other healer."

Again, Ryan found himself staring at the beautiful woman in front of him. Screw it he thought to himself, then looked her in the eye, pointed to himself and said, "Ryan."

The woman just glanced up and looked at him but did not say anything.

Nila looked at Kanti and said, "Don't be rude. Introduce yourself."

Kanti was not being rude, she was just surprised by Ryan's sudden announcement of his name.

She smiled at her mother, and then turned to Ryan, pointed to herself, and said, "Kanti." She then felt her face redden.

Ryan's eyes lit up as he thought to himself, "Great, so now I know your name." Ryan then pointed at her and said, "Kanti."

She just nodded her head, then looked down, breaking eye contact with Ryan.

Ryan was about to say something to her when he felt a tap on his shoulder. When he turned around, he saw a short, very old woman with gray hair, and deep lines etched into her face. She was not smiling, she was just looking up at him. Without warning she reached up, grabbed each side of his shirt, and pulled his face down towards her. Ryan noticed that her eyes were black as obsidian and seemed to pierce right through him into his soul. He also found that he couldn't blink or break off eye contact. The old woman stared at him intently, and then suddenly her eyes opened wide, she released his shirt and staggered backwards. As she backed away from Ryan, she raised her hand and pointed a trembling finger at him and yelled something, which he didn't understand.

Nila watched her mother let go of Ryan, then step back and yell, "You are the traveller!"

Nila became concerned and ran to her mother asking, "Mother, what is wrong."

Her mother just stared at Ryan, and slowly lowered her hand.

Kanti walked up beside her grandmother, putting her arm around the old woman's shoulder, and asked, "Grandmother, what is wrong? What is troubling you?"

The old woman just looked down at the ground and didn't say anything.

"Mother, are you alright?" Nila asked again starting to become more concerned.

The old woman nodded her head and looked up. Ryan looked over to Latona and then back to the women. He didn't know what to say or what just happened.

"Grandmother, what do you mean, he is the traveller?" Kanti asked.

The old woman just looked at Kanti, smiled and answered, "I just meant that he is a traveler from far away, and I have never seen anyone that looks like him before. I am sorry I did not mean to get excited. It's just I looked into his eyes, they are so blue. I have never seen anything like it before, and it disturbed me a little."

Nila got the feeling her mother wasn't telling the truth but couldn't see why she would bother lying about it, so she just took her word at face value. "Mother, would you like me to introduce you to this man?" Nila asked the old woman.

The old woman looked up at Ryan nodded and said, "Yes, I do want to meet this young man."

Nila walked with her mother back towards Ryan and stood in front of him, she put her hand on the old woman's chest and then said "Skyseeker,"

Ryan put his hand on his chest and said back, "Ryan."

The old woman then looked at Latona and said, "We must make sure that this man stays here with us and does not continue to travel on."

Latona was surprised by the statement and said, "I don't think he has any intentions of going anywhere right now Skyseeker. We are slowly starting to get to understand each other. He seems like a good man and is very friendly."

The old woman looked at Ryan, smiled then looked at Latona and said, "Yes, he does seem very friendly."

With that she walked over, patted Ryan's arm, then turned and walked away.

"What was that all about?" Latona asked his mate.

"I have no idea. I have never seen her act like that before. It's like something came over her briefly and then suddenly she was back to normal again." Nila Said.

"Is grandma going to be all right mother?" Kanti asked Nila.

"She will be fine dear. It's just her way and sometimes it can be strange." Nila answered.

When Kanti looked over at Ryan, she noticed he was staring at her again, so she quickly averted her eyes and asked her father, "So, is he all settled in for the evening?"

"I don't know about settled in, but he knows where his bed is and your mother has left him with some food," Latona said looking at his daughter.

Kanti looked around and noticed that the young wolf was nowhere in sight. She looked at her mother and asked, "Did the young wolf stay with the group of people at the fire?"

Nila smiled and said, "No the little one has taken a liking to Ryan, becoming his shadow, and is following him around everywhere he goes. I believe he is in the tent sleeping on Ryan's bedroll."

"That seems strange that the little one is attached itself to Ryan, as it gets along with everybody in the camp but has not bonded with any one person." Kanti said looking towards the tent.

"Well, he has bonded with Ryan." Latona said, "Ryan can't go anywhere without the little one wanting to be right beside him or climbing onto his lap."

"Well, that's good. I guess he will have something to keep him company. "Kanti said as she started to walk away.

Nila looked over at her mate, and they both looked at Kanti while she walked away and smiled. Latona turned to Ryan patting him on the shoulder, pointed to his tent and then Latona and Nila turned and started walking back to their lodge.

it was getting dark, but it wasn't totally night yet, as Ryan looked around, he saw a few people still wandering around in the camp. Ryan decided he'd had a bit of a rough day to say the least, and he would go and lay down and see if he could get some sleep. He walked into the tent, undid the flap, and let it close, then walked over to the bedroll. The pup was curled up right in the middle, so Ryan picked him up and put him down at the foot of the roll on a woven mat, he laid down on the fur and pulled the leather wrap up over himself. The dog got off the mat, walked around a little, and once Ryan got settled, came in and curled up at Ryan's feet.

Ryan laid there for a while thinking about the day's events. "What the hell is going on." he thought. "I thought maybe the movie crew just disappeared, but that's not what happened. It's almost like I've been transported back in time. What was it Johnny said, time immemorial, or something like that. Basically, meaning a really long fucking time. If Banff hasn't been built yet, I'm not even too sure how long that would've been.

I know Banff was around in the late 1800s, but I have a funny feeling this is way longer back than that, and how in the hell did I get here. The real question is, how the hell am I going to get back."

Then a horrible thought came to him. "Will I be able to get back?" He laid there with his mind going through so many scenarios and trying to answer questions that there were no answers for.

Ryan decided there was no way he was going to be able to get to sleep right now, so he thought he would just lay there for a while. As he laid there, he heard some light chanting which almost sounded like singing going on outside.

Ryan got up from his bedroll and stuck his head out the opening of the tent, he noticed about seventy five yards away, there was a small fire going with a few people sitting around it, singing quietly. Ryan decided to walk over and see what was going on. As he walked away from the tent, he heard a small yip, and the pup came running up and started to follow him. Ryan looked at the little ball of fur walking beside him and said, "You are one cute little dog. You know that, right."

As Ryan walked towards the small group sitting around the fire, he could hear a chanting melody. As he got closer, he could see three men all seeming to be a little older than him, sitting on logs around a small fire singing. Ryan recognized one of the men from the pit fire earlier, so he walked over, looked at the three men, tapped his chest and said his name.

The man Ryan recognized tapped his chest and said, "Tolbar." He then motioned Ryan to Join them. As Ryan took a seat and the other men introduced themselves as Rocano, and Skytal. Ryan sat there quietly, listening to the three men chant.

The pup crawled over the log and laid down in front of Ryan and curled up watching the fire. Tolbar reached over and took a cup and dipped it into a basket sitting beside the fire and handed it to Ryan.

It was filled with hot liquid and Ryan took a sip but couldn't quite make out what the flavour was. It was not unpleasant, it was just different, something he had never tasted before.

He held the cup up and saluted the three men as a form of thank you for the beverage. Skytel held up the cup, pointed to it and said, "Cup."

Ryan nodded his head and repeated the word, "Cup."

Skytal then pointed to the inside of the cup, looked at Ryan and said, "Tea."

Ryan looked at the man, took a sip from his cup, nodded his head, and then repeated the word back to him, "Tea."

As Ryan drank his tea, he enjoyed listening to the rhythm that the three men were creating, and after a while, found himself humming along. Rocano sitting on the right of Ryan patted him on the shoulder and looked like he was trying to encourage him to sing louder, Ryan increased his volume a few octaves, and the man smiled. Now the four of them were all chanting and smiling. In the back of Ryan's mind, it reminded him of when he, Terry, Jack, and Bill were out on the trail after a few beers and started seeing some raunchy Limerick about a girl from Nantucket.

After a while Skytal and Rocano got up and walked away, Tolbar pointed at Ryan's cup and Ryan figured that he was asking him if he would like some more. Ryan nodded his head and said, "Yes." and the man proceeded to fill the cup again.

Tolbar looked at Ryan and nodded his head then said, "Yes."

Ryan had no idea what Tolbar said until he repeated the jester and then the word.

Ryan smiled, nodded his head and then repeated, "Yes."

Tolbar smiled back and said "yes."

They both sat in silence, staring at the fire, and once they both finished their tea, the man beside him got up, smiled at him, and then headed on his way. Ryan stayed up for another hour, looking at the fire and gazing up into the sky, even though he was around the fire when he looked up, the stars were brilliant, just like they were the other night when he fell asleep beside the river. He tried again but could not see any movement in the sky other than the occasional shooting star. It was dark now, and Ryan could see one or two glows coming from the inside of some of the tents, probably from small fires and thought that maybe he should be heading back into his own tent and get some sleep. It occurred to Ryan if this is in fact, an old Indian encampment, he wondered where the horses were. They must have a corral or someplace where they keep them Ryan thought. Maybe tomorrow he'll have a look around and see if he can find it. Ryan stood up, pushed some dirt over onto the dying fire, and headed back to the tent. As he entered the tent the little pup raced past him, climbed back onto the bedroll, and sat waiting for Ryan. He Moved the pup off the bed and then got in and covered himself up. No sooner was that done when the little white pup happily jumped back on and snuggled up at Ryan's feet again. The thoughts slowly started coming back to Ryan again, and he tried to push them away so that he could get some much needed sleep. As he laid there, he could not get over how quiet it was. After a short time, Ryan eventually fell asleep.

Chapter 3

Ryan woke the next morning to the sound of children playing outside as he slowly started to open his eyes. He was hoping that the events of yesterday were just a dream, and he was going to wake up in a nice hotel room, but no such luck. He rolled on his back and laid there for a few minutes, trying to decide what he was going to do. Should he get up or should he lay here for a while. That decision seemed to be made for him, as once he started to move, the pup got up, came over and started licking his face.

"Hey cut that out." He said to the little pup, who just continued to leap up and lick Ryan's face.

"OK, OK. I get it." He said to the pup, "I'm going to get up. I need to get up now anyway because I have to take a pee." He went and opened the flap of the tent and saw that it was early morning, and that people were starting to move around the camp. Ryan left the tent and started walking to the tree line of the forest which was only about forty feet away from the tent. Once he got to the tree line, he walked in a few yards and started to relieve himself.

He turned around and he saw the pup also relieving itself against a tree and he started to laugh. "So, is this going to be our morning ritual little one?" Ryan said to the little pup, who just finished and looked up at him and then started walking beside him.

Ryan walked back towards the tent but was not too sure where to go or what to do. He was feeling a little peckish and remembered that package that Nila had given him last night and went back in the tent.

He sat on his bed and opened the package and started chewing on the meat. In no time at all, the little puppy was sitting in front of him, looking up hopefully and wagging its tail. Ryan ripped off some pieces for the little pup and put them on the ground in front of it. The pup hungrily devoured the meat that Ryan offered. It didn't take long for the two of them to consume the meat that was in the package, and Ryan thought to himself, "I'm glad that Nila had left that as it took the bit of the edge off, but now I'm thirsty. I wonder where I can get some water, or more of that tea."

He got up and headed out of the tent, stood there in the early morning sunlight looking around and he noticed a man walking towards him. When he got closer, Ryan noticed it was Tolbar.

As he approached Ryan he said, "Hello Ryan."

Ryan thought about what Tolbar had said and quickly concluded that the word in front of his name must be a form of greeting, so he looked at Tolbar and said, "Hello Tolbar."

A big smile came across Tolbar's face, and he nodded his head. Ryan was pleased with himself as he formed his first small sentence. "Baby steps." He thought to himself.

Tolbar walked up to him, looked at him momentarily like he was thinking about something then held up one finger as if he were going to show Ryan something.

Tolbar then acted like he was sleeping, then waking up, stretched, and made a movement like he was looking out of his tent or looking out of someplace. He then made a wave of his hand up into the sky and he said to Ryan, "Morning."

Ryan wasn't too sure that he understood what he meant, but then Tollbar repeated the movements and said, "Morning."

Ryan thought he got the idea, and said, "Morning."

Tolbar smiled and then added a word in front of it. Ryan thought about that for a moment wondering if that might not be the word for good. Ryan looked at Tolbar and then said, "Good morning."

A big smile came over Tolbar's face again, and he nodded his head.

Ryan thought about it for a moment then quickly turned around and started walking away. Tolbar was a little surprised at the abrupt move that Ryan just made and thought he may have done something to offend him.

When Ryan had gotten about ten feet away, he turned around and then started heading back towards Tolbar. Tolbar watched Ryan approach unsure what was happening, suddenly Ryan waved to Tolbar and said, "Hello Tolbar. Good morning."

Tolbar just started to laugh, then walked up and slapped Ryan on the shoulder and said, "Good." While he was nodding his head, confirming what Ryan had thought about the word before morning being good.

Tolbar looked at Ryan then nodded his head up and down exaggeratedly like he did the night before, and then said, "Yes."

Ryan nodded his head up and down, copying Tolbar and said, "Yes,"

Tolbar then moved his head from side to side looking at Ryan, and said, "No."

This was an easy one for Ryan to pick up. Tolbar then motioned for Ryan to follow as he started walking back to the elongated fire pit that they were at yesterday. As they got close Ryan could see Skytal and Corna sitting with some other people Ryan did not know.

Ryan looked at Skytal and said, "Hello Skytal. Good morning."

Skytal looked up at Ryan in surprise, smiled back, and said "Good morning to you, Ryan."

Ryan then looked at Corna and said, "Hello Corna. Good morning."

Corna just smiled and nodded his head. He then looked at Tolbar and said, "I see you have started to teach him early this morning."

Tolbar Just smiled and answered, "Yes, and he is picking it up quite fast, I am surprised." Tolbar looked at Ryan, pointed to a basket sitting beside the fire and asked, "Tea?"

Ryan looked at Tolbar and answered, "Yes."

Again, surprising the people sitting around the fire. Someone handed Ryan a hot cup of tea. As Ryan took a sip, he noticed that it had a different flavour than the one that he had had last night, this one tasted a little fruity like there might be some berries or something inside of it.

Ryan found the taste quite enjoyable and sat drinking his tea, listening to the people around him talk.

He noticed that he could make out a few words, but still was not able to put any sentences together. He heard Skytal mention Latona and Nila, when he looked up, he noticed Skytal looking past him. Ryan turned around and saw the man and the woman approaching the group.

As they got close, Ryan stood up, turned around and said, "Hello Latona, Nila, good morning."

Nila raised her eyebrows and smiled, and Latona looked at her and then looked at Ryan, "Good morning, Ryan." they said.

Ryan just smiled back. Latona looked at the group of people and asked, "So, who has been teaching Ryan this morning?"

Corna answered, "Tolbar and Ryan arrived this morning together, so we're pretty sure that Tolbar is the one responsible."

"Good for you Tolbar." said Latona.

Tolbar looked at Latona and said, "Last night Ryan came and joined us singing around the fire."

Latona looked surprised and asked, "He just came, and joined you?"

Skylar answered. "Yes, he came up to us with the wolf, introduced himself, and we introduced ourselves to him. He sat down and drank tea with us, and after a while Rocano asked him to join us, and he did."

"Well, it doesn't seem to be taking Ryan long to meet people, does it now." said Nila with a smile.

Ryan looked at Nila smiled and asked, "Tea?"

Again, Nila looked surprised, nodded her head, and answered, "Yes please."

Ryan seemed quite full of himself and got her a cup of tea.

Latona sat and said, "Well, everybody seems to have been busy this morning teaching Ryan how to talk."

Tolbar said, "He has a long way to go, but he has a very quick head for our language. Not only that, but his memory also seems to be very good as well."

As Ryan was sitting there drinking his tea the little girl from the night before came running up, and she was holding a big leaf in her hand.

She smiled at Ryan, pointed to the leaf, and said, "Leaf.

Ryan smiled back at her, pointed to the leaf, and then repeated, "Leaf."

A large smile spread across the young girl's face. The more Ryan looked at her the more she reminded him of his goddaughter, and he wondered if he would ever see her again. The little girl sat down next to Ryan and started petting the little pup at Ryan's feet.

"I have noticed that the little wolf does not stray too far from Ryan." Tolbar said, and then continued, "I don't know but for some reason he has now included Ryan into his pack."

I thought he would be a little young for that, would he not?" asked Latona.

I'm not too sure since this little one only wandered into our camp two weeks ago. We figured that the mother must have been killed because we have not seen her, or it was cast out because of its color. We have not seen any wolves coming close to the camp for a couple of moons." Said Skytal

The little girl was sitting on the log, dangling her legs, and looking up at Ryan. She reached up and touched his hair, and when Ryan turned and looked at her, she noticed for the first time how blue his eyes were.

Her little eyes opened wide, and she stood up and moved her face closer to Ryan, looking at the colour of his eyes, Ryan couldn't resist himself. When she got close, Ryan quickly gave her a kiss on the nose. and tickled her like he used to do with his goddaughter. The girl squealed in delight and backed away giggling. Everyone around the fire smiled.

"It looks like he is also good with children." said the little girl's Mother.

The little girl then sat down next to Ryan, looking up at him and smiling. She clapped herself on the chest and said, "I am Tisha."

Ryan saw the gesture, and heard what she said, he then looked at her and said, "Hello Tisha. I am Ryan."

A big smile came across the little girl's face, and she looked over at her mother, who was also smiling.

"What are your plans for Ryan today?" Tolbar asked Latona.

Latona looked at Ryan and answered, "We have no plans. We are just going to let him do whatever he wants to do and see what happens."

"That will be interesting." Replied Tolbar, then continued, "As he is not familiar with the language."

"That is true." Nila said, "But he is starting to pick it up quite quickly."

Ryan watched the people talk knowing that he was the subject of the discussion but couldn't figure out what they were saying. He thought, "Well at least they're all smiling so it can't be all bad."

The little girl looked at her mother, "Can I play with Ryan?" She asked looking at Ryan.

Her mother smiled and said, "Tisha, leave Ryan alone for the morning, and maybe he will want to play with you in the afternoon."

"OK mother." said Tisha still smiling and went back to petting the pup, who then rolled over on his back to get a belly rub.

The mother motioned towards Ryan, putting her hand to her mouth as if she were eating.

Ryan understood what she was asking and shook his head answering, "No." and then mimed opening a package and eating.

Nila got the idea that he wasn't hungry because he finished off the package that she left with him last night. People started getting up and walking away from the fire pit and Ryan watched them go. No one made any offer for him to follow them, so he just sat there comfortably listening to the people talk. Latona and Nila got up and started to walk away, Ryan half expected them to invite him to come along, but they did not.

"Oh well." thought Ryan, "I guess I'm on my own for today."

Tolbar Looked over at Ryan, held up his cup and asked, "More tea?"

Ryan handed Tobar his cup and answered "Yes,"

Tolbar filled Ryan's cup, and they both sat there until Tolbar had finished his tea. He then put his hand on Ryan's shoulder, got up and slowly walked away leaving Ryan at the fire with Tisha and her mother. A short time later Tisha's mother got up and motioned for Tisha to follow her, and the two of them walked away.

Ryan thought, "Well this is great. Maybe I'll just go around and explore and see what's happening.

Ryan finished his tea, put his cup with the other ones that were laying there and then got up and started walking away. He wandered out into the field and was looking at the tents and how they were constructed. He found it fascinating, almost like he was at some heritage park, but this was real. He walked to the far end of the encampment, which was the farthest point away from the river, and then turned around and started heading back. He passed the tents as well as the elongated fire pit and looked over to his right, he saw three women cutting up meat and hanging it on some form of racks. There were four small smoky fires at each corner of where the racks were located.

"Looks Like they're smoking the meat." Ryan said to himself.

As Ryan and the pup walked up, he watched the women cutting the meat into small thin strips and then hanging them on a rack made of saplings and small branches.

The women looked up as Ryan approached and stood there watching them for a while. Ryan pointed to the meat then to himself and then back to the meet again, trying to ask if they wanted him to help. The women smiled and waved their hands for him to sit down. Ryan sat down and watched the women for a few minutes, to see how they were cutting the meat, and then pulled out the knife that Latona gave him and copied their movements. The pup sat next to Ryan and then laid down. Once he had cut a small piece off the carcass about three inches wide and six inches long and relatively thin, he hung it over the rack.

He noticed that there was the young boy from last night at the fire pit who was standing there amongst the smoke, and he had a branch from some form of evergreen tree and was moving it around to keep the insects off the meat. Ryan worked with the women, taking it all in. He came to the realization that they were not smoking the meat, they were hanging the meat out to dry, and the young lad was keeping flies and other insects off the meat. The women started to quietly chant while they worked, which Ryan found quite enjoyable.

A little while later, Nila approached the group of women and said, "I came to see if you needed help, but I see you have already gotten help from Ryan."

One of the women looked up and said. "Yes, he just came upon us and asked if he could help."

Another woman looked up and said, "You know we're not going to turn down any help when it is offered for drying meat. So, if you still want to help Nila, more hands make the work go quicker."

Nila just smiled and sat down and started carving up the deer. She watched Ryan as he worked and thought how him offering to help without being asked is a good sign of a person's character.

"I will have to make sure that I mention this to Latona. He will be interested." Thought Nila.

Ryan heard the young boy starting to cough, and then a little bit more as a smoke grew thicker.

He stood up, walked into the centre of the racks, reached down and gently took the branch away from the young man and handed him his knife and pointed back to the deer. The young boy looked at him, then looked at the women and walked over and started carving up the meat. Ryan made sure to keep the bugs and flies off the meat.

The pup got up to join Ryan but decided he did not like the smoke and went back to where he was originally, laid down watching Ryan.

The women looked at each other and smiled. Nila then looked at the young boy and said, "Well Mekome, it looks like you're getting a bit of a break today."

 "Yes, I am." said the young boy, "I didn't even ask for help. He just came and offered."

One of the women looked at the young boy and said, "That's because he could see the smoke was starting to bother you and he wanted to give you a bit of a break."

 "Well, that was really nice of him." said Mekome as he started carving up the deer into small strips and hanging them.

Yes, it was." commented Nila.

 The large group made short work of getting the deer cut and hung to dry. Now it was just a matter of letting it dry and keeping the bugs from it with the smoke and Ryan. Ryan offered to stay with the smoke and take care of that job, however Nila shooed him, and Mekome away as two other young boys came up to take their place.

Ryan looked at Mekome and said, "I am Ryan."

The young boy said, "Yes, I know. I am Mekome."

Ryan nodded his head and said, "Hello Mekome."

Mekome smiled and said, "Hello Ryan."

The two continued walking towards the lodge mounds, then passed them and headed towards the river.

Ryan heard someone calling out Mekome's name and when he turned around, he saw Tisha running up to them.

"Where are you taking Ryan?" she asked.

"We were just going for a walk to the river." said Mekome."

"OK." said Tisha, "I'm coming too." As she fell in beside them.

Once they reached the bank of the river, Ryan stood there for a few moments looking up the river and then down the other way, trying to remember the last time he was here. He was sure that just to the south of where they were now standing there was a bridge that took you to the other side of the river. As he looked across the river to the east, he remembered that huge Palatial hotel that was up there.

"What was that called?" He thought to himself. "Oh yes, it was the Banff Spring".

Ryan remembered staying there once for a couple of nights with his ex-girlfriend, and how lavish it was. He felt a little tug on his shirt and when he looked down, Tisha was looking at him and pointing down towards the river. "River." She said.

Ryan nodded his head in understanding. Tisha said it two more times, and Ryan concluded she wanted him to say it. So, he repeated the word, smiled and they started walking down towards the edge of the river.

Mekome put his hand in the water, held it up and let it fall through his fingers. He did it two or three times then looked at Ryan, did it one more time and said, "Water."

Ryan Repeated the word, "Water."

Mekome wiggled his finger, then moved his arm, pointing up and down the river and said, "River."

Ryan bent down, cupped his hands and dipped them into the water, he lifted his hands up letting the water fall out of his hands and then said, "Water." Then looking at both the children pointed out towards the river and said, "River."

Both children smiled and nodded their heads vigorously. They were enjoying being able to help an adult speak. They walked back up the riverbank onto the field, and when they looked around, they noticed that the pup had a stick in its mouth. Ryan smiled, bent down and went to take the stick out of the puppy's mouth. The puppy was not having any of that and refused to let go, Ryan tussled with the little pup for a while and eventually got to stick for himself. He waved it around with the little pup jumping up and down, and then threw it a little way into the field. The puppy bounded off after it. He picked up the stick and then came running back, but not right up to Ryan or the children. He laid down about six feet away chewing on the stick and keeping an eye on Ryan.

Ryan smiled and thought to himself, "Oh, I played this game many times before, and you're not going to win."

He casually walked up to the puppy, as if he wasn't paying any attention, then he quickly reached out and grabbed the stick away from the pup. The puppy jumped up barking. Ryan threw the stick again, this time further and the puppy went running after it. This time the children went running after the puppy as well.

Ryan thought it would be interesting to see who was going to get there first, the children or the puppy. Tisha got to the stick first and held it up. The little puppy barked at her and made it very clear that he wanted the stick back. Tisha threw it towards Ryan, and the little puppy was off again. Ryan pretended to run towards the stick but let the puppy get there before him.

The puppy scooped up the stick and started running in circles with the children and Ryan running after it.

Back in the camp, Kanti, and Cita were standing on the top of Nila's lodge, watching the scene below. Nila smiled looked at Kanti and Cita and said, "Ryan seems to have a way with the children as well as the wolf.'

"The children do seem to like him." said Kanti with a smile.

Nila turned and looked at her daughter, when Kanti noticed her mothers' eyes upon her the smile left her face. She said, "But we still know nothing about this man." And then slowly started to walk away.

"He seems to be having fun." Latona said to his mate.

"Yes, he does. Their mother is probably going to be very thankful that he is wearing them out and they will sleep well tonight." Nila answered.

The group was running around the field chasing each other, when suddenly Tisha stopped and looked across the river. Her brother Mekome stopped and gazed over to where she was looking. Tisha then said a word that Ryan didn't understand. Ryan stopped then turned and looked across the river to where the children were staring, he noticed a wolf pack hugging the tree line on the other side heading down stream. Ryan looked at the children and looked over at the wolves across the river and repeated the word he had heard Tisha say.

Tisha then pointed across the river and said, "Wolfs." She then pointed down to the little pup and said, "Wolf.".

Ryan was a little confused and pointed across the river, looking at Tisha he asked, 'Wolves?"

Tisha Nodded her head and answered, "Yes."

Ryan then pointed at the little pup who was now sitting down looking up at him, and then said, "Wolves."

Tisha shook her head no, held up one finger and said, "Wolf."

Ryan couldn't believe it. He thought this was just a dog, now it turns out it's a wolf. Then he thought about it for a moment, "If I'm back as far as I think I am, I don't know how many dogs I would find out in the wilderness, if any at all." He then looked down and tussled ahead of the small pup and said, "Well, I really don't care. You are a cute little fella whether you're a dog or a wolf." The wolf just walked over and picked up the stick again, trying to get the game started once more.

Ryan decided he was going to let the children continue playing with the little pup as he was tired. He sat on the grass and watched the children chase the wolf all over the field. Ryan was surprised when it was the children that got tired before the pup and came back and sat with Ryan. The pup trotted over with his stick, laid it down and then laid down in front of it, guarding it. Ryan looked over at Tisha and Mekome and could see they were both totally exhausted. Tisha got up, said something to Mekome who then got up as well. They looked at Ryan and motioned him to follow.

As they were walking, the children were pointing out all sorts of different things and telling Ryan what they were.

Mekome and Tisha would run, come back, look at Ryan and say, "Run."

Ryan was getting the idea of what the two children were trying to do as they were walking along. Mekome said something to Tisha, and they stopped. Ryan looked at both and watched them closely. Mekome said, "Mekome." then pointed to Tisha and said, "Tisha, teach Ryan to talk."

Ryan thought about it briefly and got the gist of what they were trying to tell him, but there was a word in there that he didn't understand, he repeated that word to Mekome and shrugged his shoulders.

Mekome looked at Tisha, said something to her, and then he got down on the ground and rolled from side to side. He stood up, pointed to Tisha and she got down and rolled from side to side. Ryan still didn't quite understand what they were trying to say and shrugged his shoulders again. Mekome thought about it for a few more moments and then held his hand and closed it into a fist. He showed it to Tisha, then put up one finger, then said a word, raised another finger, then said a word, and then another finger and then said a word. Tisha looked at Mekome and then did the same thing.

Ryan clapped his hands and patted Tisha on the shoulder as their meaning came to him.

He looked at the children and then said, "Tisha, Mekome, teach Ryan talk."

Both children smiled and nodded their heads. Ryan was quite pleased that he figured it out. Ryan always was always quick at picking up other languages, but it was usually over a little longer period. He had always heard that immersion in the language was the quickest way to learn and is now finding out that it is true.

No one in this village or camp speaks English, so he is now being forced to learn their language and is putting in extra effort to do so. The children started walking and waiting for him to follow. Ryan didn't know where they were going but again had nothing better to do so he followed them.

The children walked up to a small group of people that were sitting and talking. Ryan recognized one of the women as one that was sitting around the fire this morning.

Tisha walked up to the woman and started talking to her, "Hi mother." Tisha said.

"Where have you been all morning, Tisha?" Her mother asked.

"We've been out with Ryan teaching him how to talk in our language." Tisha said with a smile.

The mother looked at the little girl sceptically, then Mekome chimed in, "It is true, and he has learned a lot of words today."

"I hope you haven't been bothering Ryan and making pests of yourself." she said to her two children. "No, we went and played with the wolf pup down by the river." Tisha said.

The woman looked up at Ryan and smiled and said, "Hello Ryan, I am Ayana."

Ryan smiled at the woman and replied, "Hello Ayana." Then because he couldn't think of anything else to say, still smiling and added, "Tisha and Mekome teach me talk."

Ayana smiled at him, then looked at the children and nodded her head.

"Is there any food or water mother?" Tisha asked, "We are quite thirsty and I am sure Ryan is probably as hungry as we are."

"I have some food left over from this morning for you." Ayana answered, then she got up and walked away. Ryan heard the word food and was hoping the conversation meant that she was going off to get some food, because he was very hungry. When she returned, she had a wooden platter with meat and some form of root vegetables on it. As well as a stomach bladder filled with water. She also had some cups, she handed one to Ryan and pointed to the stomach to see if you wanted water.

Ryan nodded his head and said, "Yes,"

Ayana poured a couple cups of water, then placed the platter down. The children started reaching for the food and Ayana said something and both the children stopped and looked at Ryan. She then looked at Ryan, smiled and pointed to the food.

"OK, I guess guests must go first." Ryan thought as he reached down, picked up a piece of meat and grabbed a piece of what looks like a cooked root.

The meat was tender, and he tore a piece off to give it to the pup. Ayana smiled, took a piece of meat from the platter, ripped it into shreds and then laid it on the ground for the pup to have. After Ryan had taken food from the platter Ayana told the children to help themselves, which they did eagerly. Ryan held up a piece of the root and tasted it. To his surprise it reminded him of something, but he could not quite put his finger on it. It was good but then again, he was so hungry, bark would have probably tasted good at that time.

Ryan looked at Ayana and said, "Food, good," and wished he knew how to say thank you.

Ryan sat eating his meal and enjoying the companionship of the people that were around him.

He even started to understand some of what they were talking about based on the amount of words that the children and other people had taught him. He couldn't understand it all, but in some situations, he understood enough where he could smile, and nod his agreement.

As Ryan was sitting there enjoying his midday meal, Cita, and Kanti were walking across the field. Cita looked over and noticed Ryan sitting with a small group of people, and said to Kanti, "Well that Ryan sure seems to be making friends, doesn't he?"

"Yes, he does. I saw him this morning playing with the children and the wolf pup." Kanti said.

Cita noticed that as they were walking Kanti was staring in that direction, she smiled and said, "He is quite an attractive man. Even though it takes a while to get used to the light hair, the white skin, but those blue eyes are beautiful."

Kanti looked at her friend and said, "You can not be serious. You could not be considering Ryan?"

Cita got a coy smile on her face and said, "He might be worth a little fun in my bed furs."

Kanti's eyes opened wide, and she exclaimed, "You can not be serious?"

"I do not know Kanti. I have listened to a few of the girls talk, and there's more than one that would not mind climbing into his tent with him." Cita said. She then noticed that Kanti was still looking over at Ryan and she could tell that she was getting upset.

Cita asked Kanti, "Do you have feelings for this man?"

Kanti turned around quickly and looked at Cita answering, "No I do not!"

Cita thought "That response was a little too quick and a little too adamant. She smiled and said, "You know Kanti, your mate has been dead for two and a half years. It would be OK for you to find somebody else."

"I know." Said Kanti, looking down then back up and over in Ryan's direction, "But I just haven't found anybody yet."

Cita saw where she was looking and said, "Really, I'm surprised. What about Stakota, he has been telling everybody that you're going to be his mate. That would not be such a bad thing, would it?"

"No, I guess it would not, except I am going to be the one who decides what mate I have, not anyone else. Stakota is a nice man, however he is very arrogant, and I have not made my mind up on him yet." Kanti answered.

"Well, he has made his mind up on you." Cita said with a smile.

"Well good for him." Kanti said.

The two girls continue to cross the field, and Cita noticed that Kanti looked back three or four times in Ryan's direction.

"Oh yes, there's definitely some interest there." Cita thought, "It will be fun to see how this develops."

Ryan sat eating with Ayana and the children, but they were not eating in silence. The children kept peppering him with words continuously, everything from the type of food they were eating. too items in the surrounding area.

Ayana finally looked at the children and said, "Let Ryan eat in peace."

Ryan just looked up at Ayana smiled and said, "No, OK. They teach me."

Ayana just smiled back at Ryan and admired how much patience he had to put up with the continuous chatter from the children who were treating it like a game. Ayana sat there and listened for a while, occasionally stopping the children, and correcting some things that they may have said wrong. She also helped put some things into context for Ryan to help him better understand what the children were trying to say. Ayana soon got caught up in the game as well and started putting words and sentences together for Ryan. They also taught Ryan how to say, "Thank you." For which Ryan was greatly appreciative.

After a while, Ryan raised both of his hands and said, "Ok, good."

The children and Anna all got the idea, enough learning for today.

Ryan stood up, smiled, and said, "Thank you."

Ayana smiled at Ryan, she was very surprised at the speed he was picking up the language.

Ayana said, "OK Ryan, goodbye."

Ryan smiled, waved, turned, and walked away. As he was walking away, it occurred to Ryan. He really had nowhere to go, or anything to do for that matter. He looked around and noticed it was hard to get a feel how many people were actually in this camp because they seem to be coming and going and doing different things. Nobody was sitting around doing nothing, that seems to be an activity for the evening.

Suddenly Ryan remembered a thought he had the night before. "Where are the horses?"

He had been to the north side of the camp, and he had been to the riverside.

He knew the trenches were to the east, so we thought he started to walk towards the west. Once he got into the tree line, he found a trail and remembered it was the trail that they came in on, so he knew there was nothing down that way. Ryan walked up to the river and then headed down in the opposite direction that he and the children were playing at earlier in the day. After about ten or fifteen minutes of walking down by the river, he turned around, headed back, came through the camp and walked ten or fifteen minutes in the other direction. He saw a few people sitting on the riverbank, weaving baskets, or doing other such things, but he did not approach them. "I don't want to become nuisance to these people." Ryan thought as he was looking around. Ryan slowly came to the conclusion, "There's no horses around here."

"How is that possible? How did they get around? There are absolutely no horses, that means…." He stopped for a second, thought hard, trying to remember what he was taught in college. Suddenly it came to him in a flash. "Horses haven't always been in North America, they weren't introduced in North America until…. Crap, when was that. Shit, that was around the 1500's. OK, well that's totally a great reason, but at least I know if there are no horses around and they don't know what horses are, we're going back past the 1500s. but I'm also getting a feeling it's going back further than that, I just don't know how far."

Ryan decided that he may as well go back to the tent, lay down and have a nap. As he was walking back, he noticed some people doing something to a hide that was tied up onto a rack. It looks like they were scraping it with some form of rock knife. He stood there and watched for a while seeing that the three women were working on what looks like a deer hide.

Ryan felt kind of silly standing there just watching them, so he turned and headed back to his tent with the little wolf pup following close behind him.

"So how was your day today?" Nila asked her daughter.

"It was good." Kanti said, "Cita and I went visiting some of our friends and helped with some baskets.

"Oh, did you bring any of the baskets back here?" Nila asked.

"No, we left them at Cita's, I will probably pick them up and bring them here tomorrow. How many do you need?" Kanti inquired.

"Two or three would be nice. Did you weave any cooking baskets?" Nila asked.

"Yes, I did. I'll make sure that we bring you one by tomorrow." Kanti said.

"Tolbar and a few of the men have gone on a hunt today, so hopefully luck will be with them, and they will come back with some more deer meat." Latona said.

"Are you going on the Buffalo hunt up the valley. Asked Kanti.

"Yes, Tolbar, Skylar, Lacano, and a few of the other men will be going as well as your mother and a few other women. Would you like to come?"

"I'm sure she would like to come to see Stakota." Said Nila.

Kanti just looked at her mother and said, "I do not need to see him."

"Well, I'm pretty sure he needs to see you." Nila said to her daughter. Then turning to Latona, she asked, "Do you think you will take Ryan with you to hunt Buffalo?"

"I'm not too sure." said Latona. "He seems like a very smart man, yet there are a lot of things I believe he does not know, and I am pretty sure he has never hunted Buffalo before."

"Well would now not be a good time to teach him." Nila asked.

"Maybe so, we will see how it goes." Latona answered.

Nila said, "I talked to Ayana today and she mentioned that in the very short time that Ryan has been here he is picking up our language fairly well."

"Well, that is good. The sooner he learns, the sooner we will be able to ask him questions, like where he is from, how did he get here, and where are his people." Said Latona.

"I don't know how someone could just travel with no clothes, no additional clothing, no knife, no companion, unless possibly he lost it all somewhere." Nila said.

"That is possible." said Latona, "But we will have to wait. I know the clothing that he has now are the only clothes that he has. I wonder if we should ask around and see if anybody has any spare clothing that they would be willing to give to Ryan to help him out."

"Are you thinking of doing a talking circle? Asked Nila.

"No." Answered Latona, "Not now, but I think we are going to have to have one sometime in the near future."

Nila looked over at her daughter and asked, "Kanti do you not have some of Toltin's old clothes?"

Kanti looked over at her mother and said, "Yes, but I am not sure if I am willing to part with them yet or not."

Mila turned, looked at her daughter and said, "You know, it has been over two years since Toltin left us."

Kanti lowered her head and said in a quiet voice, "I know mother."

"Do you not think it might be time to let go of the past and move on."

When Kanti did not answer, Latona looked at his mate and said, "Kanti, there is no need to decide now, your mother just thought it might have been a good Idea. If you're not ready, you are not ready, do not worry about it."

Kanti sat there thinking about it. It was true, her mate had been gone over two years, but she still missed him. If only he had run instead of trying to fight the great bear, he would be alive today. She smiled a little and thought that running was never anything that he would do.

The three sat in silence and then suddenly Kanti said, "You are right mother, I do have some things that I could take over for Ryan. He looks like he's close to the same size as Toltin was, so I will take some things over for him and we will see if they fit."

Nila smiled, looked at her daughter and said, "That is a good thing." and then continued in her mind. "Hopefully, you will be able to get on with your life."

As Ryan was walking back to the tent, he came upon Corna, who was talking to somebody. As Ryan walked up, that person had her back towards him, Ryan knew by the height and the gray hair who it was.

Corna looked up over the person he was talking to, smiled, and said, "Hello Ryan."

Ryan waved and said, "Hello Corna."

The old lady turned around and looked at Ryan and before she could say anything Ryan said, "Hello Skyseeker. How are you?"

The old woman just looked at Ryan and a small smile crept across her face, "Good Ryan, and you?" she asked.

"Good," answered Ryan.

"He is coming along learning the language, is he not Skyseeker?" Corna stated.

"Yes, he seems to be picking it up very fast." She said staring at Ryan. Then continued, "I have many questions to ask you, so hopefully you learned quickly."

Ryan picked up a few of the words, and was quite pleased that he could do that, even though he couldn't quite understand the entire conversation.

Ryan waved and started to walk away, turned, and said, "Goodbye."

Both smiled, looked at each other and then back at him and said, "Goodbye Ryan."

When Ryan got back to the tent the little pup went running in and sat on Ryan's bed. Ryan felt like he could use a little nap but didn't want to sleep too long. He stretched out on the bed and slowly closed eyes. and promptly fell asleep.

Ryan was lying naked in the field next to the river, coming towards him in the distance, also naked was a beautiful woman with long black hair and dark skin. As she got closer, she called his name once and continued to walk towards him.

When he got up to him, she said his name one more time, and then sat down next to him. Ryan sat up and put his arm around the beautiful woman and pulled her towards him. He looked longingly into her eyes and moved his lips close to hers.

Just then, Ryan heard the pup barking and woke up. He laid there for a few moments looking around and was incredibly disappointed that it was only a dream. He noticed a pup prancing back-and-forth in front of the tent flap. He then heard his name called from the other side of the flap.

"Coming." He called out as he got up and headed for the tent flap. As he pulled it open, he saw Kanti standing there holding a large bundle.

Instantly a huge smile broke across Ryans face, and he said, "Hello, come in," and motioned for her to come in.

Kanti noticed the expression on his face change instantly the moment that he saw her and felt her face turn red. "Don't be such a stupid little girl." she thought to herself, "You are not a young girl that gets silly when a young man pays attention to her. So, stop it now." Kanti lowered her head and walked past Ryan into the tent.

Ryan followed her and watched her take the bundle and put it on the ground, then untie the cord that was holding the bundle together. Ryan was trying to figure out what it was that she had brought him when suddenly she held up a pair of pants, and then held up another pair of pants.

"Of course." Ryan thought, "Clothes. I never even thought of that. These are the only clothes that I have, and I'm going to need other ones. I wonder why she brought them to me?"

Kanti held out something that Ryan was not too sure exactly what it was. Ryan took it from her, looked at it, and then shrugged his shoulders and then handed it back to her. Kanti smiled and wrapped it around her waist and tied it in a certain way. It then occurred to Ryan that he saw Tolbar wearing something similar the other day. He smiled, took it from her and then wrapped it around his waist and tied it the same way. She smiled and nodded her head. Kanti then pulled out a couple of tunics with sleeves and one without. Kanti then pulled out one last tunic, this one was something that pulled over your head and had long sleeves. Ryan held it out and looked at it.

It was heavily decorated with different colour beads and other items that Ryan could not identify. The decorations were beautiful, and Ryan ran his fingers over the beads and the other items. Kanti was smiling as she watched Ryan admire the garment and could tell that he appreciated the decorations on it. This pleased her because she had put many days into making that tunic for her mate and she was happy to see that the person that was getting it now was going to appreciate it as much as he did.

Kanti looked at Ryan and said, "Ryan, try it on."

Ryan didn't understand the full sentence but got his name and on, so he assumed that she would like him to try it on and see if it fit. Ryan smiled, nodded his head, and then started to undo his shirt. As he pulled it open Kanti noticed how firm Ryan's chest and stomach were, and then had to catch herself as she was staring. Again, her face started to redden, and she looked away.

Ryan caught this and smiled to himself. Ryan then removed his shirt as Kanti was turning around to look at him. Suddenly, her eyes flew open wide, and she let out a gasp. She then turned around and ran from the tent.

Ryan stood there for a moment dumbfounded. He looked down a little wolf pup and asked, "What the fuck was that all about?" The little pup just sat down, looked up at him with his tongue hanging out the side of his mouth. "Yeah, I guess I didn't really expect you to answer." Ryan added.

 Ryan listens and he could hear loud conversations happening away from the tent. He was going to go out and see what was going on, but then thought better of it and started to put his shirt back on. Suddenly, the tent flap opened and Skyseeker, Latona, Tolbar and another elderly gentleman man that Ryan had never met before walked into the tent. Skyseeker walked up to Ryan and took the shirt away from him, then grabbed his left arm and stared at his tattoo.

 "Shit." thought Ryan. "I never thought of that. I've had it for so long. I forget that I even have it. These people would've never have seen a tattoo that looks like this."

 The old woman had a firm grasp on Ryan's wrist and was pulling his arm straight so she could get a good look at the tattoo. She then licked her thumb and rubbed it on the tattoo to see if it would come off or smudge. When it didn't, she stared up into Ryan's eyes, the same as when he first met her. Ryan could feel her eyes pierce into him and decided this was not the time for him to capitulate and stared right back at her. The two locked eyes for what seemed like an eternity, but was only a few seconds, then the old woman nodded her head once, said something to the other elderly man that was with him, and the two of them walked out of the tent.

 Latona walked up to Ryan and stood there looking at the tattoo.

Nila came into the tent and asked Latona, "What is Kanti so upset about?"

Latona looked at his mate and motioned her to come over. "Have a look at this." He said to her.

Nila looked at the tattoo on Ryan's arm and sucked in her breath. "It is like somebody captured the spirit of the great brother bear and put it onto Ryan's arm. Is it painted?' she asked.

"No, Skyseeker tried to wipe it off and it looks like it is permanent." Answered Latona.

"Another mystery from our new strange friend." Latona said.

Ryan didn't say anything and let them look at the tattoo. He knew at some point they were going to ask him about it, and he was going to have to find a way to explain it, along with a lot of other things.

Ryan decided to lighten the mood, smiled, slapped his right hand across the tattoo a couple of times and said, "Tattoo."

Latona looked at the rendering of the bear and marvelled at how precise it was. He then looked at Ryan questioningly and asked, "Taboo."

Ryan shook his head, tapped his arm again and said, "No, tattoo."

Latona nodded his head and then repeated, "Tattoo."

Ryan smiled and then tried on the decorated outfit that Kanti had brought him, both to see if it would fit and to cover up the tattoo and hopefully end the conversation. The tunic fit like it was made, especially for him. Nila looked at it and motioned him to put his arms out so she could see how it hung. She then said to Ryan, "Very good."

Ryan just nodded his head in agreement and ran his fingers across the beads that were decorating the front of it. He looked at Nila and said, "Tell Kanti thank you."

"We will," said Latona. Then turned to his mate and said, "I can not believe she parted with Toltin's meeting tunic."

"Neither can I." said Nila, "But then what reason would she have to continue to keep it. I'm hoping that maybe by doing this and giving away some of these items she could start forgetting a bit of the past."
I don't think she will ever forget Toltin." said Lakota.

"I do not want her to forget her past, what I want her to forget is the grieving that she's been going through for the last two years, and for her to start living her life again. Nila said as they both left Ryans tent.

Once everyone had left the tent, Ryan sat down on his bed roll and looked around. The little wolf pup came over and stretched out next to Ryan, looking up at him. Ryan reached down and started scratching the little wolf behind his ear and said, "Well that was interesting, wasn't a little guy. I keep forgetting where I am, or when I am for that matter."

Ryan continued to pet the little wolf and then went on. "I know at some point I'm going to have to explain where I come from as well as this tattoo on my arm. These people have been more than gracious. They have welcomed me and are treating me like one of their own.They are feeding me. They are teaching me and supplying me with all the things I need. I wonder if the roles were reversed if my kind would be as gracious. I'd like to think we would, but somehow, I doubt it."

The little pup just continued to enjoy getting scratched and then rolled over to get his stomach rubbed. "Well, you're a spoiled little thing, aren't you?" Ryan said to the wolf. "Well, what do you think? Should I just tell them I'm from the future and have no idea how I got here, or should I come up with some other explanation that maybe easier for them to understand? I'm definitely going to have to give it a lot of thought. As I'm starting to understand their language and they realize it I'm going to be getting more questions. The old woman Skyseeker seems incredibly sharp. It's almost like she knows what's going on but isn't letting on."

Ryan stopped rubbing the wolf's belly and it let out a little yip, then stood up and faced the flap of the tent entrance of the tent. Ryan heard someone scratching on the flap and then heard his name called. The pup rushed to the flap and let out a few yips. Ryan got up and opened the flap and saw Tisha there smiling up at him.

Ryan smiled and said, "Hi Tisha."

"Hi Ryan." Tisha answered, "You come and eat with us?"

Ryan thought that sounded like a pretty good idea because he was starting to get hungry, "Yes." Ryan said,

Tisha smiled up at Ryan and said, "Come on let's go. Everyone is at the fire. I think we are having moose today." Ryan understood some of it, but not all of it so he just looked at Tisha and said, "Good." and then continued to follow the little girl to the fire pit.

As they were walking towards the pit, Ryan noticed that it was starting to get dark. He must have been sleeping for a while. He thought, "No wonder I'm hungry."

When they arrived at the fire pit Ryan saw Tisha's mother as well as Lakota, and Nila. He looked over and saw Kanti there as well. He smiled at her, and she just lowered her head.

As he got closer to the fire, she got up and walked over to him. She looked up at Ryan and said, "I am sorry Ryan, I did not mean to run away. It was rude of me."

Ryan understood that she was saying she was sorry but did not understand some of the conversation, so he just looked at her, put a broad smile on his face and said, "It Ok. Good."

Kanti looked up at Ryan, smiling at his attempt to tell her it was Ok, nodded and her head said, "Thank you." Then turned around and walked back towards the fire.

Ryan followed her with Tisha at his side, when he got to the fire pit Tisha sat down and grabbed Ryan's arm so that he would sit down next to her.

Tisha's mother Ayana smiled at Ryan and asked, "Are you hungry?" She then rubbed her stomach while asking the question.

Ryan nodded his head and answered "Yes!" a bit too loud.

The people around the fire smiled seeing that Ryan was starting to understand their language a little better.

Ayana handed Ryan a wooden cup and said, "Tea."

Ryan took the cup and said, "Thank you."

He sipped the tea and found this one similar to the one that he had the other day that seemed to have a hint of berries in it. He was beginning to think that this was his favorite. Ayana then handed him what looked like an antler platter that had a generous slice of meat on it with some cooked greens on the side.

Ryan started cutting the meat and sat and listened to everybody's conversation. Ryan was pleased at how much he could understand. He felt that if he could understand three or four words in the sentence, he could almost make out what they were talking about, but knew it was going to take a lot longer before he could carry on a full conversation. As Ryan sat there listening, he cut up some of his meat and gave it to the little wolf pup. Tisha also cut up some of her meat and fed it to the little Pup. Ayana, seeing this, cut some meat into small chunks and placed it in front of the little wolf, which the little wolf devoured eagerly.

When they were finished eating, Ryan fell to tug on his arm. He looked down and Tisha was looking up at him and asked, "Can I see your tanoot?

Ryan smiled. I was about to answer when Ayana said, "Tisha do not bother Ryan. It is not polite to ask such things."

Ryan got the gist of what Tisha's mother was saying and looked around at the rest of the crowd, who looked at him expectedly. A lot of them had been wanting to ask to have a look at it, but didn't want to be impolite, and we're now happy that the child had brought it out into the open.

Ryan looked at Ayana and said, "It OK." Then looked down at it and started to remove his tunic. Once she had his shirt off Tisha looked at his arm and started to giggle.

She said delightedly, "It is so pretty." Then, with her index finger started tracing the outline of the bear.

Ryan was looking down at her smiling and corrected her, "Tattoo." He said to the little girl.

Ryan then noticed several other people sitting around the fire straining to get a look at it. Ryan looked up, smiled at everyone, and then turned his body to the right so that everybody could get a look at it. People were smiling and nodding their heads with some saying, "Good." and he heard other people talking but could not quite understand what they were saying. As he looked over at Kanti, he noticed she was looking at it as well. As he looked past Kanti, he saw Cita coming towards him. Kanti shifted to see what Ryan was staring at. She saw Cita walking towards the group with a coy smile on her face, Kanti also noticed that she was walking in a very sensual manner. She walked past Kanti and around to where Ryan was and sat next to him on the right hand side.

"Could I have a look at that? Cita asked with a very friendly smile.

Ryan had to turn his body to face her directly so that he could show her his left arm. she continued smiling and with one finger delicately tracing the outline of the tattoo. A movement Ryan was finding quite pleasant. As she looked up into his eyes. He heard Kanti say something, but couldn't understand what she said, but noticed Cita smile, stand up, and walk over and sit next to Kanti.

Tisha asked Ryan a question, so he turned his attention to her.

Kanti looked at her friend, saying under her breath, "You look like you are throwing yourself at him."

"What if I am, you are not showing any interest in him are you?" Cita said with a smile then looked over at Ryan with his shirt off and continued. "You must admit he has a very nice body, and that drawing on his arm just makes him more interesting. Don't you think?"

"I will agree with you. He does have a nice body, but when I first saw the drawing on his arm, it scared me. We do not know how it got there, so we will have to wait until we can ask him, but that could take some time." Kanti said.

"A few other young women and I are wondering what he would be like." Cita said smiling at Ryan.

Kanti looked at her and was going to ask what she was talking about, but then it struck her. "You don't mean?" Kanti asked.

"Why not? You can see that he is not unattractive, he just looks different. He is handsome in a strange way and you must admit those blue eyes are something. Also look at him sitting there with the shirt off. He looks like he is definitely all man."

"Sometimes I do not know how your mind works." Kanti said.

Cita just smiled looking at her friend and observed her looking at Ryan talking to the young girl. "Just as I thought, she is interested in him, but not willing to do anything about it. I wonder how long that will last." she thought.

Ryan sat there quite a while enjoying the camaraderie of being with these people. After a while he started to get tired, so he stood up to excuse himself. He said good night, and then slowly started to turn to walk back to his tent.

Cita looked at Kanti and said to her, "Maybe I should offer to walk him back to his tent tonight, Don't you think that would be a good idea?"

Kanti Just looked at Cita and replied, "You can do what you want. I do not care."

Cita just smiled thinking "Yes you do." But said, "No, I was just teasing. You know I am not that bold."

When Ryan got back to the tent, he was surprised at how tired he was. He put the package that Ayana gave him underneath the bed roll hoping the little wont be getting its paws on it. However as soon as Ryan laid down, the little pup curled up beside him and was soundly asleep in no time. Ryan laid there for a while looking around and was surprised how dark it was. When he held his hand up in front of him, he could not see it. It's amazing when there's no light how eerie the blackness could be when there was no glow coming through the flap from the outside as the fire was too far away. Ryan laid there and went over the day's events. He thought again, "If the situation was reversed, would his people be so accommodating to a stranger that seemed to come out of nowhere." He knew what the answer was, but he just couldn't bring himself to say it. He heard a little pup let out a little yip and move around. Ryan felt around for the pup and found it was asleep. Ryan figured it must be having an exciting dream about chasing rabbits. A short time later Ryan joined the little wolf in sleep.

Ryan slept well at night and when he woke up in the morning, he was incredibly relaxed. He enjoyed the fact that he could get up whenever he wanted as there were no alarm clocks, as a matter of fact there were no clocks anywhere. Most people got up when they wanted, which was very early in the morning, and went to bed when they were tired, which was usually when it got dark.

Ryan smiled as he thought about this, and then looked around and noticed that the pup was nowhere in sight.

"He must be out taking care of business." Ryan thought to himself as he sat up on his bed. He was starting to feel a little hungry, so we reached for the package that Ayana had given it to him the night before and opened it up. There was a fair piece of moose meat in it, so Ryan took out a knife and carved off a piece and started chewing. Ryan smiled to himself as he looked at the knife and then the meat and thought how easy it was to fall into the habits of his hosts, even though he has only been here for a couple of days. Ryan heard a little yip and looked up as the pup came bounding into the tent from outside. It rushed up to him and sat down in front of him staring up at him expectedly. Ryan looked down at the little animal, smiled and said, "You are such a little mooch. You know that right?"

The pup just sat there wagging his tail and sticking his tongue out while panting at Ryan. Ryan cut a few pieces of meat off and fed them to the dog. Once they ate their share, Ryan put the leftover meat back into the package and put it under his bed roll. Ryan then stood up and started walking to the opening of his tent as he stepped out into the sun in the early morning sunshine Ryan thought to himself, "I could really go for a cup of tea. I really should learn how to make it, so I don't have to rely on everybody else's generosity."

Ryan started walking with no destination in mind when he heard his name called. Ryan turned towards one of the tents and saw Tolbar standing there beckoning him to come over. Ryan smiled, waved back, and started over his direction. As Ryan got closer a woman stepped out of the tent.

She was shorter than Tolbar with long black hair, high cheekbones, slender waist, looking to be in her late thirties or early forties, Ryan was terrible at guessing ages, especially of women.

Tolbar looked at the woman beside him, then Ryan and said, "Hello Ryan. I would like to introduce you to my mate Kiona."

The women just turned, looked at Ryan smiled and said, "Good morning, Ryan."

Ryan looked at the woman and replied, "Good morning, Kiona."

Kiona sat down and scooped something out of a basket and handed it to Ryan. Ryan took it thinking it might be tea but realize that this is not a cup that was handed to him, it was a bowl. He looked over at Tolbar was holding a bowl of his own up to his lips, sipping from it. Ryan did the same and realized that it was some sort of meat flavoured drink he also noticed there was a good supply of greens mixed in with it. Ryan drank the soup and use knife to pick up the greens. He didn't know what they were, but overall, it was very tasty. Ryan thought about it for a few moments and realize since he's been here, he has had a pretty balanced diet of both meats and greens. He was quite surprised, but then looking at how healthy and lean most of these people were he could understand it.

Ryan held the bowl up to Kiona and said, "Good."

She smiled and said "Thank you. It's just some soup. I had leftovers and warmed up for the morning meal."

Ryan did not understand most of the conversation but just nodded and smiled. Tolbar looked over Ryan's shoulder and saw two boys walking past them.

He got up, looked at Ryan and said, "Excuse me Ryan." And then stepped away. Tolbar walked up to the two young men and started talking to them.

Ryan finished the soup and put the bowl down, looked over at Kiona and smiled.

Kiona looked at Ryan, held up an empty cup and asked, "Tea?"

Ryan smiled and answered "Yes." Then remembered and quickly added, "Please."

Kiona smiled and went to a small basket that was sitting next to the fire. Ryan watched her stick her finger in the water to test it, then pull it out. She then took two rocks out of the basket and put them into the fire, then took two rocks that were in the fire, brushed off the ash and dropped them into the basket with a sizzle and a hiss. She left them in there for a few moments and then added two more stones. Ryan noticed steam starting to come from the water. She quickly touched the water with her finger, smiled and then took two of the stones out of the basket, replacing them with hot stones from the fire. There was the sound of hissing and steam rose from the basket. Kiona left the stones in for a while and then took out a very small basket that was only about four or five inches.

Ryan looked at it, noticing it looked like it was woven the same way that the basket with the water had been, except the leaves that were used to weave the big basket had been shredded into much smaller pieces to make the small basket. Kiona picked up a leather pouch loosening the leather thong that held it closed, reached in, and pulled out a pinch of the contents and put it into the basket. She repeated this action two more times. She noticed that Ryan was watching her intently, and took another pinch out, held her hand out and got Ryan to do the same.

She poured some into his hand and spread it around with her finger. Ryan looked at the contents in his hand and could not identify it. He saw that there were dried berries, some other dried items and something that looked like it might have been Pine needles. He wasn't sure but it really didn't matter as he enjoyed the tea. He just smiled and poured the contents back into Kiona's hands. She then added the mixture back into the small basket, sealed it, and then dropped two more stones into the cooking basket along with the small basket containing its dry tea.

Ryan smiled to himself and thought, "Well I guess Tetley wasn't the first one to invent the teabag." With a stick, she pushed the small basket down to the bottom and then let it float back to the top several times. Once the basket became saturated, it slowly started to sink to the bottom and Kiona just left it and then looked up. Tolbar was walking back towards the tent with his arm around one of the young boys.

"Ryan." He said once he arrived, "This is my son Sakta." Tolbar then looked at his son and said, "Son, this is Ryan."

Ryan smiled at the young boy and said, "Good morning, Sakta, good meet you."

Sakta smiled at Ryan and said, "Thank you Ryan. Good to meet you."

Ryan noticed that he said this last part slowly and realized that he was correcting his grammar. Ryan just smiled and nodded his head once.

Tolbar then asked, "Ryan would you like to come with us and watch the wrestling?"

Ryan had no idea what Tolbar asked but got the impression that he was being invited somewhere, so he nodded his head and answered "Yes." He thought, "What the heck, I don't have anything planned, so let's see what's happening."

The three of them started walking towards the river. When they got close to the river Ryan noticed there were some other men and younger boys standing around on a grassy area next to the river. As they got closer, Sakta said something to his dad and then jogged ahead to meet with the other boys. As Ryan got closer, he could see Corna, Latona and a few other men. Ryan also noticed Mekome standing watching with his little sister Tisha standing beside him. As they walked up to where everyone was standing, Ryan looked at Latona and shrugged, hoping that someone would be able to explain to him what was going on.

Latona got the idea, smiled, and waved his hands over at the young boys and said, "the young men are going to be wrestling for fun."

Ryan understood fun and he understood young boys, but everything else was lost. He repeated the word, "Wrestling?"

Latona thought about it for a moment then looked at Tolbar who was smiling as they both got together in a clinch and started play wrestling.

Ryan got the idea and then said, "Oh, wrestling." and then mimicked what they were doing.

Both men stopped what they were doing, smiled and nodded their heads.

"This should be interesting." Thought Ryan, "It must be a good way for the young boys to blow off steam.'

Ryan stood there with the group, then one of the men who he didn't know said something and two boys came forward and faced each other. Ryan heard the man say something and thought that it almost sounded like a countdown and then dropped his hand quickly in a chop. Both boys moved forward and started grappling with each other, neither boy was wearing a shirt so there was nothing to grab onto. Finally, one of the boys dropped down, grabbed his opponent by the waist, lifted him up and dropped him onto the ground. Once this was done the boy that picked him up and dropped him, stood up quickly, the boy that was on the ground smiled and started to get up. That's when his opponent reached down and offered a hand to help him up. The men watching started clapping and nodding their heads. Two more boys came forward and the countdown was done again, and the hand was dropped. Both boys moved in this time. One of the boys dropped down low wrapped his arms around the other one's feet, tumbling him backwards and then jumped on top of him. He then quickly stood up and backed away. Again, when the boy went to get up his opponent smiling reached out his hand and helped him up. Ryan watched Tolbar's son and the young man that he was walking with earlier square off. Both boys were bigger than the other boys and Ryan could feel that this was going to be a bit of a different match. Ryan was right, both boys circled each other and we're very strategic in every move they made. Sakta faked a move a couple of times to the right, but his opponent was not taking the bait. His opponent tried the same thing, but this time to Sakta's left, with the same result. Both were smiling and you could see that they were enjoying this, and there was no real animosity towards each other.

Suddenly Sakta's opponent dropped down low and made a lunge for his legs. Sakta saw it coming and jumped up over his opponent landing on his feet as his opponent sprawled out on his stomach.

He quickly rolled over and got up on his feet. Sakta's opponent made the same move again and started to dive towards his feet. Sakta started to jump over him again but time his opponent stood up, catching him by surprise and Sakta crashed down to the ground. He quickly got up again before his opponent could get on top of him and pin him. Ryan looked over and smiled and nodded his head. Ryan then noticed that Cita and Kanti had walked up and were watching the wrestling matches as well.

The two boys went back to circling each other at this time Sakta went down to grab his opponents' legs at the same time his opponent did the same thing. The two boys crashed together, and both hit the ground laughing. Sakta looked over and noticed that his friend was favouring his shoulder, the one that he just crashed into.

"Are you Ok?" Sakta asked.

"Yes, but I seem to have caused some damage to my shoulder I think." His friend answered.

"Let's call this draw, and we'll do it again when your shoulder is better." Sakta said.

His friend just smiled and nodded his head and came over rubbing the shoulder.

"Why did you quit?" Tolbar asked his son.

"Barcal hurt shoulder when we collided. So, there was no point in going on and injuring his shoulder further, so we decided to call it a draw." Sakta answered.

Tolbar Just smiled at his son, patted him on the shoulder and said, "A draw is good. You don't want to hurt your friends over a friendly competition, so a draw is good."

Mekome walked over to Latona and asked, "May I try?"

Latona looked down at the young lad, smiled and said "I'm sorry but you are too small right now. And we have no body size to match you with right now."

The young boy just lowered his head and turned to walk away. Ryan could tell that the young boy was very disappointed and wanted to participate like the older boys. Everyone started to break up and Ryan looked over at the young boy and thought why not?

He walked over to Tisha and Mekome and said, "You want wrestle. I teach. Ok?"

Mekome looked at him, shook his head and said, "No, I'm too small."

"Not too small." Ryan said," I teach."

Tisha looked at her brother and said, "Why don't you let Ryan teach you? If he thinks he can, maybe he can."

Mekome looked up at Ryan then said, "OK, if you can teach me that would be great."

Ryan smiled and said, "Good."

Once everyone had left and it was just Mekome and his sister, Ryan looked at them and thought about it for a few moments. He had known that in a lot of his judo classes, as well as some of his other martial art classes there was a lot of smaller people that were quite good at fighting. As a matter of fact, when he was training and just starting to learn, he got his ass handed to him by a young man who is only about four foot seven inches. So, he should be able to train this young boy to be able to handle taller opponents. Ryan walked with both children to the edge of the field and then stopped, turned, and looked down at the young boy.

"I'm going to have to combine the number of disciplines because it appears the goal is just to put your opponent down and not to cause them any bodily harm or physical injury." Ryan thought.

Ryan said to Mekome, "Ok. I teach Mekome wrestle."

With that Ryan got down on his knees and started to go through a few movements showing the boy a few moves that he wanted him to do. Mekome was confused but copied what Ryan was doing. After Ryan figured that the young boy had those moves down properly, he told him to stop. He then moved in like he was attacking him, but very slowly so Mekome could try using the moves that Ryan had shown him. He managed to knock Ryan's hands out of the way and get his leg behind Ryan to be able to push him down. Young boy was pleased with this and kept practising the move. Ryan then taught Mekome a couple of other moves and made him do those repeatedly until he felt the Young boy had them down pat.

Tolbar and Sakta came walking across the field towards the small group.

"What are you doing?" Asked Tolbar

Tisha looked up and answered, "Ryan is teaching Mekome how to wrestle."

Ryan looked over at Tolbar and smiled.

"So, Ryan, you wrestle?" Tolbar asked Ryan.

Ryan just nodded his head smiling and answered. "Yes."

Sakta looked over at Mekome and asked, "What have you been taught so far?"

Mekome said, "Let me show you." And with that went to stand in front of Sakta, then got into position and said to Sakta, "Ok, let's go."

Sakta smiled, got into a crouched position, and then launched at the boy.

Mekome pivoted on his right leg and swept his left arm in front of him from right to left knocking Sakta's arms out of the way. He continued pivoting and put his left leg behind Sakta's legs and with the upper portion of his body pushed him down to the ground. Sakta went down easily and laid there for a moment looking up at Mekome, suddenly a big smile crossed his face, and he started to laugh.

"That was great." He said and jumped back up. "What else did Ryan teach you?"

Mekome smiled, then went back into the position he was before, so Sakta adopted a similar position. They both stood there for a few minutes and then Sakta realized that Mekome was waiting for him to make the first move.

He looked at Mekome and said, "You won't trick me this time."

He then fainted like he was going to attack, and then backed up again. Mekome did not move, he just kept his eyes on Sakta. Suddenly, Sakta came in low, looking to grab the young boy around the waist and take him down. Mekome dropped to one knee so that he was lower than Sakta and when he ran into him, he grabbed him by the legs and carried him over top of him onto the ground.

Sakta laid on the ground with Mekome on top of him. Sakta did not move and Mekome was worried he might have hurt him. He quickly got up and looked down to see Sakta with a broad smile on his face, nodding his head.

That was a good move." Sakta said to Mekome.

A smiling Mekome reached down to help him up.

Sakta then walked over to Ryan and asked, "Ryan, can you teach me how to fight as well?"
Ryan nodded his head and answered, "Yes."

Tolbar walked over and put his hand on Ryan's shoulder and asked, "Could you teach me as well."

Ryan looked over and shrugged his shoulders and said, "Yes."

So, for the next hour, the four of them were practising, and learning a variety of moves. Tisha even asked if she could get in on the fun and paired up with her older brother for a little bit. Everybody was laughing and having a good time, and Ryan enjoyed the fact that he could partner with Tolbar as they were close to the same size. Tollbar on the other hand was not as happy, as Ryan kept putting him down on the ground. But he was taking it in a good-hearted manner and was learning quite a bit from this blonde haired, blue eyed stranger. A few other boys drifted over and got in on the training as well.

The group was unaware that they had an audience, Skyseeker, Kanti, and another young woman were watching them from the distance. Skyseeker was watching Ryan, but then continued to keep looking over at her daughter's child and noticing that she was paying quite a bit of attention to what was going on out in the field.

"It seems Ryan has hidden talents." Skyseeker said with a smile looking at Kanti.

"Yes, he full of surprises." She answered not looking at Skyseeker.

"I noticed you looking at him." said Skyseeker. "Perhaps you are interested in him?"

"No!" answered Kanti a little too quickly. "I am just watching him teach the boys how to wrestle."

"Oh, I see." Skyseeker answered, continuing to look at her granddaughter.

Once everybody was quite tired and slightly bruised and battered, Tolbar said, "Well, Ryan, I think that's enough for today."

Ryan got the gist of what he was saying and nodded his head in agreement. Tolbar then said something to the group, and they all started to walk towards the river. Ryan thought he might as well follow.

When he caught up, Tolbar looked at him and said, "We should bathe, as we smell." and with that he pinched his nose.

Ryan smiled nodding his head in agreement as they walked down to the river. When they got there, Ryan noticed there were some young women bathing in the river already and thought that maybe they were going to wait till the women had finished. However, the group of men just started stripping off their clothes and walking into the river.

Ryan thought, "What the hell." and stripped off and followed them in. The young ladies finished what they were doing and came out of the water heading up to the bank to grab their clothes. They got dressed and slowly left. The men were splashing around, swimming and washing the dust and sweat from their bodies. The wolf pup played at the edge of the water running in and then running out, not trusting its swimming just yet.

The two young women started walking away from the river and ran into one of their friends and stood there talking and pointing back to the river. They then continued back into camp, and they saw Cita and Kanti walking towards Latona and Nila's Lodge. One of the girls called out to the pair to wait up. The three girls then hurried to catch up to the two women.

Kaya said to the two women, "You two should go down to the river and have a look."

"What will we be looking at?" Kanti asked.

"The men are down there having a wash." Answered Kaya

"Why would we want to go down and watch the men bathing?" Kanti asked, looking at the three women.

"Well Ryan is down there bathing with them. Kaya said.

"So!" Said Kanti, "It is not polite to stare at people while they're bathing."

"It may not be polite". Said to Kaya. "But well worth it. And in case you're wondering that blonde hair is everywhere, and I do mean everywhere."

"Well, I'm not interested." said Kanti.

"Well, you should be, because believe me, he is every bit a man." Kaya said looking at Kanti.

Cita raised one of her eyebrows, smiled and said, "So, tell me how much of a man is he?"

Kaya got a big smile on her face and answered, "He is very, very, much a man."

The girls all started to chuckle. Cita looked at her friend and said, "Do you know, I am feeling particularly dirty, maybe we should go and bathe in the river now."

Kanti looked at her friend and said, "We just bathed this morning. We do not need to go down again."

Cita nodded her head and said, "You are Right, that's too bad."

Shinta chimed in, "You girls really should go and have a look because I will tell you Ryan is a very good looking man. It could be interesting to take him for a ride. "

Kanti looked at Shinta with a shocked expression on her face, "But what about Droon, she asked.

"What about him?" Shinta answered smiling, "There are no commitments or promises." Ryan could be a very good distraction and a bit of fun."

"I don't know what is up with you all. You watch men bathing, and you turn into little girls." She then turned and started to walk away.

Shinta, Kaya, and their friends seemed a little surprised at this and Kaya asked Cita what's the matter with her.

Cita smiled watching her friend walk away and said, "I think she likes Ryan but does not want to admit it."

"I Can not say that I blame her." said Kaya. "He is a very good looking man."

"I agree, and I also agree with you that he would be good for a bit of a diversion." Said Cita. She then turned and left to catch up to Kanti. As she got close, she called out to her friends to slow down.

As Cita caught up to her friend she said, "You know you keep saying you have no interest in Ryan, but when any other woman starts talking to him or about him seem to get very jealous."

"I do not!" Kanti snapped.

"Yes, my friend you do. You can keep telling yourself that you are not interested, but I think deep down you just might be. You just have not convinced yourself yet."

"Well, I really do not think I am going to need to convince myself." Kanti said.

Cita just smiled as they continued walking to the pit house.

Chapter 4

When the men finished bathing, they came out of the water and started up the bank towards the field. The little pup followed right behind them. Ryan had to help him over the bank to put them up on the field and he bounded away, stopping, and turning around to make sure that Ryan was coming. All the men laid their clothes in the field and sat down as it was a beautifully warm day, and they would let the sun dry them off. Ryan felt a little uncomfortable sitting there with no clothes on but noticed that it didn't seem to bother anyone else in the group, so he just went with the flow. Once the men had sat there for a while and dried off, they got up and started getting dressed. They all started to go in different directions and Ryan was not too sure where to go. Tolbar and Sakta started walking away when Tollbar turned around and waited for Ryan to follow. They headed back towards Tolbar's tent and when they got there, Tolbar's wife was sitting there smiling at them as they entered the campsite.

"I hear you had an exciting day." She said to her mate and her son.

Sakta answered, "Yes, we did. Ryan was teaching us new ways to wrestle and fight." She looked at her mate curiously.

Tolbar smiled nodding his head. "Yes, Ryan is very capable when it comes to wrestling and has taught us a lot of things that we have never thought to try before, and some of them are very effective."

His mate smiled at him and then said, "They must be. I see you have some new bruises on your body."

Tolbar Just smiled and said, "Yes, that is thanks to Ryan. He is a good teacher and very thorough."

Kiona looked at Ryan and asked. "Would you like some tea, Ryan?"

Ryan smiled and said, "Yes."

She poured him a cup of tea, which he took and started to sip. Ryan looked at her, thought about what he wanted to say, and then gave it a try by saying, "You make gooder tea I have."

Kiona smiled at him and shook her head and then said very slowly. "You make the best tea. I have tasted."

Ryan thought about it for a second then nodded his head and said back to her, "You make the best tea I have tasted," and then added, "Thank you."

Kiona smiled and looked at her mate and then said, "See, I told you I made the best tea in the camp."

Tolbar smiled, putting his arm around her and said, "I had never doubted it. You know that."

"Ryan is going to teach us more over the next little while." Sakta said to his mother.

Kiona looked at Ryan and then said to Sakta, "You can not take up all his time. He may not want to spend that much time teaching."

Ryan figured that they were talking about him and the teaching and thought he needed to let them know somehow that he enjoyed it. He looked at Tollbar, smiled and said, "Teaching wrestling fun. I like."

Tolbar said, "Good. You can continue to teach us if that's OK."

Ryan got a little bit of the conversation, and they just decided to nod his head yes.

Tolbar smiled knowing that he did not quite understand, but that he was willing to agree. Kiona asked the group if they were hungry and all three men nodded their heads yes. so, she went and brought out some meat and some leftover soup that she had. She put some hot rocks from the fire into the soup to warm it up, and while that was happening, she cut some of the meat into small pieces and put it into the soup as well. Kiona purposely dropped a few on the ground for the wolf pup to pounce on. In a very short time, the men were sitting around with warm bowls of soup with a good helping of meat in it. She also cut up some meat into strips, put them on the platter for them to pick at. Ryan didn't realize how hungry he was and had two bowls of the soup as did Sakta and Tolbar. The trio devoured the meat that was on the platter. Kiona smiled and went and got some more meats and prepared it for the men. When they were finished, they sat around drinking tea, in companionable silence.

Kiona said to Ryan, "I have something for you." and she then went into the tent and brought out a small leather pouch.

Ryan thought it might be food for later or tomorrow, but when he opened the pouch, he found that it was full of dried ingredients and realized that it was tea. There was also a very small basket in the pouch, like the one that she used this morning when she made the tea.

Ryan smiled, looked up at her and said, "Thank you." Ryan thought, "This is great, now I have my own tea. The only problem is I have no basket for water, I have no way to carry water up from the river, and most importantly I have no idea how to start a fire to heat the rocks. Ryan thought about it for a few moments and then concluded he was definitely going to need to learn how to start a fire, as he was pretty sure no one here had a lighter.

Kiona and Tolbar were deep in conversation about something, and Ryan decided that he should excuse himself and give the couple some time on their own. He didn't want to make a nuance of himself, so we stood up, thanked them, then started to walk away with no destination in mind. Ryan thought that you might like to take a walk along the river so started to head in that general direction. He hadn't gotten too far when he heard his name called. When he turned around, he saw Tisha running up to him.

"Where are you going?" She asked when she caught up to Ryan.

Ryan looked down at the little girl, smiled and answered, " Going for a walk to river."

Tisha just smiled back at him and said, "OK, I will come with you."

Ryan and the little girl started walking towards the river followed by the little wolf pup. when they got close to the river Tisha pointed to the east and said, "Let's go this way."

Ryan looked out at the little girl and said, "OK." And off they went. After they walked for a while, Ryan noticed that the riverbank was higher on this side than it was on the other, and it was quite a way down to the river. He also noticed that the river was starting to get a little narrower and was starting to flow faster. Ryan looked down the river towards the east. He noticed what looked like rapids, which surprised him because the river when he was following it a few days ago seemed to be calm, flat with no rapids. As they got closer, Ryan noticed that the rapids carried on for about three or four hundred yards and then the river went back to being calm.

"This is dancing water." Tisha said to Ryan.

Ryan understood the word water but not the other one and repeated it to Tisha as a question, "Dancing?"

Tisha thought about it for a moment, then started dancing. She stopped, looked at Ryan and said, "Dancing."

Ryan nodded his head in understanding and said, "Dancing water."

Ryan thought about going down to the river but did not want to climb down the steep cliff to the water's edge. So, Ryan and Tisha sat on the high riverbank, looking down at the fast-moving water below them. Ryan heard a noise behind them and quickly turned around seeing the young wolf chasing a squirrel around the log. The squirrel would get the wolf running around the log and then jump to the top of the log unnoticed by the wolf who continued to run around the log chasing nothing. Tisha and Ryan watched the spectacle for a while, laughing pointing at the wolf chasing the squirrel that he was not going to catch.

After a while the wolf gave up, sat down and just stared at the squirrel sitting on top of the log looking back at the wolf.

"Well you are just a great hunter? " Ryan said to the little wolf.

The little wolf turned, looked at Ryan and then padded up and sat down beside him looking over a Tisha.

"We should get back now." She said to Ryan and got up and started walking. Ryan got up to follow up a little girl with the pup at his side. When they reached the camp Ryan noticed that the light was starting to dim and realized that they had been on the walk down the river for quite a while.

He saw Latona and Nila walking towards him, and Latona smiled and waved. "Hi Ryan, we are on our way to Corona and his mates fire for a meal. Would you like to join us?" He asked.

Ryan smiled and nodded his head and said, "Yes, thank you."

Nila looked at Tisha and asked, "Would you like to come as well Tisha?"

Tisha just shook her head and answered, "No I have been way longer than I should have been, and mother will be getting worried, so I'm going to go home."

Nila said, "That's probably a good idea." Then asked, "When is your father getting back from Three Sisters camp?"

"He should be back either tomorrow or the next day. Mother said he went to trade some of his furs for a buffalo hide, which mother wants to make a jacket out of for winter. He's going to check his trap lines on the way back, so hopefully he comes back with more small animals." The young girl said excitedly.

"That would be good, it would mean someone will be getting some new winter mittens soon." Latona said to the young girl with a smile.

"I hope so. Mother said she will make me some if father is lucky with the traps." she said, and then turned around and bound it off towards her tent.

As the three adults and one pup walked across the field to Corna's tent Latona asked Ryan, "Was it a good day for teaching wrestling today."

Ryan understood most of what he asked, so he just smiled and said, "Yes it was fun."

"You know you are going to have more people asking you to teach them now." Latona said.

Ryan wasn't too sure exactly what he said, so Latona said it again, much slower and with more emphasis on certain words.

Ryan got the gist of what Latona said and answered, "That OK. I like teaching."

Latona smiled and said, "That is good because you are going to be doing it for a while. I was thinking of coming and you could teach me as well." Pointing to himself.

Ryan nodded his head and said, "I teach Latona wrestle."

Latona smiled, nodded his head, and said, "Good. I look forward to it."

As they approached a tent that Ryan had never been to before he heard someone call out to them. "Latona, Nila, we are so glad you could make it tonight and I see you brought us an unexpected guest."

"Yes, we did. I hope you do not mind Suna, but he had nowhere to go for a meal tonight." Nila said to the woman.

"He is more than welcome." Suna said back to Nila. "a lot of people have met him, but as of yet I have not been introduced."

"Let me fix that mistake right now." said Latona, turning to Ryan and saying, "Ryan this is Suna. She is Corna's mate."

Ryan smiled, looked at the woman and said, "Hello Suna. I am Ryan. Good meet you."

Nila touched Ryan's arm and corrected, "Nice to meet you."

Ryan thought about it for an instant and then repeated, "Hello Suna, nice to meet you." He then turned and looked at Nila who was smiling at him.

Suna looked at him, smiled and said, "It is nice to meet you as well Ryan."

Corna looked at Latona and said, "He is picking up the language quickly, isn't he?"

"Yes, he is." answered Latona. "I wish I had that ability. It's only been a few days and even though he can not understand full conversations, I get the impression that he understands a lot of what the conversation is about. In the short time he's been with us he has picked up quite a lot."

"I hear he was teaching some of the boys and a few of the men how to wrestle." Corna said to Latona.

"Yes, and from what I hear he has a lot of new methods that are quite effective. You can ask Tolbar, I understand he was on the receiving end of a lot of the training today."

"I know." said Corna. "I saw him later this afternoon and he has a few bruises that he didn't have this morning. He did say that he enjoyed the training. I can tell that Ryan is going to be quite busy training the young boys, as well as some of the men once they see what he can do. He taught Mekome some moves, and he managed to put Sakta down a few times."

"That is amazing." Latona said, "He is at least a good head and a half taller than Mekome.

"Yes, he is." Latona agreed, "But apparently, it is not the size. It's the technique according to Ryan."

"Have you discovered any more of where he is from, or where he was going." Corna asked.

"No." said Latona, and speaking with the Skyseeker she said that we should just let it be until he has a much better grasp of our language. She feels that if we start asking too many questions right now, he may just decide to leave, and she would like him to stay around for a while for some reason.'

"Well, she must have a good reason for wanting that, but I would never ask her what that reason is." Corna said.

"I am not going to ask her either." Said Latona.

"Are you men coming to eat any time soon?" asked Suna.

"Yes, we are." Corna replied. "Sorry, we were off talking to ourselves, we did not mean to be rude."

"We were just telling Ryan that we are having fish for dinner." Nila said.

"Fish, what a nice treat. Said Latona

"I know." said Corna. "With all of the game that we have around and how plentiful it is, fishing is not something we do often."

"Where did you get the fish?" Nila asked.

"I set fish traps up just before Dancing Water on the river and was quite lucky. I got several fish and gave three to Lacano." Said Corna.

"He was quite surprised at how many he caught, but I expect nothing less from my mate. He is a great hunter and now he is showing off being a great fisherman." Suka said, smiling at her mate.

"Quit teasing Corna, Suka, or he will get a big head and there will be no living with him." Nila said with a laugh.

Ryan listened to the exchange picking up bits and pieces of the conversation, and he thought fish sounded delicious.

Suka brought out a large cut down antler with fish on it. It smelt delicious, and Ryan noticed some green herbs, or something had been sprinkled on the top of them. Suka picked two pieces and put them on another plate and handed them to Ryan. Ryan thanked her and took the plate but did nothing with it. He watched as a plate was handed to Corna, Lakota, as well as Nila. Ryan observed Latona, cutting the fish into strips, then cubing it, sticking it with the knife and popping it into his mouth. Once Ryan knew how to eat it, he copied the movements and did the same thing. The fish tasted delicious. He ate both of his large pieces and Suka put another one on his plate.

Ryan noticed they were including him in the conversation by asking very simple questions that were easy for him to answer.

Suka asked, "Did you teach the men wrestling today?"

Ryan answered. "Yes. I enjoyed it."

When they finished dinner Suka scooped out some tea and started passing it around. Ryan noticed that both Nila and Latona had their own cups with them which Suka filled. Knowing that Ryan would not have a cup Suka grabbed a cup for him and filled it with the tea.

"Thank you for the tea." Ryan said, taking a sip. He was surprised that this tea was not the same as Ayana's tea. This tea had a different taste to it, it had a mild minty taste. Ryan was sipping his tea and pondering the taste when Suka looked over and asked, "Do you like it, Ryan."

Ryan smiled nodding his head answering, "Yes, I do. It good." Ryan then stopped and tried again, "It is very good."

Suka smiled and went back to drinking her tea. A few other people drifted around the fire and Suka welcomed them offering them tea as well. Ryan noticed after time it was starting to get dark and he was starting to get tired. He stood up and said good night to everyone and started to walk away. He turned around, looked at the little wolf and whistled. The little wolf was laying in front of the fire almost asleep. His head popped up at the sound of the whistle and he saw Ryan was not there. He spotted Ryan walking back to the tent and started trotting after him.

When Ryan got back he decided to call it an early night. He stripped off his clothes and got into his bedroll, quickly falling asleep, with a little wolf curled up at his feet.

Ryan heard something and woke up. Opening his eyes Ryan realized that he must have been asleep for a while because it was pitch black, and he could not see his hand in front of his face.

He felt the little pup stirring at his feet and he heard the flap to his tent open and somebody step inside. He couldn't make out the shape, but he could hear somebody walking towards him. His body tensed, but he laid there pretending he was asleep, but he was wide awake. Ryan then heard some rustling and then what sounded like clothing or something hitting the ground. He then felt the top cover get lifted and a warm body climbed in beside him. Ryan was surprised and quickly sat up still not being able to see who was right next to him.

"Who are you, and what do you want?" Ryan asked into the darkness.

He felt a finger being pressed against his lips as if trying to silence him, then another hand crept under the covers moved towards his manhood, then he felt fingers wrapping around it. "Whoever this is, they were very good at what they were doing." Ryan thought, as in no time at all Ryan had an erection. Ryan heard a giggle and then in one movement the person that was laying beside him, climbed on top of him and mounted him. As she came down on him, both Ryan and the stranger moaned together. The woman on top of him started rocking back and forth, and Ryan reached around grabbing her by the waist. The woman's momentum started to pick up and Ryan's rhythm matched hers. Ryan couldn't believe this was happening to him, but at this point he didn't care. He moved his hands around the woman's waist and moved them up to her body, taking a breast in each hand and gently massaged each in turn. They were full and a good size Ryan thought to himself as the woman was sitting on top of him increased her motion and started going faster and faster. Ryan tried to keep up with her but knew that he could not hold on for much longer.

Just as Ryan was feeling it was going to explode soon, the woman started moaning loudly.

This excited Ryan even more and the two of them reached their full passion together. The woman on top slowed her movement until she just laid on top of him. Ryan had his arms around her, hugging her softly. They laid like that for a few moments then the woman then kissed Ryan, sat up abruptly, got up from Ryan, picked up her clothes and left.

Ryan laid there for a few moments thinking, "What the hell just happened. Who was that girl." Ryan laid back with a smile on his face, trying to figure it out. The little pup who had moved over against the wall of the tent once all the action started, came back and again curled up at Ryan's feet.

"Well, boy, what do you think about that. Please tell me that this happens all the time because I could get used to that." He said to the little dog in the darkness.

Ryan slept in the next day and woke up both relaxed and content. He laid there for a while, thinking about the strange events of the night before decided it was time for him to get up as he climbed out of his bed. He noticed that the little pup was nowhere to be found, he looked around and could not see the little wolf anywhere.

He heard some laughter and squealing coming from outside in the field and when stepped outside the tent he noticed Tisha and another little girl about the same age chasing wolf around the field, they would stop and start running away, and the wolf would turn and chase them. This went on for a while and Ryan decided that he needed to relieve himself, so he walked to the back of the tent and into the little ways into the forest. When he was done, he returned and as he rounded the tent the pup looked up noticed him and came running over to greet him with Tisha following.

"Come for a morning meal" she said to him.

Ryan looked down and asked. "Is it OK with your mother?"

Tisha looked up and answered. "Mother sent to me ask, but we started playing with wolf."

Ryan thought about it for a few moments and figured he was quite hungry as he had worked up an appetite the night before, "OK, let us go." He said walking towards her.

The other girl came running up to join them as they walked towards Tisha's tent.

Ayana, and Nila were sitting out front of the tent having tea when they soon looked up and noticed Ryan and Tisha walking towards him with Tisha holding Ryan's hand.

Is Ryan coming from a visit for a visit?" Asked Nila.

"He is coming for a morning meal." Ayana answered.

"Really, that is interesting." Said Nila.

"He has been here a few times." Ayana said with a smile. "It was Tisha's idea. I am not too sure if it's just a young girl crush or if she thinks that Ryan is now one of her playmates. But she really likes to be around him."

"And what about Ryan? How does he feel about having a child hanging on him all the time?" Nila asked.

Ayana smiled and answered, "He is really quite good with her. He is very patient and lets her get away with more than she probably should, you know how full of energy she is and how exhausting she could be sometimes.

"Well, it could be young girl attraction, and I guess I could see it. He is a rather handsome man once you get past his skin colour and his hair colour, however those blue eyes are piercing. They are probably best feature." Nila said.

"I'm not too sure about that. Have you seen him with the shirt off?" Ayana asked.

Nila Just smiled and said, "No, I have not but I will take your word for it."

As the group came to the fire pit. Ayan said, "Good morning Ryan, would you like something to eat or some tea perhaps."

Ryan smiled and said, "Thank you Ayana, tea would be good." He then looked at Anya waiting to see if she was going to correct him.

She just smiled and said, "You are learning our language very well." She turned, got some tea and handed it to Ryan.

Ryan sipped the tea and decided that he did like the different teas that he had been trying, but Ayana's tea was his favorite. As he was pondering this Ayana put a bowl in front of him with meat and greens and it smelled great. Ryan tasted it, finding that it was not hot, but it was quite warm and very tasty. The wolf sat down beside him, looking up at Ryan and whining a little bit.

Ryan looked down at a little wolf, shook his head and said, "Sorry buddy, this is for me."

Ayana smiled, went into a pouch, and pulled out some dry meat, then broke it up into small pieces and put it down in front of his small pup. The pup started wagging its tail, then pounced on the meat.

Nila looked at Ryan and asked, "So, Ryan what are you going to do today?"

Ryan listened carefully and found that he understood the question, smiled, and said, "Some of the men wanted me to teach wrestling today. I do morning."

Ayana looked at Ryan smiling and corrected, "I will do that this morning."

Ryan smiled, nodded his head, and then said. "Some of the men wanted me to teach wrestling. I will do that this morning."

He then looked at Ayana who was smiling while nodding her head. Ryan found that he did mind when the people corrected him, because he knew they were just trying to help him get a better grasp on the language. It also helped him understand what people were talking about better.

Tisha looked at Ryan and asked. "Can I come when you teach everyone to wrestle?"

Ryan smiled and looked down at the young girl and answered, "Yes you can."

She thought about it for a moment then looked up at him and asked, "Can I wrestle too?"

Ryan looked at her and said, "We will see."

It was very noncommittal, but she was happy with the answer.

Ayana looked at Ryan and asked, "Ryan are you sure it will be OK? She is very small."

Ryan smiled at Tisha's mother and answered, "I will not let her wrestle big, will I need be somebody her size."

Ayana was going to correct him, but then decided not to as she got her answer. Ryan was not going to have any larger boys wrestle with her. It would have to be somebody her size and she was OK with that.

While Ryan sat there Sakta and Tolbar came walking by and then noticed Ryan sitting there, so they came over to join the group.

"Good morning, Ryan." Tolbar said.

Ryan looked up and said, "Good morning, Tobar."

"Will you be teaching wrestling today?" Tolbar asked.

Ryan nodded his head and answered "Yes. When we do?"

Tolbar thought about it for a few moments and then said, "I will gather everybody in the practice area where we were yesterday."

"OK." said Ryan. "When"

Tolbar said, "Shortly." And then walked away.

It suddenly struck Ryan that the concept of five minutes or twenty minutes does not exist. It will either be now, shortly, or later. He thought "Well I guess that makes things a lot easier."

Ryan was sitting and listening to Nila and Ayana talk about mundane things and didn't notice Latona walking up until he sat down beside him. "Good morning" he said to Nila and Ayana, then turned to Ryan and added, "You as well my friend."

Ryan nodded and said, "Good morning to you Latona."

Latona looked at Ryan and said, "I hear you are teaching wrestling today? Tolbar is walking around asking anybody that might be interested if they would like to join in the training. You are going to have a lot of people showing up" he said with a smile.

"Why do you think there are going to be so many?" Ayana asked.

Latona looked at her and said "A number of people came in last night from Three Sisters Valley and have not met Ryan and have only heard of him when they arrived last night. There are a number of people that are interested in seeing if the stories that they are hearing about him are true."

"Well Ayana." said Nila, "It looks like we are going to have to go down and watch. It will be interesting to see how people that have not met Ryan yet react when they see him for the first time."

"That should be quite interesting." Ayana said. Tisha looked at Latona and said, "I get to come too. Ryan said I could even wrestle."

Latona looked skeptically at the little girl then at Ryan.

Ryan smiled and said to Tisha, "Only if I can find someone the same size as you."

Latona smiled and said "Why not? If she wants to do it." He then asked Ayana "How do you feel about your daughter wanting to wrestle?"

"Well, if she wants to wrestle and Ryan said that he will pair her up with somebody her own size, why would I stop her. She will either like it or she will not, the decision is going to be hers."

Latona nodded his head in agreement and then patted Ryan on the shoulder and said, "Well Ryan let's go, people are starting to gather already."

Ayana looked at Latona and asked, "Are you in such a hurry that you cannot sit and have a cup of tea with us?"

Latona looked at Ayana and sat back down and said, "Of course. How rude of me. I would love a cup of tea." he then looked at Ryan and said, "Once we finish our tea, we will then head to the practice field."

Ryan smiled and sipped his tea. Once they were done, they headed towards the field and when Ryan looked over, he was surprised at the amount of people that were there he figured there had to be forty or fifty people. He didn't know there were that many people in the camp to begin with as he never saw them all come together like this.

Ryan looked at Latona and asked, "Where all people come from?"

Latona looked at the crowd and said all the people are from the camp or have come in from the three sisters camp, which is to the east, and he pointed in the general direction. People came last night, and you have not met you." Latona spoke slowly hoping that Ryan would understand, which he did.

Ryan just nodded his head and watched as more people started to come and join the group of people that were milling around.

As they got closer, Tolbar broke away from the group and walked up to Ryan and Latona. "We have quite a crowd today. Both watch the wrestling and participate." he said to Latona.

Latona could understand this as it was a break from their daily routine and something exciting and different was happening. He also knew there were several people in the crowd that were wanting to get a look at Ryan. Nobody openly stared at him, but there were several sideways glances, or looking at him when he was looking at something else.

Corna walked up to join the group and said to Ryan. "I think I will join you today."

Ryan smiled and said, "Good." and nodded his head. Ryan looked at the amount of people and wondered how many of these men were here for wrestling.

He asked Latona, "How many people wrestle today?"

Latona got the gist of the question and turned to the crowd and said in a loud voice, "All those that are here to be taught today please stay where you are. Those of you are just here to watch. Please come towards me and sit over there."

Better than three quarters of the crowd broke away to sit down and Ryan was looking at about thirteen or fifteen people. Some young boys, some young men, and some men. Tisha and her little friend were standing there looking hopeful that they would be allowed to join in.

Ryan looked at the little girl, smiled thinking to himself, "She so reminds me of Niki, just a little troublemaker."

Ryan proceeded to walk amongst the group pairing people off based on their size. It seemed to him to be a good idea if they could get pairs that were roughly the same size and the same weight. Tolbar's son Sakta said that he would wrestle with Mekome, which made Mekome very happy, but Ryan thought it would be better for both boys if their partner was the same size. Once he broke everybody into pairs, he told all the boys and men to remove their shirts. As they were doing this, he removed his. He could hear people behind him, gasping and then murmurs of excitement as people noticed his tattoo.

Ryan just smiled to himself and thought, "We might as well get this over with quickly and I can answer all the questions later."

Ryan then proceeded to look at Tolbar and Latona. He looked at Latona and said, "You with me."

Tolbar padded Latona on the shoulder, smiled and said, "I'm glad he picked you. I was getting tired of getting thrown around yesterday. So today it is your turn."

Latona wasn't too sure if you liked this arrangement but just smiled at Ryan and walked up beside him. Ryan started the training by going through a lot of the basic moves that he went through the other day, as he had a lot of new people here today. After a while, he started getting a little fancier and was showing people how to do flips, knee blocks, and other moves. He had noticed that Cita and Kanti were sitting down watching, but then also noticed as he was doing the training. The two women were facing each other while sitting down and looked like they were trying to mimic or copy some of the moves. Ryan decided to give the men a break and told him to keep practising amongst themselves. He walked over to Cita and Kanti and asked would you like to wrestle.

Kanti looked up at him and said, "Women do not wrestle."

Ryan was surprised and asked, "Why?"

Kanti really didn't have an answer for him, so just repeated, "Women do not wrestle."

Ryan smiled, looked at the two women and again asked, "Why?"

Cita smiled at her friend and said, "Yes why do women not wrestle Kanti? We could wrestle. It's not like it would be scandalous or anything. We do not wrestle because nobody has ever asked us."

Kanti thought about it for a few moments and then said, "Cita, you are right. Do you want to try?"

Cita just nodded her head, smiled, and said, "Yes, why not."

Both the women looked up at Ryan and in unison said, "OK."

Ryan was a little surprised they agreed but happy they decided to participate. Both women stood up and went over next to Tisha and her friend who were doing quite well Ryan noticed.

Ryan walked over to Latona and was about to show everyone another move, when Latona stood up and put his hands out in front of it and said, "I'm getting tired of getting thrown to the ground. How about you let me throw you down for a while."

"But you fall so well." Tolbar shouted out and everybody started to laugh.

"That may be so Tolbar, but I am starting to get more bruises on me than you had yesterday from your lesson."

Tolbar just smiled back and nodded his head. Ryan thought that giving Latona the lead would probably be a good idea. So, the next move he went over slowly with Latona and then let him perform the move on him. Latona flipped Ryan over his hip, and he landed on his back on the ground.

Ryan laid there looking up at Latona and asked, "Feel better?"

Latona smiled, looked down at Ryan, then offered his hand to help Ryan up and said, "Yes."

They repeated the move again to show the group, but this time as Ryan hit the ground he rolled over and came back up quickly.

Latona was surprised but still smiled because he was not the one getting up off the ground.

Ryan looked at the group and said, "when you go down get up as quickly as you can."

They practiced that move several more times with Ryan getting tossed to the ground much to the delight of Latona. Ryan decided to let everybody practice on their own while he walked around helping them out in improving their technique, their hold, or where to place their feet. When you got to Cita and Kanti, he noticed that Kanti was not in the proper position she needed to be in. Ryan asked Cita if he could show Kanti how it's done.

Cita said, "Yes Ryan, you should show Kanti how it's done." And with that turned and smiled a big broad smile at her friend who was starting to turn a little red in the face.

Ryan got down in position and put one hand behind her head and the other and he grabbed her shoulder and then looked at her deep in her eyes and realized that he couldn't help himself staring.

After a few moments Kanti smiled at him, raised one eyebrow, and said, "Are you just going to look at me all day, or are you going to teach me how to wrestle?"

Ryan started to blush but increased his gaze towards her and said, "I could stare into your eyes all day long and love it."

This time it was Kanti's turn to Blush, and when she started to blush, Ryan twisted, put his foot in behind her and down she went.

She looked up at him surprised and said, "No fair, I was not ready."

Ryan smiled, looked down at her and said, "Must be ready all time." Then reach down to help her up.

He continued going around and helping everybody practice. He also noticed when he looked out at all the other people watching their friends or relatives as they were eating. It was almost like a festival, or a show and they were the entertainment. As they were finishing up, some of the young boys came up and asked Ryan what happens if you have multiple people wanting to wrestle you?

Ryan thought about it for a moment and saw where this was going and asked, "How many people?"

One boy looked around at his friends and answered, "Five."

Ryan then noticed that there were five of them. He said to the young lad, "Would you boys like to try to wrestle me down?"
The young boy looked at his friends who were nodding yes, and without a word they came rushing in. Ryan took a stance and pushed the first boy aside and he went down as he was off balance. The second boy came in too fast and too anxious, and Ryan put him on the ground. The third boy came up short, but unfortunately got too close to Ryan who was able to grab his arm, pivot himself in and flipped the young boy over his shoulder. Ryan then stood facing the two young lads who are now thinking that this was a bad idea.

Ryan held up his hands and said, "OK."

He reached out his hand to shake with one of the young boys. The young boy reached out to take it, and Ryan quickly spun him around into the other young fellow, and both boys went to the ground.

Ryan looked at the young boys and said. "You must be ready all time."

He looked up and saw Kanti walking towards him.

She smiled at Ryan and said, "Now it's my turn."

Ryan was a little surprised but watched her come forward. As she got within about five feet of him, she made a quick move as if she was going to do something but then twisted her ankle. She stumbled and Ryan leaped forward to help her. Ryan caught her and she fell against him. She started to stand up on her one good leg with both of her hands on his stomach, slowly and seductively sliding them up his chest. She leaned against him, and he could feel her warm breath on his neck, Ryan could feel her hands climbing up his chest, he felt her kissing his neck. Ryan was totally taken back and started breathing a little faster, then suddenly she shifted her position to where her bad leg wasn't bad anymore. It was behind him, and she was pushing him over. Ryan hit the ground on his side and rolled onto his back. There was laughter from the audience as well as the other young men around wrestling.

Kanti looked down at Ryan with a broad smile on her face and raising one eyebrow said, "You are right Ryan, you must always be ready." With that she turned and walked over to her friend chuckling.

Ryan got up with nothing more than a bruised ego, looked at her and said, "You tricky. I must watch you. With that Ryan smiled and turned back to Latona who was wiping tears from his eyes and still laughing. "Do you think funny?" Ryan asked.

"Oh yes!" replied Latona, then continued. "Is this a move that you will be teaching us Ryan?"

Ryan just smiled, looked at him and said, "Yes right now." He then looked at Tolbar and said, "Tolbar, you and Latona do the move that we just saw.

Latona's eyes opened wide and then he started smiling. He looked over at his friend Tolbar who started walking towards him exaggeratingly swinging his hips like a woman and blowing kisses at him. The crowd around broke out in loud laughter. As Tolbar got closer, Latona started blowing kisses back. When Tolbar reached Latona, he put his head on his shoulder and rubbed his hand on Latona's chest. The two men could not keep it up any longer and both broke down in hysterical laughter.

Ryan who was now also laughing said "OK let's go. More practice."

Once all the laughter had faded, everybody got back to practicing. They stopped for a meal midday and then continued practising some more with everyone enjoying this entertainment. The people loved to be entertained and when something spontaneous like this happened, they treated it like an event. Some of the people were cheering on friends and family that were wrestling with other people. It was quite an eventful afternoon.

Once everybody had had enough Latona said to the crowd. "I believe we should give Ryan a break today, and maybe he will teach us some more over the next few days."

Ryan nodded his head and said to the crowd, "I would like that."

Latona continued, "I think though we all now need to go have a bath at the river, as we look like we've been on a major buffalo hunt."

All the men nodded in agreement and started walking towards the river. Latona walked over to his mate, smiled at her, was a gleaming her eye and said, "We are going to the river to bathe, why don't you come with us, and you and I can go further down the river and…." He hesitated then continued, "Bathe."

His mate looked up at him, smiled, put her hand on his chest said, "No, I bathed this morning, so I do not need to bathe now. However, you are dirty and smelly, so you need to go bathe."

Latona looked a little disappointed, but then Nila continued, "However tonight if you still have that look in your eye, we can definitely do something about it."

Latona smiled and kissed his mate on the cheek and then turned to catch up with the others heading down to the river. Once he got to the river, everybody stripped off their clothing and waded in. Ryan was still not comfortable with this, but nobody else seemed to mind at all. Even Cita and Kanti stripped off and went into the river to bathe. This was just natural for them. Ryan was going to have to get used to this he thought. He tried not to stare at Kanti but glanced over at her when she wasn't looking in his direction. He didn't want to stare because he knew that was considered rude, but he just couldn't take his eyes off her. Latona and Tolbar noticed Ryan looking at Kanti when she wasn't looking and then noticed her looking back when Ryan wasn't looking, and both smiled at each other. When everybody was finished bathing, they all came out of the water and shook her clothes to get the dirt off and brushed off as much dirt as they could. They then got dressed and headed back into camp, everybody going in different directions.

As Ryan headed back towards camp, he saw Tisha running towards him with the little wolf following behind.

Ryan smiled as the two approached looking at a little wolf and saying, "I wondered where you got too."

He then turned and looked at the little girl but before he could say anything to him Tisha said, "Mother asked me to come and find you and see if you wanted to stop by for tea."

Ryan thought that sounded like a great idea because he did like Ayana's tea. Ryan nodded his head at the little girl, and they started to walk towards her tent. When they arrived Ayana had a cup of tea in her hand ready for Ryan.

"That was fun watching the wrestling today." She said to Ryan.

"I was surprised so many people come. " Ryan said.

"Entertainment." Ayana said with a smile.

Ryan didn't quite understand the word and shrugged his shoulders to indicate that he did not understand the word.

Ayana thought about it for a moment, and then said, "Something people like to watch, fun, exciting."

Ryan got the gist of what she's saying and nodded his head in his head.

"Thank you for teaching Mekome and including Tisha." She said to Ryan.

Ryan looked at the little girl and then up at her mother and said, "She is a good wrestler. She will give boys a challenge."

Ayana just smiled and sipped her tea.

"Where is Mekome?" Ryan asked.

Tisha answered, "Him and some other boys are across the field target practicing."

Ryan didn't fully understand and looked at Tisha and repeated, "Target practicing?"

Tisha smiled and then mimicked firing an arrow from a bow.

Ryan nodded his head in understanding and thought that might be interesting to watch. "Where are they doing this?" he asked the little girl.

She said, "I will show you after you finish your tea, " and then took a piece of dried meat out and gave it to the pup which he took, then went over in the grass laid down and started chewing on it. Ayana and Ryan talked for a while about the day's events.

Ryan had barely finished his tea when Tisha grabbed his arm and said, "OK you are finished. Let's go now." and started pulling Ryan.

Her mother scolded, "Leave Ryan alone! You can not be pulling adults like that. It is rude."

Tisha put her head down staring at the ground and then glanced at Ryan looking as she was getting ready to start crying. "I s am sorry Ryan." she said, choking back a soft sob.

Ryan patted her on the head and said, "That is OK." Then looked at Ayana and said with a smile, "I did tell her we could go after the tea was finished, so I guess I am done. Thank you so much for the tea." Ryan then leaned close to her and said in a conspiratorial voice, "I do not want to tell anybody, but your tea is the best I had." He then got up and let Tisha lead him.

This brought a smile to Anaya's face as she watched Ryan being pulled across the field by her daughter with the little pup following close behind. "That man has such patience with that little girl. He is going to make a good father someday." She thought.

The trio walked across the field until they came upon five boys with bow shooting at a target which was just a hide stuffed with grass. Ryan stood and watched them for a while, and then Mekome noticed him and his sister standing there.

"Hey Ryan!" he shouted over. "Would you like to try?"

"Yes, I would." Ryan called as he strolled over to the group of boys. He noticed all the boys from the wrestling earlier on in the day.

"How can you have energy to do this after wrestling all morning?" Ryan asked.

The boys just smiled and one of the boys handed Ryan a bow. Ryan examined the bow, it looked like it was cut from a tree, it was straight and about tree feet long. He wasn't too sure exactly what it was strung with but when he pulled it the bow flexed nicely. The handle of the bow was wrapped with a piece of leather to show where the hand should go. Ryan held to bow up, feeling it had a good weight to it. Ryan had taken lessons on shooting a bow for a movie that he was doing some stunt work in, but that was a compound bow made of fibreglass and carbon fiber. It shot fibreglass arrows with razor tips on the end of it or in the case of the movie rubber tips. Ryan examined the arrow and noticed it was a piece of wood sharpened at the tip and it had feather fletching on the end.

Ryan put the arrow in the bow, pulled it back and let it fly. It flew faster than he thought it would, but he missed it by about six feet. All the boys started to laugh and give Ryan a hard time. Ryan smiled, took another arrow loaded into the bow and shot again this time he was only about two feet short. Ryan figured this time for sure he had the range, so he loaded a third arrow and cited down range and let it fly. This arrow hit the target true.

The boys all cheered and told him what a great job it was and what a great shot it was.

Ryan felt that they were just trying to encourage him and smiled and said, "Well maybe one day I get as good as you boys."

He looked and noticed that there were two types of arrows, one was a sharpened point to the wood and another one had a chiselled piece of stone in a triangle that was inserted into the tip and wrapped with leather stipes. Ryan looked at one arrow, then the other. He then looked at Mekome and held out the two arrows with a questioning look on his face.

Mekome knew what Ryan was asking and pointed to the one arrow that was just a sharpened tip and said, "That one is for small prey, Rabbits, birds. Fox, the occasional deer." He pointed to the other one and said, "This one is for much larger animals, moose, buffalo, elk."

Ryan nodded his head in understanding. He stayed with the boys for a while, practising with them, and became quite good and precise once he had got the range figured out. He could also hit the target more frequently and only missed a couple of times, and even then, not by much.

He noticed Tish sitting with the little wolf watching and asked Mekome, "Why not let Tisha try?"

Mekome looked surprised and answered, "Why, she will not want to try?"

"Have you ever asked her?" Ryan questioned.

"No," Then looking at his sister he called out, "Tisha, would you like to try?"

Tishia's face lit up. She had always wanted to learn but people kept telling her that she was too young, and now her brother is willing to teach her. "Yes." she called out excitedly.

A few of the other boys started to object but stopped when Ryan said that he thought it would be a good idea, then pointed out how well she did at wrestling earlier today. Mekome and Ryan taught her the right way to hold the bow and load an arrow. Tisha even managed to hit the target several times and when she did the boys gave her encouragement. When they were done, the boys all started breaking up, Mekome and Tisha started walking back with Ryan. Tisha was excited and ran ahead to tell her mother about Mekome including her in the practice.

When they were halfway there Ryan got an idea, stopped, and looked at Mekome and asked. "Can you make fire?"

Mekome looked at Ryan, seemed a little surprised and answered "Yes."

Of course, he could make fire everybody could make fire he thought why is he asking me this?

"Could you teach me how to make fire?" Ryan asked.

Again, Mekome was surprised. "How could this man not know how to make fire?" he thought but he didn't want to say anything so he just nodded his head and said, "Yes of course I will teach you."

Ryan smiled nodding his head and then put his finger to his lips then said. "Tell no one, please."

Mekome looked at him for an instant and then thought, "If I did not know how to make fire, I would not want anybody to know either." so he just smiled and said, "OK Ryan, I won't tell anyone." Then asked. "When would you like start?   "

Ryan looked at Mekome and asked, "Can you teach me today."

Mekome nodded his head and answered, "Yes, I could teach you after the meal if you wish. It is not hard and should not take us very long."

Ryan smiled and said, "That will be very good."

They continued walking back towards the tent and when they got there, the wolf came out to greet Ryan. Ryan waved at Ayana and her mate as he started to walk away, but they called him back and asked if Ryan would like to join them in an evening meal.

Ryan thought about it for a moment and then answered. "Yes, I would." thinking to himself how he still couldn't believe how accepting and giving these people were.

Ayana introduced Ryan to her mate, "Ryan this is Neudal my mate. He has been at Three Sisters camp and checking his trap line but is home now."

Ryan smiled and said, "It is good to meet you Neudal. I saw you watching wrestling today."

"Yes, it was fun. I may join in on your next practice if that would be, ok?" he said with a smile.

Ryan smiled and said, "That would be good. The more people the good."

Ayana looked at Ryan and corrected, "The more people the better."

Ryan smiled and then repeated the sentence back. He then looked at Neudal and said, "Ayana is helping me to talk …" He thought about it for a second and continued, "Better."

He turned to look at Ayana who just smiled and nodded her head.

Neudal smiled and said, "She is patient that way."

Ayana looked at her mate smiling and said, "But not as patient as Ryan is with our children."

Neudal looked at Ryan nodding his head and said, "Yes I understand Mekome and Tisha have made you their best friend."

Ryan just smiled and nodded and answered. "Yes, they did. Your children are great."

Both Neudal and Ayana smiled at Ryan, then Ayana said, "Tisha came running into camp all excited about the boys teaching her to shoot and letting her practice with them. I am sure that was you doing."

"No." said Ryan looking at the young boy, "It was Mekome's idea to let his sister practice."

Neudal looked at his son and said, "That is good that you would include your sister."

"Yes, it was." added Ayana, not quite believing it.

After they had finished eating Ryan got up and thanked them for the meal and announced that he was going to have an early night. Ryan turned, looked at Mekome and Tisha wishing both a good night. He noticed that Mekome winked at him as he turned and walked away. Ryan Headed back to his tent with the little pup following closely behind. Ryan had a very active day and was tired, but he hoped that Mekome would remember his promise and come by to teach him how to make fire. Ryan laid down on his bed and quickly fell asleep. He was awoken by somebody by the entrance outside his tent, calling his name and tapping on the leather.

Ryan recognised the voice and told Mekome to come in. The young boy came in with something wrapped in a small package of leather and placed it on the ground.

"Do you still want me to teach you how to make fire?" he asked Ryan.

"Yes please." Ryan answered.

Unable to control his curiosity, Mekome had to ask, "How come you do not know how to start fire?"

Ryan didn't want to be explaining his history to the young boy right now, so he looked at him and said, "It is a long story, tell you later."

That seemed to satisfy the young man as he opened the leather packet. Ryan noticed it contained a piece of bark, a straight piece of wood which looked to be about the dimension of a drinking straw, but it was about two feet long. There was a piece of wood with a notch, cut in it and the V point of the notch with a burn mark. Also in the package were some pieces of wood and something that looks like fluff or dry vegetation.

Mekome stepped out of the tent for a few moments, and when he came back, he had some twigs and dried branches which he broke up into small pieces. In the middle of the stone fire pit, he placed some of the dry vegetation and made a small pyramid with the small sticks around it. He left one side open so that he could get at the dry vegetation inside.

Ryan pointed to the dry ingredients in the twig and asked Mekome, "What is?"

Mekome looked at Ryan and answered, "Dried moss. But cattail fluff works as well."

Ryan didn't understand what that meant, so Mekome told Ryan to follow him and led him to the trees behind the tent. He took him over to a fallen tree with moss growing on the side, picked it up and showed it to him. Ryan quickly got the idea of what it was and nodded his head.

They went back into the tent and Ryan closed the flap. Mekome took the piece of bark and laid it on the ground. Ryan noticed it was only about six inches square, he then watched Mekome lay the piece of wood on top of the bark. He then took a pinch of moss and put it just underneath the Vee that was cut into the notch of the wood. Ryan then watched him take the rod and place it right at the tip of the vee. Mekome then started at the bottom, rubbing back and forth, and working his way up to the top and then dropping his hands and working them back up again so that the rod was continuously spinning. Ryan watched with fascination as the very tip with the rod rotating into the wood was starting to make slivers which after a while started smoking. Mekome continued rubbing the stick up and down in one fluid and continuous motion. Ryan did notice that some wood shavings were falling onto the bark through the notch and onto the bark. In what seemed to be just a little over a minute the embers and the moss were smoking. Mekome quickly stooped, lifted the wood board, and pulled out the bark while starting to blow on the moss. Ryan noticed the bright orange glow of the embers. Mekome continued to blow and put a pinch of dry moss on it, while starting to walk it over towards the fire, blowing to keep the embers alive. Once he got to the fire, he tipped the piece of bark and the embers into the dried moss Inside the stacked sticks. He continued to blow and in a very short time he had a small fire going in the fireplace.

Ryan was completely amazed at how quick this process was. In his mind Ryan somehow thought that you would have to be doing that for at least five or ten minutes to get it started, yet this young lad had a fire going in under a couple of minutes.

Mekome handed the piece of bark to Ryan and said, "It is your turn to try."

Ryan smiled and thought, "Why the hell not. I'm going to have to learn to do this sometime."

He prepped everything the same way that he saw Mekome do it, then he put the wood down, took a pinch of moss, put it in underneath the notch, put the stick where it needed to be and then started the rubbing process.

This is where things got interesting for him, he was finding it hard to get his hands up to the top and then back down again quickly. There were a few false starts and Mekome was very patient with him and showed him how to hold his hands, and how to rub them together to work his way up to stick and then back down again. After a while Ryan finally got the rhythm that Mekome had, he thought this time he is going to do it for real. He concentrated and started rubbing the stick vigorously with his hands going up and then coming back down to go back up again. Eventually, he saw the embers starting to smoke Within the Vee and kept going for a while longer.

Mekome tapped Ryan on the shoulder and pointed to the embers and said, "Start to blow."

Ryan stopped, put the stick down, took out the birch bark with the embers and moss on it and slowly started to blow. He was pleased to see a slight glow start a blue more, and then went over to the second set of stacked sticks and moss that Mekome had shown how to set up and transfer the embers onto the dry off and slowly started to blow.

Ryan smiled as a small flame caught the moss and a short time later he heard the crackle as its sticks started to ignite. It had taken him longer than Mekome, but he was just learning. Ryan was pleased with what he had accomplished.

Mekome smiled, nodded his head, and said, "You did good Ryan."

Ryan smiled and said, "Thank you."

Mekome looked at the fire and said, "Now, do it one more time."

Ryan was a little surprised, but then thought the young boy was right. He extinguished the small fire and made another stack of sticks with moss in it then sat down in front of it and started the process all over again. This time he had a fire going quicker than he did last time, but still nowhere fast as Mekome. Mekome smiled as Ryan sat in front of his small fire and then said, "There you go, you know how to make fire now."

Ryan smiled and nodded at the young boy then looked at him and said, "Please do not tell anyone you teach me fire, OK?"

Mekome smiled, nodded, and said, "Ok I will not tell anyone."

Ryan just smiled thinking to himself, "Well, this is great. I can now make fire. I have a water basket and a bladder. I can make my own tea. It would have seemed like a small thing from where he used to come from, but it was a big thing now, and something that could help keep him alive.

Mekome looked at Ryan and said, "I must go now. I will see you at practice tomorrow morning."

Ryan said, "After the morning meal, we will all start practising but not as long this time."

"I don't think you have to worry about that. People are going to be sore tomorrow I bet." Mekome said as he got up and started to head out of Ryan's tent.

"Wait." Ryan called out. "You forgot your fire making stuff."

Mekome just turned and looked at Ryan and said, "Not mine, yours now."

Then starting to leave but remembering something, Mekome turned around and took a small pouch from his belt, walked over and emptied it out onto the leather that was stretched out with the fire making pieces on it. He emptied out dried moss, and some white fluff.

He looked at Ryan and said, "Fire starting Material."

Ryan smiled and said, "Thank you, Mekome."

As Mekome started across the field, he was wondering where Ryan was from and how come he could not make fire. "He knows so much, yet knows so little." He thought to himself.

Suddenly Mekome looked up and his eyes widened as he almost bumped into someone.

"Skyseeker, I did not see you there." He quickly stammered.

"Yes, I noticed that you almost walked into me. I see you were visiting with Ryan." The old woman said.

"Yes." he said a little too quickly, adding "We were just talking about wrestling."

"Indeed." said Skyseeker, "Just talking about wrestling, were you?"

"Yes, that is all." Said the young boy starting to squirm under Skyseeker's gaze.

She was trying hard not to smile. She knew the young boy was lying but did not want to call him out on it. "Will you be doing some more practising with Ryan tomorrow?" she asked.

"Yes, I think there is going to be more people tomorrow because a lot of people that were watching today said that they would like to try it and learn some new things." Mekome said.

"It is always good to learn new things, is it not young man?" Skyseeker said, looking directly at him.

Again, the young boy started to squirm a little and answered, "Yes, it is Skyseeker."

"It is good to learn things, and it is good to teach new things." she said to the young boy. "Would you not agree?"

"Yes, I would. Skyseeker." said Mekome, quickly looking at her, and then looking around for an escape. Skyseeker decided to let the young boy off the hook. "You should get going now. I am sure your mother is wondering where you are." She said with a smile.

"Yes, thank you Skyseeker." he said, and then quickly hurried away.

Skyseeker stood there for a few moments looking at Ryan's tent, she had been watching Ryan over the last few days and had been noticing a few things. She was surprised when she walked by tonight and heard Mekome teaching Ryan how to make fire. This made her very curious. "How can a man that age have survived this long without knowing how to make fire. Without fire you will die."

As Skyseeker stood staring at the tent she thought, "Soon Ryan, we shall travel together, and all the questions will be answered." She then turned and walked away from the tent.

Inside, Ryan sat there looking at the small fire that he had started earlier. He then went over, knocked all the sticks down and put the fire out. He walked outside behind the tent to the forest and gathered more wood. He came back into the tent and set up a small pile in the hearth. Once it was in place, he sat down, grabbed the rod, put the wood with the notch over the piece of bark and started working the stick back-and-forth, as well as up and down the shaft. This time with no help or encouragement, he got a fire started. He took the bark with the ember over to the kindling and blew the fire up. Ryan was very pleased with himself at this time. He had done it solely by himself and knew that, if need be, he could start a fire on his own. Ryan thought that he would keep a small fire going tonight, not for the heat, but just for a light in case his mystery woman came back to visit him.

He had not been able to see who it was the other night and thought if she came tonight, he would be able to see who it is. As he looked over his bed, he saw the wolf curled up, chewing on one of his moccasins. He went over and wrestled it out of the pup's mouth. The young pup thought this was a great game as he had played it with Ryan on a few occasions. Ryan looked at the small wolf sitting there staring at him expectantly like they were going to play some more.

"You can be a little demon," he said to the pup. "I think maybe some training is in order."

Ryan thought about that for a few moments and thought, "Why not. I think maybe we should start with basic training."

Ryan looked at the little wolf and said, "First of all we're going to have to give you a name. I can't keep calling you little one or little wolf." Then the idea hit him, and he thought, "Why not?"

he looked at the little wolf and said, "Guess what your new name is?" He waited for a few moments as if he was almost expecting the wolf to answer him then he said, "Zeus, I'm going to call you Zeus."

The wolf let out a little yip and then tried to sneak around him to get the moccasin that Ryan had put on his bedroll.

Ryan picked up the little pup, then put it down and firmly said, "No!"

The pup looked up at him that scooted around behind him and grabbed the moccasin again. Ryan caught a little wolf before it could take off with his shoe.

"This is going to take a little bit." Ryan thought as he was wrestling the moccasin out of the little pup's mouth.

Ryan spent a little bit of time teaching Zeus some of the basics. He then concluded that it was going to take quite a while for him to get even the basics down with his young and hyper little pup. Ryan was quite tired because the day had been very active so he put a few more logs on the fire, climbed into his bed after putting his moccasins underneath them so that Zeus couldn't get at them. Zeus curled up at the foot of the bed roll and was quickly asleep. Ryan went over the events in his head thinking about how much fun he had training all the boys and a few of the women on how to wrestle.

He also enjoyed shooting the bows with the boys and then having Mekome teach him how to make fire. Ryan was also happy that he had picked up on it and was able to start a fire on his own, he couldn't believe that Mekome would just leave his fire-starting kit for him to keep. It made him think again how caring and giving these people are. Ryan tried to stay awake for a while, hoping that his mystery woman would show up, but he quickly fell asleep. No one came into his tent that night and he woke up refreshed the next morning.

Ryan laid there thinking about what he's going to do today. That was one of the nice things about being here. You didn't have to make any plans if you didn't want to, you can just carry on and see where the day leads you. Ryan heard a very faint tapping on the side of the tent and his name being called.

"Come in." Ryan said.

The flap opened and Tolbar's mate Kiona entered. "We are just getting ready to have some leftover soup from last night for our morning meal and we were wondering if you would like to join us."

"I would love to join you." Said Ryan, as he threw back the cover and got up out of his bed.

Kiona had seen Ryan without his shirt several times, but it still surprised her every time she saw the tattoo. She thought maybe at some point she would get used to it, but right now it was so rare that she had to stop herself from staring at it.

Ryan threw on a shirt it started towards the opening, he turned back and saw that Zeus was still curled up on the bed. He thought to himself, "What the hell." and said, "Zeus come on."

Zeus raised his head, stood up stretched and then trotted after Ryan and Kiona. as they headed across the field. Ryan was pretty sure that little wolf would have followed them whether he called or not, but he decided to take this as a win and say it was because he called him by name.

As they were walking to Kiona's camp, Ryan asked, "Where is Tobar or Sakta?"

"Tolbar has a bad back and Skyler knee is bothering him a little bit." Kiona answered.

"I can understand that, because my shoulder is hurting me today." Ryan said.

As they walked into the campsite, Ryan saw Tolbar and his son sitting there.

Ryan smiled and asked, "Ready for training today?"

Tolbar look up at Ryan not too sure whether he was serious or not, and said, "I don't think I will make it today."

Sakta looked at Ryan and shook his head and said, "I will not be joining you today either."

Ryan just laughed and said, "I think we went too hard yesterday. We are all sore me too."

Kiona just smiled and corrected Ryan by saying, "Me as well."

Ryan smiled, noted the correction but did not repeat it. "We can give it a day or two and then start training again." Ryan said with a smile, massaging his shoulder.

Both Tolbar and Sakta nodded their heads in agreement. Kiona served the soup from the cooking basket, and they all sat around eating.

Ryan looked over and noticed four small baskets with steaming liquid in them of different colors. One was blue, another red yellow and then green. Kiona put a cooking stone in the red one.

Ryan looked at Kiona and asked, "What are you cooking?"

Kiona let out a little chuckle and answered. "I am not cooking anything Ryan, this is color for beads."

Ryan looked at her a little confused and said, "I do not understand."

Kiona smiled and showed Ryan another basket that had small bird bones in it. Next to it was a basket that had porcupine quills. Ryan picked out one of the little bones and held it up and noticed that it was hollow. He then looked at the porcupine well and then back questioningly at Kiona. Kiona took a knife and cut a porcupine bill in half, handing it back to Ryan, who then noticed that it was hollow as well. Kiona took a few of the bones and then dropped them into one of the baskets that had the red liquid in it. She let it sit for a while, then reached in with two twigs and pulled them out. Ryan noticed that the bones were now red. Ryan did not fully grasp the meaning of this until it suddenly struck him. The shirt that Kanti gave him with all the bead work and the designs on it. This is how they made the beads. Of course it's not like they have plastic beads.

He looked at the bubbling liquid and asked, "What makes color?"

Kiona answered, "Berries, blueberries for blue, red berries for red, flower petals, and other things. for the yellow. The yellow and blue get mix together or the green."

"That is great." said Ryan. "What do you do once you have colored?"

"We stored them until winter" Kiona answered. Ryan looked a little puzzled, so Kiana continued. "We are very busy visiting, hunting, and doing other things in the summer so we do not have time. But in the winter when the snow is coming, that is the time that we need to keep busy and we keep busy by making our clothes, doing craft work, making knife handles that sort of thing."
Ryan understood ninety percent of the conversation and thought to himself, "That's smart. Not like you could watch TV or curl up and watch a movie. You would have to keep yourself busy and engaged or you would go crazy."

Ryan smiled and nodded his head in understanding and asked, "Do you have a lot already done?"

Kiona smiled and answered, "Yes, and we will continue to do this right up until the season starts to turn. We also keep our eyes open for clear rocks and other things that we could turn into earrings as well."

Ryan was becoming more and more amazed with the way these people live. They live simply but they have their ways and traditions. Kiona made sure that Zeus got a deer bone with a little bit of meat on it that was used in making the soup the night before. The little pup was ecstatic and dragged the bone away just in case somebody decided to try to take it back from him. When Ryan had finished his morning meal, he thanked Kiona and Tolbar and decided to go for a walk. Ryan called Zeus, but the little wolf was not going to leave its prize bone.

Kiona said, "Just let him be. I will keep an eye on him."

Ryan's smile thanked her and then started walking across the field. He had not gone too far when he noticed two couples with hides stretched on frame, and they were scraping the underside of them.

Ryan stopped and observed for a while. He noticed that they were using a rock that had been chiselled down on one side. It resembled the head of a hatchet but made of stone. They were holding it with two hands, one hand on top of the other while scraping the underside of the hide. Ryan thought this looked like hard work and decided to see if they would like any help.

Ryan walked up to them and said, "Hello, would you like some help?"

 A young woman looked up, nodded her head in the affirmative, then stood up and handed Ryan the stone scrapper. Ryan got down on his knees in front of the frame and started repeating what he saw the woman doing. The young woman tapped him on the shoulder and got him to reposition his hands which he found were a lot more comfortable, and it made it easier to control the stone. With the extra set of hands, everybody managed to get spelled off and it made the work go a lot quicker. When they were done, they took the hides from the frame and started rolling them up. They thanked Ryan for the help and then started walking away.

Ryan headed off in the different direction and when he looked up, he noticed Latona's friend Corna and five other men carrying poles that were sharpened at one end as well as something that looked like shovels and they were heading towards the woods.

Ryan caught up with him and asked, "What are you all doing?"

 Corna looked at Ryan, smiled and answered, "We are heading out to dig new trenches."

Ryan was a bit surprised, as he used the trenches yesterday and they were far from being full. Ryan looked at Corna and said, "Trench is not full yet. Why dig new one."

Corna smiled and said, "It is best to have the new ones dug before the old ones fill up, then all you have to do is fill in the old one and change the location."

Ryan thought about it for a moment and decided that sounded like it was a smart idea. The men started to walk away, and Ryan asked, "Do you need help?"

Corna turned to look at Ryan a little surprised because nobody wanted to dig trenches, it was hard and dirty work. You were battling bushes, roots and could take you quite a while to get it done. If they could build the trenches in the field that would be great, but that is where they live and they need to keep the trench as far enough away from that as well as from any source of water.

Corna smiled and said, "Yes, you could help if you want."

Ryan smiled and took one of the long poles that Corna was carrying and started following them into the forest. They walked aways in and came to a very small natural clearing. That was about one hundred yards from where the original trenches were currently. Ryan watched as the men started taking the larger poles with the points in them and pounding them into the ground, holding them with two hands and thrusting them into the ground, breaking up the dirt. Ryan quickly got the idea and joined them. He then saw that what he thought were shovels were in fact moose antlers that were cut down and slightly sharpened to make shovels.

While they were breaking up the dirt other men were coming along behind them and digging the dirt out. It was hard work. They would only go a couple of inches, and they would run into a root which had to be hacked out with a stone axe. After a few hours, they had about a third of the trench done and Ryan was getting quite thirsty. They heard a noise coming through the bush and Ryan looked up to see Nila, Ayana, Kiona, and some other women walking towards them, and then noticed that they were carrying platters with food with them and had water bags as well.

Nila looked at Corna and said, "We figured you would be hungry and thirsty from the hard work of digging the trenches, so we thought that we would bring you some food and water."

She then looked over and noticed Ryan and was a bit surprised. "Hello Ryan." she said, "How did they talk to you in helping them with this?"

Corna looked at Nila and said, "We did not have to talk him into anything, he volunteered."

She looked surprised and asked, "You mean he just asked to help."

"That's exactly what he did." Corna said with a smile. then looking at Ryan he added, "He is very helpful. Just not too bright."

All the men around started to laugh including Ryan, who then looked at Corna and said, "If you want, I go now."

Corna just laughed and said, "No, you have to stay now."

Ryan just smiled and said, "OK then. But can I have something to eat first?"

Everyone laughed, then climbed out of the trench, gathered around, and started to eat. The women turned and started to walk back, Corna's mate stopped, turned, and asked, "When do you think you will be finished?"

He thought about it for a moment and said, "It will be a while."

Ryan smiled to himself, thinking, "There was again. Shortly, a while, and later. No ten minutes, two hours it was a very eloquent measurement of time."

As the women were walking back to camp Suna said. "I'm surprised Ryan volunteered to help them."

"I am not. "Nila said.

Ayana added "I'm not surprised either. A lot of people have been telling us that he has no problem stepping into help. Keeley was coming back from the river yesterday carrying two heavy bags of water when Ryan ran up to her, took one of the bags to help her so she was not carrying such a heavy load."

"Yes, and I noticed him helping Kaiman and his mate scrape those hides today." said one of the other women.

Nila nodded her head and added, "Yes, he is more than willing to help anybody that needs to help. It is funny though that when he arrived here, he had no clothing or provisions. The clothing that he has now is only because Kanti gave it to him because it was her former mates. I know Latona helped with a knife and Ayana has given him tea and a cooking basket but other than that, he has nothing."

"He seems eager to help everyone else out." Said one of the women, "Maybe we can see if we can help him out."

"That's a good idea Suna. What do you have in mind?"

The women continued talking as they headed back into the camp. Late in the afternoon the men finished the trench and stood back looking at it.

Corna then turned to Ryan and said, "Now you see why we would like to do it. Now it is done and when the other one is full, we will not be under any pressure to get dig new one as it is already completed."

Ryan smiled and agreed with him saying, "It is very smart. Get the work done when the weather is good, and the time is permitting so you have the time to do other things."

Corna put his hand on Ryan's shoulder and said, "Now you are learning."

Ryan smiled as all the men headed back towards the camp. A lot of the people knew the men were out digging the trenches so when they came into the field, they were called over to the long fire pit Where a haunch of venison was being cooked.

"That smells really good." said Ryan as they walked up to the fire.

"Well, we figured you would be hungry." Said Kiona as she started, carving off pieces of meat as the men sat down.

Ryan enjoyed the meal as well as a companionship with his new friends after a while, though Ryan excused himself saying that he was feeling rather dirty from digging the trench and was going to head down to the river for a quick swim to clean himself off. A few of the other men that were digging the trench with Ryan thought that sounded like a good idea saying they would join him. As he started to walk down towards the river, Ryan heard a little yip and turned around to see Zeus chasing after him. He slowed down and let the wolf catch up and then they all walked down to the river.

They stripped off their clothes, jumped in the river and started swimming and splashing around. Ryan looked at the bank and saw the little white wolf pacing back-and-forth, putting a paw in the water, taking it back out and whining looking at Ryan's direction. Ryan got out of the water, picked up the little wolf and carried it into the river.

Ryan only went out a little way and then he sat down holding the little wolf out in front of him. "OK Zeus, let's see if you're a swimmer or not."

A little wolf's legs were paddling underneath him and Ryan holding onto him moved him around in the water. Occasionally, he would loosen his grip with a little pup would start to sink, so Ryan quickly grabbed onto him and kept him on the surface of the water. After a few moments, Zeus seemed like he was enjoying it and kept trying to swim towards Ryan. Ryan figured that they both had enough and picked a little wolf up, stood up and carried him back to the bank of the river. Put the little wolf down and immediately Zeus started shaking to get the water out of its fur.

Ryan walked up the bank, got dressed, waved at some of the other men that were still swimming and walked back to the camp with Zeus following close behind. On their way back, He passed Ayana and Neudal's camp and they asked if he would like to come in for a tea. Ryan accepted and sat for a while, sipping tea talking with whoever and whomever. He noticed he was starting to get tired so again he excused himself and headed back to his tent.

Zeus had run ahead and wiggled his way inside the flap of the tent before Ryan got there. As he pulled the flat way, he said to the pup, "You better not be chewing on any of my clothes."

But when he went in the little pup was curled up on his bed. Ryan noticed a few parcels there that were not there when he left. He walked over to one, and it was a small leather pouch with something inside of it when Ryan opened it up, it had a wooden cup inside. He realized the pouch was like the pouch he saw a lot of the other people wearing around the camp that had their own personal cup in it. Ryan was very surprised that somebody would leave him a cup, but thankful as now he had a cup of his own for drinking water and for tea. He opened one of the other bundles and found that it was a cooking basket with cooking stones inside it. Another bundle, a leather vest with a wooden bowl wrapped up inside. Ryan sat there looking at the items in front of him.

"I can't believe this" he thought to himself, "They are so giving of themselves. I never asked for any of this but somehow, they knew that I needed it. I'm going to have to try to find out who gave me these so I can thank them personally."

Ryan thought about starting a fire, but then decided that he was too tired. It was still a light out when he climbed into his bedroll getting Zeus to move down to the end of it by his feet. Ryan was asleep in no time.

Ryan thought he was having one of those really good guy dreams but then realized he was actually awake at somebody was stroking his penis. Ryan smiled to himself thinking that his special friend had come back. He stared into the darkness, still unable to make out her form or her face and said, "Hello."

A finger, then pressed against his lips which he took to mean no talking. His cover was flipped to the side, and the woman climbed on top of him, guided his member inside of her and started rocking back-and-forth. Ryan held firmly to her hips and matched her rhythm.

She seemed hungrier than she was before and was moving a lot faster. Ryan slid his hands from her waist up her back and pulled her closer to him. He moved his hands around to cup those firm full breasts but was surprised to find these we're much smaller. The realization then hit him that this was not the same woman that to visit him the other night, but somebody totally different. She started rocking harder and Ryan decided he didn't care. He just tried to match her rhythm. After a short time, he could tell she was getting ready to climax and he was ready to join her. She started moaning loudly slowing down her movement. Ryan started moaning and picked up his. The woman on top of him moaned loudly and then laid across his chest as Ryan enjoyed his own orgasm. She laid there for only a moment, gave Ryan a quick kiss on the mouth, then jumped up, grabbed her clothing and left. Ryan called after her, but she continued out of the tent. Ryan laid there exhausted trying to figure out who that was but came up empty.

Ryan slept in the next morning and was awakened by Mekome sticking his head in the tent calling his name.

Mekome noticed that Ryan was still in his bed and said, "I an sorry Ryan, I did not mean to wake you, but it is mid morning."

"I know." said Ryan, "I had a late-night last night and was more tired than I thought."

Ryan looked at Zeus who is still curled up at the foot of his bedroll and watched the little pup stretch then look over at Mekome.

"We were just wondering if you would like to join us this morning. We are going to practice with the bows again." Mekome said.

"That sounds like fun." Said Ryan as he got up out of his bedroll. "Let me get ready and I will join you outside soon."

Mekome waited outside for Ryan to join him when the little pup came out, ran out into the field, relieved himself, and then came bounding back for attention from Mekome. Ryan emerged from the tent, and the two of them followed by the little wolf started over towards the practice field. As they were passing close to Mekome's tent, his mother called out for Mekome to come over.

Mekome looked at Ryan and said, "I will go see what mother wants and I will meet you at the practice area."

Ryan answered, "That ok, I will come with you and say good morning to your mother."

"Good morning, Ayana." Ryan said as they entered the campsite.

"Mekome said he was going to get you to see if he wanted to practice with them this morning." She said.

Ryan smiled, nodded his head, and said, "Yes I thought that might be fun, so I am going to go over and practice with the boys."

Ayana looked at Ryan and asked, "I was just wondering if you would like some tea before you go, and have you had a morning meal yet?"

Ryan's smiled and answered, "No, I was still sleeping when Mekome came and got me. I guess I was a little more tired than I thought, and I am not really that hungry this morning. I will practice with the boys and then see about getting a midday meal."

Ayana smiled and then asked if he would like some tea.

Ryan answered, "Yes." then remembered and reached into the pouch, tied to his belt, and took out a cup.

"Oh, you have your own cup now I see."

Ryan smiled and said, "Yes, I do. Somebody left me this cup, a nice bowl, another cooking basket, a carrying basket, and some more cooking stones. I am not too sure why though."

"Well, Ryan. You have been helping a lot of people out, well not asking anything in return. I think people gave them to you just to show their appreciation." Ayana said.

"Would you know who they are? I would like to thank them." Ryan asked.

Ayana just smiled said, "Sorry I do not."

Ryan was pretty sure that she did, but just decided not to tell him and he decided not to press her anymore.

"I think I am going to take my tea and go meet the boys. Thank you very much." Ryan said as he stood up.

Ayana reached it into a pouch and pulled out a piece of dried meat and handed it to Ryan. "Just in case you get hungry while you are practicing."

Neudal who had come out of the tent asked his Mate, "What about the Pup?"

Neudal tore another piece out of the pouch and handed it to Ryan to give to the little wolf. Ryan thanked him looked down at the pup, said, "Zeus, sit."

To Ryan's surprise the little pup sat down, took the meat then walked a little way away, laid down and started chewing on it.

"Zeus?" Neudal asked Ryan.

"Yes, I named the wolf Zeus." Ryan answered.

Neudal thought about it for a moment, smiled and nodded his head. "It is as good a name as any." he thought to himself as he watched the man in the wolf walk away to the practice area.

When Ryan joined the boys, they had already set up the target now we're taking turns shooting at them. Ryan joined them and found that this day his aim was a lot better than it was the last time they practiced. After a while unnoticed by anyone Latona walked up and stood there watching the group firing arrows into the target.

Latona smiled and then walked up to the group. Looking at Ryan he said, "I see you are not bad with a bow and can hit what you are aiming at.

Ryan looked at Latona and said, "I try."

Latona looked at Ryan and said, "We are expecting a large group of people in from Three Sister Valley in three days. We are heading out tomorrow to do some hunting to get meat for a feast. Would you like to join us?"

Ryan was a little surprised at the offer but thought it sounded like it would be a lot of fun and said, "Yes I would like to come, thank you."

Latona just looked down range at the target, that at Ryan and said with a smile, "You keep practising, and we will talk later."

Ryan smiled and said, "I will keep practicing."

As Latona started to walk away. Ryan thought of something and called out his name. Latona stopped and turned around. Ryan looked at the boys and thanked them for letting him practice with them today, but said he needed to talk to Latona about something and started to walk towards Latona.

The two men started walking together. Ryan turned rubbing his chin and said to Latona, "You have no hair face."

Latona wasn't too sure what to make of that. He just looked at Ryan and said, "No Ryan I do not."

Then Ryan asked, "Why?"

Latona looked at Ryan and noticed that he had a lot of hair on his face and realized why he might be asking the question. "I do not grow much hair on my face, but when I do..." he made a pitching motion with his fingers and continued "I pull it out."

Ryan thought about that for a moment and then asked, "So you pull out the hair?"

"Yes, I do not grow much hair now, but when I get the occasional one, I pluck it, or Nila plucks it for me."

Latona then noticed how much hair Ryan had on his face and realized that he might not pluck out the hair, so he decided to ask, "How do you get rid of your face hair where you are from?"

Ryan thought about it for a moment thinking how he was going to answer. Then looked at Latona ran his finger across his face and said, "I cut off hair, but I need very sharp knife."

Latona thought about it for a moment, nodded at his head and said, "Yes you would. I don't know where to get a knife that sharp." he said to Ryan Then quickly thought of something and added, Skytal had some flint that he traded from a traveller that came up from the south and I believe he made some very sharp knives. Let's go see if he possibly still has them around."

"Flint from the south?" Ryan asked.

"Yes, when people come up from the far south, they sometimes bring flint with them. It is unlike any that we can get around this region and it can be napped very fine, and it makes very sharp knives."

Ryan thought about that for a moment and asked, "People come from the south too here?"

Latona smiled and said, "Yes, from south, north, east, and west. We have people come from far away as a great ocean to the west, that is how we have things like shells to trade with them as they come through."

"Why do they come?" Ryan asked.

"They are just on journeys for one reason or another. Some travellers just pass through and some stay. We enjoy it when they stay as they have all new stories, and languages that we can learn." Latona answered.

Ryan had not noticed, but as they were walking Latona Had led them to Skytal's tent. As they approached, they saw him sitting outside his tent with his mate drinking tea.

"Hello Sita, Skytal." Latona said as they approached. "How are you both today?"

"We are well, and how are you and Ryan today?" Skytal asked.

"We are good as well." Latona said and then continued, "Ryan has a bit of a problem that you may be able to help us help with."

Skytal was immediately interested. "A problem?" He asked.

"Yes Skytal, if you take a look at our friend's face you will notice it is quite hairy." Latona said pointing to Ryan and smiling.

"Yes, we have noticed that, and some have commented on it but we just thought that might be the way of Ryan's people." Skytal said.

"Well apparently, he would like to get rid of the hair." Latona said.

Ryan watched Skytal cringe and said to Latona, "That is a lot of hair to pull out. Even if we were to use shells."

Ryan looked at Latona and asked, "Shells?"

Latona smiled and said, "Some travellers from the great water to the west on their way through, had connected shells That we could use as tweezers to clamp on the air and pull it out."

Ryan could understand why Skytal cringed and said, "I do not want to pull them out like that."

Latona just laughed saying, "I imagine not. It would hurt." He looked at Skytal and added, "Ryan's people scrape the hair with a very sharp knife, but I do not have anything like that, and I remembered that you traded that flint a while back and I was wondering if you had any sharp knives or pieces left over."

Skytal smiled and said, "I do have some knives, but I have something that might work a little better. There was this nice one I was knapping, but it split so I have a long piece that's only about a finger and half wide and tapered at the bottom due to the way it fractured. Let me see if I can find it." He went into the tent and came out a short while later, holding up a piece of flint. Ryan noticed it's about eight or nine inches long, two inches at the top with tapering down to about three quarters of an inch at the bottom. Skytal handed it to Ryan who examined it and then held out his arm and ran the sharp portion against his arm watching hair fall away.

"That is very sharp." he said to the two men. "I think it will work."

Skytal took the piece of flint back from Ryan and pulled out a thin piece of leather cordage and started wrapping it around the bottom of the flint and worked his way up. When he had wrapped half a handle, he tied it off and then handed it back to Ryan. Ryan felt it in his hand and thought that is going to make a great razor. Looking at it, it reminded him of a straight razor which he had used a couple of times in the past, or should he say in the future he thought.

Latona rubbed his face and then looked at Ryan and asked, "Are you going to try that now?"

Ryan answered, "No, I will do it later this afternoon because I'm going to need to heat water up to soften my beard."

Latona nodded his head and said, "That makes sense, the softer the hair, the easier it cuts." Latona then looked at Skytal and said, "I have asked Ryan to join us on the hunt tomorrow and he has accepted."

"He did, did he." Skytal said looking at Ryan, "That is good, then we will now get to see what kind of hunter he is. Are you a good hunter Ryan?" He asked.

Ryan just smiled and said, "You will have to wait until tomorrow to find out."

Latona smiled and said, "Good answer Ryan."

Ryan thanked Skytal again for the flint shaver and tucked it into the pouch that held his cup. "I'll have to be very careful when I take it out that I don't cut myself." he thought.

Latona and Skytal got into a conversation about the logistics of having so many people coming in from Three Sisters Valley. Ryan decided that now is probably a good time as any to try to get the hair from his face. He excused himself and headed back to his tent.

Once he arrived, Ryan started a small fire and started heating up the cooking stones. He took the water bladder down to the river and got water while the stones were heating up. When he came back, he filled a small basket with water and then dropped a few cooking stones which hissed as they hit the water. He left them in for a while and took them out and replaced them with fresh heated ones from the fire. In a relatively short time he had the water extremely hot. Ryan dipped his hand into the water and splashed some on his face. He did this several times in one area to soften up the beard. He took his razor out and slowly started to scrape away the hair. It was made more difficult by the fact that Ryan had no mirror and had no way of seeing how well he was doing and had to rely on the feel of how smooth his skin was. Ryan nicked himself two times and drew blood but pressed on. Ryan had about a quarter of his face done When he heard someone at the entrance to the tent calling his name.

He looked up and said, "Come in!" and was surprised when Kanti walked through the opening. Holding a bundle. Ryan went to get up, but she motioned him to stay where he was.

She put down the bundle and walked over and sat down in front of him looking at him and said, "You are bleeding." she said to Ryan.

"Yes, I know. I'm trying to cut off my face hair." he said looking at her.

Kanti smiled and said, "Good."

Ryan was a little surprised and asked, "You don't like face hair."

She looked at him, crinkled up her nose and answered, "No, it makes the face look dirty."

Ryan nodded his head and said, "I am not doing well because where I come from someone else helps cut the hair off my face." He did not add that the person was a barber.

She thought about that for a moment and asked, "Would you like me to do it for you?"

Ryan looked at her and asked, "Have you done this before?"

Kanti shook her head and said. "No, I have not but I will try."

She took the flint razor and splashed a handful of water onto a section of Ryan's face then with great concentration started scraping the hair away. Ryan was looking at her as she concentrated at the task in hand and tried not to chuckle when he noticed that when she was really concentrating the tip of her tongue poked out of the corner of her mouth a little. Kanti was doing a good job and had been working for a few moments when suddenly she got an idea.

She put down the razor, looked at Ryan and said, "I will be right back. Do not continue. I will finish when I get back." With that she got up and walked quickly out of the tent.

Ryan sat there wondering where she had gone but found that he likes getting the attention from her, so he was going to sit there and wait till she came back. When she came back, she had a small pouch in her hand and a wooden bowl, as well as a rock that fit in the palm of her hand. Ryan looked at the items but couldn't make any sense of them. Kanti went over to the basket and put two more cooking stones in it from the fire to really heat it up. Kanti placed a handful of something that she pulled from the pouch into the bowl, then took the rock and started grinding it up. Once she was satisfied, she took some hot water from the basket and scooped it into the bowl. She then took a twig and stirred the mixture briskly. Ryan noticed that the concoction in the bowl was starting to froth and looked like she was making a foam of some kind. After a moment she stuck two fingers into the bowl, scooped up some of the foam and rubbed it on an area of Ryan's face. She took the razor and started working on that area. The hair came away a lot easier and smoother with the addition of the slick foam. She did nick Ryan at one point and tried to apologize.

Ryan smiled and said, "Do not worry, if I was doing it, I would've cut myself a lot more than just the one time."

Kanti looked at the nicks he had on his face from when he was doing it by himself, smiled and nodded her head in agreement. It is short time Ryan was clean-shaven. Kanti reached out and rubbed her hand gently over Ryan's face. She looked him in the eye and said, "Much better. Smooth."

Ryan looked at her and said, "Thank you for the help. Can I ask for help again next time I need to be shaved?"

Kanti just smiled and said, "If it means I do not have to look at your face hair, then yes."

Ryan laughed a deep, happy laugh, and decided that he felt very comfortable around this woman, and she seemed to be getting a little more comfortable around him. Ryan then looked over at the package and asked, "What is in the package?"

Kanti's eyes opened in surprise because she had forgotten that she had brought in the package. "It is a few more clothes from my former mate that I no longer need and thought you might be able to use." She answered.

Kanti looked over and noticed that the tunic with all the fine bead work on it that was her former mate's favourite was hung over a frame in the corner up against the wall of the tent. She looked at it and smiled.

Ryan noticed where she was looking and said, "I hung it up. It is too beautiful to fold and not be shown."

Kanti could not believe how happy that statement made her feel. She just smiled and proceeded to open the parcel that she had brought. There were some more shirts in it as well as some pants and a pair of summer moccasins, and some winter footwear that look like thicker moccasins that went up your leg to just below your knee.

Ryan smiled saying, "Thank you so much for the clothes."

She just smiled back, looked down and said, "I have no further need for them. I have more but I am not ready to part with them right now."

Ryan reached out and put his hand on her knee and said, "Thank you again for everything."

Ran removed his hands from her knee and started to get up. "I wish he had kept that there a little longer" she thought to herself. Then looking at Ryan she continued thinking, "He really is quite handsome once you get past the skin colour and the hair color.

"Oh yes." she said, "Mother asked me to come and see if you want to join us for an evening meal."

Ryan looked at her, smiled and said, "Yes I would like to."

"Good, then you can come back with me. Now that you have no face hair, I guess it's OK to be seen with you." She said with a smile.

Well, we can not have you seen with a hairy guy." said Ryan as he started to follow her to Latona's home.

As Ryan and Kanti started walking away from the tent, Ryan heard a little whimper and turned around to see the wolf sitting at the opening wagging its tail.

"Come on Zeus!" he said to the little pup and watched as it came running up to join the two of them. They continued to cross the field, and then Ryan heard his name being called. He stopped, turned around and saw Tisha running up towards them.

"Hi Ryan." she said out of breath as she caught up to them, Neudal and Mekome were wondering if you wanted to come by and have an evening meal with us? Mekome has something that he wants to give you as well."

"I'm sorry Tisha." Ryan said, "I will not be able to make it today as I am going to share an evening meal with Latona, Nila and Kanti."

A look of disappointment came across the young girl's face and she looked down at the ground and said, "Ok I will let them know."

Ryan looked at Kanti then back the little girl smiling and said, "Could you do me a favour, and look after Zeus? Mabey take him back to your camp and when I am finished my evening meal, I will come visit you and pick up the little one."

A huge smile flashed across her face, and she said, "OK, that would be good." Then looking at the little wolf said, "Come on Zeus, let's go." and started running off.

The wolf turned and looked up at Ryan and then back at the little girl. "Go on. He said to the wolf and took off in a flash. Ryan looked at Kanti and said, "He is going to be much happier with her because she plays with him and spoils him."

Kanti looked at him and said, "I think someone has a little crush on you."

Ryan looked at her questioningly and asked, "Crush?" because he didn't understand the word.

Kanti thought about it for a moment and then said, "She really likes you."

Ryan just smiled, looked at her and asked, "What about you?" expecting her to go red.

She tilted her head, looked at him and took her finger and thumb and put it about an inch apart and answered, "A little bit."

"A little bit is better than no." Ryan thought as they continued to walk towards Latona's lodge.

Once they arrived Kanti went down the log ladder first with Ryan following closely behind her. When he got to the bottom, he could smell something wonderful cooking.

Ryan smiled, looked at Nila and said, "I do not know what you are cooking but it smells great."

Nila looked up at Ryan and said, "We are having grouse tonight. Latona needed some feathers for arrows and managed to kill three grouse."

"You are right Ryan they do smell good, don't they." Latona said looking at his mate.

Ryan turned to look at Latona, and for the first time noticed that Skyseeker was there as well. He was a little surprised at first and then realized, "Of course she would be here, she is family after all."

Skyseeker walked up to Ryan, reached out with her thumb and four fingers and grasped Ryan lightly on the chin, turning his head to the left and then turning it to the right before letting go.

"I see that you finally got rid of your face hair." She said to him with a smile, "You did a good job."

Ryan smiled at Skyseeker and then pointed to the three nicks that he had on his face and said, "These are by me. Then ran his hand over the rest of the smooth face, looked over at Kanti and said, "The rest Kanti has done."

Skyseeker looked over at her granddaughter and said, "You did a good job."

Kanti smiled and said, "He was having trouble doing it himself and kept nicking himself, so I decided to help him out."

Skyseeker just nodded her head looking at her granddaughter and smiled.

"Would you like some tea? "Nila asked.

"Yes please." answered Ryan as he reached into his pouch and pulled out his cup.

"Oh, you have your own cup now." stated Latona.

168

"Yes. When I arrived last night back to my tent, someone had left a cup, a bowl, and some other items. I'm not sure who it was. Do you have any ideas?" Ryan asked, looking at both Latona and Nila.

Nila looked up, smiled and answered, "Sorry, Ryan I have no idea. But somebody must have appreciated some help that you gave them at some point."

"That is funny." Said Ryan, "That is what Ayana said. I think you all know who gave them to me but you are just not telling me.'

Skyseeker looked at Ryan and said, "That is a possibility."

"Where is Zeus?" Latona asked.

Before Ryan could answer Kanti cut in and said, "Tisha is looking after him. She wanted Ryan to come for an evening meal tonight and was very disappointed when he could not make it. So, Ryan suggested that she could look after the pup, and he would pick him up later. It made her happy."

Skyseeker smiled and said, "Yes, she has become quite attached to our yellow haired friend here."

Ryan laughed and said, "She is a smart little girl, and I like her and her family very much. She reminds me of someone I used to know."

Kanti smiled and looked at her mother and said, "I think she has a little crush on Ryan."

"I do not think so." said Ryan smiling, "I think I am more of a playmate for her."

"That could be it, but I think it probably is that she has grown attached to our white skin friend here. I have heard there is a few other women around the camp that are a little smitten with Ryan." Nila said, looking at her daughter.

"Well, I do not know why." Kanti said, "Those blue eyes do look very different.

Nila just smiled and went back to preparing the meal.

I like your pit house Ryan said to Latona looking around.

Latona looked at Ryan and said, "It is called a lodge."

Ryan smiled nodding his head and then asked, "Why is it that some people live in a lodge and others live out in the field."

Latona answered, During the winter season everyone lives in their lodge. We have whole families staying in them, that is why they are so large. In the summer some people prefer to live out on the field in their tents and move out there in Spring but move back in with their families in the lodge when the snow starts."

"Have lodges always been around." Ryan asked.

Latona shook his head and said, "No they have been around for many, many, many seasons, but stories say that it was people from the west that showed the elders how to build them when some travellers passing through decided to stay. That is why we like where we like living in this location as it is a crossroads for people coming from the west, north, south, and east. So, if they stay for a while, we get great stories and learn new things."

Skyseeker looked over at Ryan and said, "It is very important for our people to learn new things."

Ryan got the feeling she wasn't talking about the same thing that Latona was, but just decided to nod his head instead of answering or saying anything.

Ryan was surprised that the meal that smelt so fantastic exceeded his expectations. "This meal is great Nila." Ryan said to Latona's mate.

Latona looked at his mate and said, "I must agree with Ryan. These birds were cooked to perfection and whatever herbs you used with them just enhanced the flavor."

Nila beamed at her mate's praise and said. "I just added a little of this and a little of that, plus a pinch of salt."

Ryan was unfamiliar with the last word and asked, "Salt?"

Nila went to a small container and took a small pitch and placed it in Ryan's palm. Ryan studied it for a moment and then tasted it, smiling as he recognised the taste.

"Salt." He repeated nodding his head and smiling. Then asked, "Where do you get it?"

We trade it with travelers that come from the great water to the west, it is very rare, and we use it sparingly when we can get it. We also get some from travellers that come from the west as well. They claim there is a lake there where they can get it from. Some also claim That it could be dug out of the ground as well, but we believe that is just a story."

Ryan smiled and said, "I do not think it's a story. I have seen it many years ago."

Skyseeker was surprised and intrigued by that statement but did not ask any questions.

After dinner, they sat around talking about the hunt tomorrow. Skyseeker asked, "Ryan are you excited about going hunting tomorrow?"

"Yes." said Ryan. "I am looking forward to it."

Kanti added, "Yes, it is going to be fun."

Ryan was a little surprised and looked over at Kanti and asked. "Are you coming with us?"

She stared back at Ryan and said. "Yes, I do hunt. Are you surprised?"

Ryan felt a little embarrassed and quickly looked at Kanti and said, "I am sorry."

Kanti just smiled at him and said, "I will not be hunting tomorrow because some of the women are going to go along with the hunting party and do some gathering."

"Gathering?" Ryan asked.

"Yes, we look for Berry's, greens, bullrushes, all those things and bring them back. This is the time that we need to be gathering and storing them because when the winter comes, it will be harder if not impossible to find them."

"That makes sense." Ryan thought to himself. "When are we leaving tomorrow?" Ryan asked Latona.

"We will be going out mid morning." Latona said, "We will be gathering in the field where you were practising the other day. Do not worry if we do not see you there, we will not leave without you. I will send somebody to your tent to get you."

Ryan smiled and said, "I do not think you are going to have to worry about that. I'm looking forward to it, so I'll make sure that I am there."

"Good." said Latona.

Ryan remembered that he had made a promise to Tisha to go back and pick up Zeus and meet with Mekome and his father. He thanked Nila for the wonderful meal and then excused himself. Ryan got up to leave and as he was walking over towards the log to climb out, Skyseeker came up and touched him on the shoulder to get him to stop. Ryan stopped and turned around and looked at the old woman.

"You and I will need to get together sometime, maybe the day after the feast. We have things we need to go over and some questions that need to be answered." She said to Ryan.

Ryan didn't say anything but nodded his head in agreement and then climbed up the log and onto the field.

As Ryan started to walk towards Neudal and Ayana's tent, he noticed Tisha out in the field with Zeus chasing him around. He stopped and watched for a while with a smile on his face as the little girl would chase the wolf around in a circle, then stop and start to run away and when the wolf noticed this it would turn and start chasing her. Tisha looked up and noticed Ryan and then came running over to him.

"You did come!" She said excitedly.

Ryan smiled at her and said, "I told you I would, and here I am."

Tisha took Ryan's hand and started to lead him towards the tent. Ryan smiled, thinking how much she reminded him of his goddaughter Nina. As they walked into the camp, Ayana looked up and smiled watching Tisha lead Ryan in and scolded, "Tisha, leave Ryan alone."

Ryan looked at Ayana and said, "That is OK. She was making sure I got here safely."

Neudal looked at Ryan and said, "I am glad you could make it. Mekome has something he wants to give you and he has been dying to do it all day."

Ryan looked around and then asked, "Where is Mekome?"

"I am in here." Came a voice from inside the tent. "I will be out shortly."

Neudal smiled at Ryan and said, "He went in to get your surprise as soon as he saw you walking in with Tisha."

Mekome emerged from the tent, holding a bow and a leather elongated pouch with arrows in it. He handed the bow to Ryan and said, "Here, I made this for you, so you will have something to use on the hunt tomorrow."

Ryan looked at the bow and admired the work that went into it. The bow was similar to the ones that they used in practice however, all the bark had been removed from it, and he noticed that there were some carvings etched into the wood up and down the shaft. There was also a bone mounted in the centre portion of the bow as a hand grip and guide that was held in place by a wrapped leather strip.

"This is beautiful." He said to Mekome.

"Thank you." Mekome replied happy that Ryan liked it. "It is my way of thanking you for helping me by teaching me all the new wrestling moves."

Ryan held the bow up and tested the tension and said, "This is a good bow. I look forward to using it tomorrow while hunting."

Mekome then hand it over the leather quiver with the arrows in it saying, "I gave you the two types of arrows one with the pointed tip for birds and small game, but more of the ones with the stone tips on them for larger game because I think you are all going out after deer and elk tomorrow. I also marked the arrows for you."

Ryan wasn't too sure what that meant and asked Mekome, "Marked the arrows?"

174

"Yes, all of the arrows and spears have a hunter's mark on them so that they know which arrow or spear killed the animal, and that hunter is the one that gets credited with the kill." Mekome explained.

Ryan took one of the arrows out of the quiver and examined it, noticing a carving of a triangle with two lines through it. He pulled out another arrow and saw the same marking.

"Is this my Mark?" He asked Mekome.

"Yes, it is. I was not too sure what your mark was, so I came up with that one. I hope it's OK." Mekome replied.

"It is perfect, thank you." said Ryan with a smile, "I am really surprised, but very happy for this gift."

Neudal smiled at Ryan and said, "He wanted to do this for you because of you teaching him to wrestle he has now been accepted more by some of the older boys who are coming to him and asking him for tips with their wrestling. Also, he knew you did not have your own bow or arrows for hunting tomorrow."

"That was very thoughtful of you." Ryan said to Mekome, "And I look forward to seeing if I can get anything with it tomorrow."

While Ryan was sitting there, Zeus came over and climbed up on his lap. Tisha asked Ryan for his cup, which he gave to her, and she went over and got him some tea.

Ayana smiled as he was sipping his tea and Ryan asked, "Have you found out who gave me the cup and other gifts."

"No, not yet." She answered with a smile, "But I'll keep asking."

This time Ryan felt certain that she knew more than she was telling and concluded that he was never going to find out who had given him the gifts. He sat with the family for a while and as it started to get dark, he thanked Ayana and Neudal for the tea.

"Thank you for the special gifts. I really…...." He stopped and looked over at Ayana.

She smiled and said, "I think the word you're looking for is appreciate."

Ryan then looked at Mekome and said, "Thank you Mekome. I really appreciate the gift."

Mekome just sat there smiling and nodded his head.

Ryan excused himself and said, "I'm going to go turn in now. I want to make sure that I'm up and ready to go on the hunt tomorrow." he looked at Neudal and asked, "Are you coming tomorrow as well?"

Neudal nodded his head and answered, "Yes. But don't worry we won't let you sleep in. We will come and get you."

Ryan smiled and said, "I keep telling everyone I will be there." Ryan got up, waved, and then headed back to his tent, followed closely by Zeus.

Chapter 5

Ryan woke up early, excited about going on the hunt that day. He was a little disappointed that he didn't have any female callers in the night, but in a way was glad because now he was awake and fresh and not worn out. Ryan quickly got dressed and headed out of the tent with Zeus close behind. As he was leaving, he thought to himself how different it was to just get up and do things without worrying about the time, if it's light you get up, if it gets dark then it's time to go to bed. As Ryan walked across the field, he saw up ahead in the distance Neudal, Latona, Skytal, Nila, Tolbar, Corna, Kanti, Cita, and a few other men and women that he had not been introduced to yet.

As he walked up to the group Latona smiled and said, "Nice to see that you did not sleep in today."

Ryan looked at him and replied, "I told you I would be here on time."

Tolbar looked at Ryan, then at Latona and said, "The young man must be excited about going hunting for him to be up this early."

Smiling Ryan padded Tolbar on the back and said, "You are right. I am very excited about going hunting."

Neudal looked at Ryan and said, "You are excited now, let us see how good of a hunter you really are."

Tolbar looked at Ryan's bow and said, "I see you have your own bow. May I look at it?"

"Sure." Ryan said and took it off his shoulder and handed it to Tolbar.

Tolbar took the offered bow and started examining it, turning it over to see the markings and admiring the workmanship. "This is a good bow. Did you make it yourself?"

"No, I did not. Mekome made it for me as a gift for teaching wrestling." Ryan said smiling at Neudal.

Tolbar looked at Neudal in surprise and asked, "Did Mekome make this by himself?" showing the bow to Latona.

Latona examined the bow, nodding and agreeing.

"Yes, he did, and he worked hard on it to surprise Ryan, and I think he did a good job" Neudal answered with obvious pride in his voice.

"He did more than a good job my friend. I may have to get him to make a bow for me." Tolbar said with a grin.

Neudal's chest swelled with pride from the high praise, and he wished Mekome was here to see how much Tolbar and Latona liked the Bow. He would be sure to tell him later.

As they started walking away Ryan Noticed Mekome and Tisha and called out to them.

As they joined the group Ryan asked, "Would you mind looking after Zeus while we are Hunting? I do not want him getting in the way."

Both children nodded their heads and Tisha called out to the little wolf, "Come on Zeus, let's go play." And with that she started running into the field with Zeus running behind her.

"We will look after him until you get back." Mekome said, and then followed his little sister.

Ryan turned and started walking to catch up with the rest of the group. Ryan had shot a bow many times and learned how to shoot proficiently so that he could use it in the movies and filmmaking. However, he had never been out bow hunting and hoped he did not embarrass himself in front of his new friends.

The group started following the river on the north bank heading west. Ryan wasn't too sure where they were going, but just decided that he would follow along, pay attention, and try not to screw up too badly. He noticed it as they were walking, occasionally, the women would break off, go to some bushes and pick some berries or stop and pick some mushrooms off some fallen logs or around the bass of some trees and wondered to himself how they knew what was edible and what wasn't.

Then thought to himself, "What a stupid question that was as they've been probably gathering their own food for generations."

The group noticed a lot of game, but it was all on the other side of the river, Latona pointed out a herd of elk grazing in a field across the river, turned and looked at the group and said, "It looks like the animals are lucky today. We are on the wrong side of the river."

Tollbar smiled and said, "I am sure they did not all cross the river because they knew we were coming."

"I know." said Latona, "But two or three of them would have been good for the feast.'

Tolbar smiled at his friend, "I am sure we will run into some at some point. If need be, we may need to work our way up into the tree line a little. Let us keep going and see what we can find."

Latona nodded his head in agreement and continued walking, smiled and said, "The women are having much more luck gathering than we are at hunting."

Kanti looked up at her father and said, "Then you had better get at it, because how embarrassing would it be to go back with all of us women, baskets loaded, and you hunters with nothing."

Cita laughed and said, "I think that would be great. It would be quite the story to tell around the campfire tomorrow when there's no meat for the feast."

"There will be meat for the feast Cita." Latona said mock scolding the young woman.

"We shall see." Cita said with a smile as the woman headed into a patch of wild berries.

Ryan and the men continued walking, with Ryan listening to a conversation between Tollbar and Neudal, when suddenly he heard a scream. When Ryan turned around, he saw that Kanti was standing rigid and had dropped her picking basket with the contents falling out onto the ground. He could see no immediate danger as he looked around, then he noticed across the river, the biggest grizzly bear that he had ever seen in his life. It was walking between the tree line and the bank of the river on the other side with its head moving from side to side as it scented the air. Ryan quickly walked up behind Kanti to watch the big bear lumber along its way across the river.

The bear seemed to catch a scent, which Ryan assumed must be that of the group of people on this side of the river. Suddenly, the great bear stood up on its hind legs, and Ryan could not believe how tall it was.

"That bear must be close to thirteen feet standing like that." he thought to himself.

When he looked at Kanti, he noticed that she was visibly trembling and looked like she was about to collapse. Ryan instinctively put his arm around her shoulder and she immediately turned and hugged Ryan. He could now hear that she was crying but Ryan didn't understand what was going on, as he held the sobbing woman close to him. He looked over at Latona and was about to ask what was going on when he noticed Latona shaking his head and putting his finger to his lips, signaling Ryan not to ask any questions. Ryan got the hint and just stood there holding Kanti in his arms while she wept. The grizzly on the other side of the river went back down on all fours, raised its head, growled at the group across the river, and then continued on its way, turning, and then heading into the woods.

After a short while, Kanti stopped crying, wiped her eyes, looked up at Ryan and said, "I'm sorry, I do not mean to be such a little girl."

Ryan smiled at her and said, "It is OK you were upset."

Kanti continued looking up at Ryan, smiled and said to him, "You can let me go now."

Ryan grinned at her with a twinkle in his eye and said, "But what if I don't want to."

A beautiful smile came across Kanti's face and then turned into a mischievous grin. She said, "Then I will have to put you down on the ground again, like I did before."

Smiling Ryan released the young woman and said, "Well, we do not want that to happen now do we."

Cita said, "No you do not. It was embarrassing enough for you the first time, if she did it to you a second time you would never live it down."

Ryan could see that the jokes were bringing a lighter mood to Kanti and whatever was bothering her was slowly ebbing away. Ryan walked back to the group of men looking at Latona questioningly but didn't say anything.

Latona just looked up at Ryan saying, "Later."

Ryan said nothing, just nodded his head and the group carried on with Ryan walking at the rear with Tolbar listening as he pointed out several landmarks around the area. Ryan didn't notice Latona slowing down until he was level with both Ryan and Tolbar. Latona looked at Tolbar who nodded and started walking up into the middle of the group. Ryan looked over at Latona.

Latona said, "Thank you for being so kind to Kanti back there." Ryan didn't say anything and just nodded his head and Latona continued. "We see this big brother bear from time to time, and she can still not get over what it took away from her."

"I do not understand." said Ryan.

"Of course you do not." said Latona. "You were not here." His face got serious, and he looked up at Ryan. "Big brother bear is the bear that killed Toltin, Kanti's mate."

"What. How?" Ryan asked.

"He was out with the hunting party going after mountain goats as it was getting close to winter and Kanti wanted one of the hides, also the meat is good as well.

They were walking along between the tree line and the mountain slope with their attention up on the slope looking to see if they could find any goats. Kanti's mate was in the lead, and suddenly the bear rushed out of the bushes and in one movement swiped at him. The bear's paw was huge, and its claws were long, it struck him in the head knocking him to the ground. It then started to maul him. The rest of the hunters started attacking the bear to drive it off. Apparently, it did not take that much time to run the bear off, but the damage was already done and Toltin was dead. Most of the people there believe that he was dead before he hit the ground after the first swipe of the giant bear's paw. They brought his body back to the camp and Kanti did not handle it well. She mourned for many years and Nila, and I felt that she would continue to mourn and never take another mate or even look at another man."

"I am so sorry to hear that." said Ryan, shaking his head and looking at Latona. "It must have been terrible for her."

"It was, but Nila and I have noticed lately that she is starting to come out of her shell and become more like her old self again." Latona said.

"Well, that is good then, is it not?" Ryan asked Latona.

Latona smiled at him and answered, "Yes, it is. We think it's because of some tall white-haired man."

Ryan looked surprised and asked, "What do you mean? Me?

Latona smiled and nodded his head.

"No, you have that wrong." Ryan protested. Ryan looked up and saw Kanti walking with the other woman and then turned to look back at Latona. "You are wrong. She is not, as you say interested in me."

"Are you so sure Ryan?" Latona asked, smiling.

"Yes, I am sure." Answered Ryan.

"Interesting." Said Latona. "In talking to Kanti, you both say the same thing. I think you can both see certain things, but you can not see that you may be good for each other."

Ryan looked at Latona as he started to walk away and said, "She is not interested in me, do not worry."

Latona stopped, turned around smiling and said, "Are you sure about that, and who said I was worried Ryan." He then turned and continued walking into the group.

The group continued to follow the river for a while when suddenly Latona who was at the front of the group raised his hand for everybody to stop. As they looked ahead, they saw a small herd of elk coming up from the river and heading into the trees. Latona talked to Kanti and some of the other women, then they started walking ahead.

Ryan looked at Neudal and asked, "Are we going to follow them into the woods?"

Neudal looked at Ryan and shook his head. "No, the women are going to walk ahead and walk past where the elk have gone into the woods, making noise to drive them a little further into the woods. We are going to go in at an angle up here and try to cut them off. I hope you know how to move quietly through the woods."

"I'm not too sure I know how to move quietly through the woods." Ryan thought to himself, "But Let's give this a try."

Following Neudal and the other men as they walked one hundred yards up the tree line and then started heading in at an angle. He watched the man in front of him and he noticed that they were incredibly quiet. Ryan watched Neudal, the man in front of him and noticed they were very specific about where they placed their footing.

They did not step on any branches, they searched for preferred ground, and they moved swiftly. After what seemed like a long time to Ryan, but in fact was only a short while, Latona held up his fist for everyone to stop and then motioned for everyone to come closer. As they came close, they noticed a young elk eating some foliage in front of a large bush about thirty feet away.

Latona looked at Ryan smiling and whispered, "It is time to see what type of hunter you are." and pointed in the direction of the elk.

Ryan knew that he was being tested and just smiled back at Latona. He took the bow from off his shoulder and pulled out two arrows from his quiver. One which he stuck in the ground in front of him and the other he loaded into his bow. The hunters were surprised with this move but just continued to watch. The second arrow was a trick that one of his instructors taught him just in case you missed with the first arrow, you have quick access to the second one. That advice had always stuck in his mind. Ryan drew back the bow and took careful aim at the beast in front of him. Ryan then took three short breaths and then released the arrow. The men watched the projectile sail towards the elk, and then go above its back by about a foot and into the dense bush behind it. The men were about to start laughing at Ryan's terrible aim, when a loud bellow sounded, and the bush started to shake. An incredibly large male elk with a full rack of antlers started to bolt from the bush with an arrow in its side. Before anyone could react, another arrow hit the elk halfway up and just behind the shoulder, piercing the elk's heart. The huge elk took three more steps, fell on its front legs, and then toppled over. The hunters were stunned and turned to see Ryan standing there with his bow.

"I' have never seen anything like that!" Tolbar said with a surprise expression. "I did not even see the elk in the bush."

"Ryan how did you know it was there, and how did you get off the second shot so quickly?" Latona asked, just as surprised as the other hunters.

"I just wanted to prove to you all that I was a good hunter." Ryan said with a smug look on his face.

He decided not to tell them the truth. That truth being that Ryan did not see the elk in the bush. He totally missed the first elk he was shooting at, and then quickly loaded the second arrow as he was going to take another shot at the elk that he had missed in the first place, but when he saw the big elk start to move out of the bushes he aimed and shot and was lucky enough to hit it in a vulnerable spot.

"I think I'll just keep that little bit to myself." Ryan thought. Still smiling at the group who were looking at him shaking their heads.

in the commotion the small elk in the front of the bush bolted

Latona called to the group, "Skytal, Neudal, Tolbar, Ryan and me, will look after this, and get it dressed out so we can take it back. If a few of you want to see if you could track down any of the other elk that scattered."

The men nodded their head and silently headed off into the direction they felt the elk should be. Ryan Helped the men gut the elk, and then watched as the men removed the head and took the antlers. It took a while to get the job done and then the men attached poles to the elk's legs and the four of them started to carry it towards the river.

"It is best to get away from these entrails, because we're going to have predators here very quickly. Said Latona.

186

As the men came into the clearing the women crowded around to see what the men had got. The story of Ryan's hunting prowess was quickly related to everyone, and he noticed Kanti smiling at him.

She looked at him and said. "Well, I guess you are quite the hunter."

He smiled and asked, "Was there any doubt?"

Kanti looked at him and answered, "Yes there was a lot."

With that everybody in the group laughed. The other hunters showed up and to everyone's delight, they had taken down a young elk. It was dressed and mounted on a pole being carried back.

"This male is heavy and we're going to have to stop several times so we should head back now." Skytal said.

With that they turned and headed back towards the camp. On the way back the men spelled each other off, and even some of the women took a turn carrying the kill. On the way back Ryan noticed that Kanti had bundles of bullrush tied onto the pack on her back. As they continued on their way, she veered off to a batch of what looked to Ryan to be thistle. She then took out two pieces of leather, wrapped them around her hands and started digging at the thistle and putting it into her basket.

When she was done and started back, Ryan moved in beside her and asked, "What did you need the thistle for?"

She looked at him and answered, "Once it's cooked it's very good to eat."

Ryan looked a little surprised and said, "But it's prickly."

"Not if you cook it properly. Kanti said with a smile.

"And the bulrushes?" he asked.

"We use the bulrushes for a lot of different things. The leaf's can be used for weaving, mats, baskets, and such. The stems or stock when dried out can be used for arrows, fire starting sticks. At certain times in the year the brown the top carries a lot of pollen which is good, or near the end of the year it could be broken up and explodes with a white fuzz that could be used for fire starting, or absorbent material for baby's waste. Finally, the root can be ground up to make flour and is edible and tastes good, so we use for food.

Ryan looked at Kanti and said, "I do not think I could ever eat that."

A smile crossed Kanti's face and said, "You already have. When you had mother's stew. Did you not like it?"

Ryan thought about it then answered, "Yes, it was good."

Konti continued, "Well, there was thistle in that as well. Some of the greens that you ate at different camps could have been thistle as well."

Ryan just smiled and said, "Well, I will now shut up and always eat what is in front of me."

Konti smiled at Ryan's joke, and they walked in silence for a few moments, when Ryan looked at her and said "I'm very sorry to hear about your mate. Latona told me, so I understand why big brother bear upset you so much."

Kanti just looked at the ground as she was walking, then looked up at Ryan and said "It should not still bother me after all this time, but it does. We are supposed to live in harmony with all the animals, the earth, wind and the air, but I wish that animal dead." She then looked down again.

"That is understandable." Said Ryan. He then noticed a butterfly and it made him think of his goddaughter. He would call her butterfly, and she liked the name.

Kanti noticed the look that came over Ryans face and asked, "Are you Ok Ryan? It is just a butterfly"

Ryan smiled and repeated "Butterfly." Good to know the name in their language he thought.

They walked in silence for a little more and she looked up and smiled at Ryan and asked, "So what are you going to do with your hide?"

"Hide?" Ryan asked.

"Yes, from what I hear you are the one that killed the elk, so the meat will be shared with everybody, but the hide is yours."

"I don't know." Said Ryan little confused.

Well, you are going to have to cure the hide." Kanti said.

"Cure?" Ryan asked.

Kanti looked at Ryan thinking, "How can this man not know these things?" She then smiled and said, "Do not worry about it. I will help you with it. It does not need to be done right away, but make sure you put the hide in the cool storage."

"OK." said Ryan with a smile. "Where is that?"

"I will show you when we get back." Said Kanti.

"Good." said Ryan.

"The men are going to want to butcher this as soon as we get back to camp and store the meat for the feast tomorrow, so we will just roll the hide up after that and do it in the next day or so."

An idea came to Ryan so he said, since you have given me many beautiful clothes would you like the hide? I am sure you could make something out of it."

She was surprised at his offer, smiled and said "We shall see."

The men didn't get back into camp until late in the afternoon and Kanti was correct, they went right to butchering the meat.

Ryan helped with the butchering of the elk as he had done it before when he had hunted with Bill and the boys back on the ranch. He had to watch how they removed the hide because back then they didn't bother saving it. Once the hide was off, Neudal rolled it up and handed it to Ryan.

"You can store that in the cold storage with the meat if you want, before you cure it." He said to Ryan.

Ryan just nodded his head, picked up some packages of meat and followed the men across the field to a much smaller mound that Ryan had noticed but had never paid any attention to. As they neared it Ryan noticed there was no hole in the top. There was a hole in the side with a lashed log door over it. Once it was open Ryan could see there was a passageway going down. The men entered. They went down about ten feet and then there was a room with log walls all the way around and a log ceiling, reminding Ryan of an old root cellar like the one back on the ranch. Ryan noticed that the temperature in this room was very cool, he also noticed that there was another doorway covered with a buffalo skin. The men started placing the packages of meat on shelves attached to the wall.

Latona and Skytal took their larger packages of meat and pulled back the buffalo hide and disappeared behind it.

"What is behind there?" Ryan asked.

"The ice room." Neudal answered.

"Ice room?" Ryan asked.

"Yes, there is a passage, it continues going down for about ten strides with another room at the bottom a little smaller than this one. We have blocks of ice in there that we cut and brought up from the river last year covering it with long grass. Putting the meat in there will freeze it so that we will have access to it in the wintertime." Neudal explained.

Ryan nodded his head and thought, "Wow, how clever is that. A natural freezer that requires no power."

"Do you not hunt in the Winter?" Ryan asked.

"We do." Replied Neudal, "But sometimes the winters are harsh, and we can not. It is always good to have a cache in case."

"Makes sense." Said Ryan as Latona and Skytal returned.

"Why don't you join us for an evening meal before you turn in?" Neudal asked Ryan.

"I would love too," said Ryan, "I have to try and get Zeus away from Tisha as well"

"Good luck with that." Neudal said with a smile as both men headed off.

Ryan woke up next morning looking forward to the day ahead. So many people have been talking about the people coming to visit from three sisters that he thought it sounded incredibly interesting and fun.

Ryan got up, put on some pants and a sleeveless vest, then started to head out of the tent. He heard a little yip and turned around seeing Zeus sitting up on the end of his bedroll.

"Come on." he said, motioning with his hand to the door. The little pup jumped up and passed him on the way out. "Well, it looks like some of the training is starting to pay off." Ryan thought to himself as the pair started walking across the field.

Ryan looked up and noticed Kanti and Cita walking towards him. As he drew closer, Ryan smiled and waved saying, "Good morning."

The women stopped and smiled back at Ryan and said, "Good morning to you Ryan."

"I am just off to the river to clean up, so I look good for when the other people get here." Ryan said.

"That is a good idea." Kanti said with a smile, "We do not want you showing up dirty. Do we?" she continued looking at Cita.

Cita smiled and answered, "No, that just would not do."

Ryan knew he was getting teased and decided not to take the bait but just stood there smiling at the two women.

Kanti looked at Ryan and said, "Mother asked me to ask you if you want to come by for some tea and a morning meal."

"That would be wonderful." said Ryan, "I am a bit hungry."

"Then we will see you later on this afternoon." Kanti said to Ryan.

Cita grabbed Kanti's arm, and they started to walk away. Ryan stood there for a moment, watching her walk away, realizing that he really did enjoy the view. He then turned and headed towards Latona and Nila's lodge. When he got to the log that went down, Ryan realized he didn't know what the protocol was. There was nothing to knock on to announce that he had arrived, so he decided to just call out.

"Hello." he called down.

He heard Nila answer back. "Ryan is that you?"

Ryan called out, "Yes, it is. Kanti said that you invited me over for a morning meal."

"Yes, we did, come on down." Nila called back.

Ryan climbed down the log and into the lodge and halfway down, you noticed a wonderful smell and then realized he was hungrier than he thought he was. He had no sooner hit the bottom when he looked up and saw the wolf looking down at him whining.

"You had better go get him and bring him down." Latona said with a laugh.

Ryan went back up the log, picked up the pup and carried it down with him.

Nila asked. "Did you bring your cup with you?"

Ryan shook his head and said, "No I was going to bathe and did not bring anything with me."

Nila quickly grabbed a cup and filled it with tea for Ryan then handed it to him.

"Thank you." Ryan said, taking the cup.

"I have some meat left over from last night as well as a little soup that I could heat up for you." Nila said.

"That would be wonderful, if it is not too much trouble." Ryan said to Nila and turned to see Latona sitting down in front of a small fire.

"Good morning, Latona." Ryan said as he walked over and sat down across from the man.

"Good morning to you, Ryan. So, are you looking forward to the feast tonight?" Latona asked.

"Yes, I am." answered Ryan with a smile "Everybody has been talking so much about it. I am looking forward to getting to meet new people as well."

Nila came to the fire with a set of tongs and picked up a cooking stone and walked back and put it into the cooking basket. Ryan could hear the hiss as a stone was lowered into the liquid. She then came back and got another stone and repeated what she had done before.

Nila Looked at Ryan and said," Latona tells me that you were very quick with your bow yesterday, and got two arrows off before any of the other hunters could even fire one."

"Well, I think I was just lucky." said Ryan with a smile.

"Latona looked at him and said, "I do not think luck had anything to do with it. You got those arrows away very quickly, and now some of the other hunters are talking about the way you put one arrow in the ground for a quick access before you fired the first one. They are now thinking that on the next hunt they may try the same thing. The story of how well you did is being told all over the camp and I am sure that it will be told to all the new people that are coming in."

"It was not really all that special." said Ryan.

"Yes, it was." said Latona. Then he started to laugh. "Looks like we are going to have to start calling you the great white hunter."

Ryan wasn't too sure he liked that and said, "Please do not do that."

Nila just chuckled, looked at Ryan and said, "Don't worry, Ryan. He is just teasing you.

Ryan looked over at Latona who was nodding his head smiling, "Do not worry, we will come up with a better name for you than great white hunter."

"Why do you need to come up with a name for me?" Ryan asked. "What is wrong with my name?"

"Nothing is wrong with your name Ryan." Latona answered. "It is just from time to time someone does something extraordinary or special and they are given an additional name for it."

"Oh." said Ryan. "I wonder why some people had names and other people had names such as Calling Bird or Skyseeker"

Latona nodded his head and said, "We have had names for many, many seasons, but people travelling through have different names as well as different customs, and different ways of naming people. We have adopted some of those ideas from time to use them ourselves."

"That is right, I forgot you have many people from all different directions passing through your camp." Ryan said.

"Yes, we do, and if we are lucky, some people will stay and make their home here, and we will have new stories and new ways of doing things."

Ryan thought of something and changed the subject by asking, "You mentioned the feast, that I know about, but you also mentioned a gathering what is that?"

Latona looked at Ryan and then nodded his head. "That is when we have groups of people visiting the camp. We sing and dance and tell stories, the young men have competitions such as bow shooting, spear throwing, wrestling, and such. It is a good time for all and a lot of fun. We get to meet people that we have not seen for a while and new people as well."

"It sounds like fun." said Ryan, "What should I wear?" He asked.

Nila looked at him and said, "We all wear our finest on the first day. I would suggest that you wear that nice tunic with all the bead work on it that Konti gave to you."

Ryan smiled and said, "That would be good. I have been waiting for a reason to wear it because it's so beautiful. Kanti must have put a lot of work into that, with all the bead work and decoration on it."

Nila smiled and appreciated the fact that he realized how much work went into it and said, "Yes, it took her quite a while, and she was very proud of it. Both Latona and I are surprised that she gave it up."

"Maybe not too surprised." Latona said, looking at his mate, who just smiled back at him.

Nila handed Ryan a bowl of soup and a platter with some sliced meat on it. She heard a little yip, and when she turned around, she saw the pup sitting down, looking up at her, wagging its tail.

"Don't worry little one I have not forgotten you." she said as she handed the little wolf a bone with a good amount of meat still on it. The little wolf dragged the bone a few feet away and proceeded to gnaw on it.

Ryan enjoyed the company and conversation while he visited with Nila and Latona but didn't realize how long he had been there until Kanti showed up to pick up her outfit that she was going to wear.

"Are you still here?" She asked Ryan, "I thought you would be getting ready by now."

Ryan looked at Latona Nila and said, "I am sorry. I have stayed too long." Then he started to get up.

Nila looked at him shaking her head and said, "Nonsense. There is plenty of time."

"I still have to go to the river and get cleaned." He said to them." Can I ask a favor? Could you look after Zeus, and I will pick him up on the way back from the river."

They all turned and looked over at the little wolf who was laying down feasting on his huge bone.

"I do not think he is going to be wanting to leave that anytime soon, so go ahead and we will see you on your way back." Latona said.

With that Ryan turned and started up the log steps.

Ryan walked across the field down to the river where he noticed a lot of other people had the same idea as him and we're swimming. Ryan took off his clothes, left them on the bank and waded into the water. The water was incredibly cold, but he found that he was starting to get used to it. Ryan swam for a while and tried to clean himself off as best he could.

"I'm really going to have to talk to Kanti about getting some of that soap plant that she used on my face for shaving." Ryan thought.

Once he was finished, Ryan got out of the water, dressed and headed back towards his tent. As he passed the lodge, he remembered that he had to stop in and pick up Zeus. Zeus was not too happy about leaving his new prize bone so Kanti suggested that Ryan take it with them back to his tent and he could finish devouring it there. Ryan thought that was a great idea and carried the little pup and the bone up out of the lodge starting on his way to the tent. Ryan put the little pup down and the little wolf was following behind Ryan and yapping at him to put his bone down. Ryan just kept telling him that he would get it once they got back to the tent. Upon arrival Ryan opened the flat of the tent and dropped the bone down inside, the little pup quickly ran and grabbed it, and then tried to start dragging it outside. Ryan decided that it would be better for the little one to eat it inside, so no other animals would come along and try to take it and possibly hurt him. He picked the bone up, threw it to the far end of the tent and the little wolf went running over and started gnawing at it.

Ryan felt refreshed after the swim and looked through the clothes that he had. He had a nice pair of pants that somebody had left him that he had not worn yet, so he tried them on, and they fit just right. He then looked at the tunic that Kanti gave to him and smiled to himself, because he was finally getting a chance to be able to wear it.

Ryan thought about shaving but since he had done it the other day, he thought he would be OK. He picked up the tunic and put it on. It fit well and was very comfortable. He noticed that with all the decorations on it, it had a bit of weight to it but not too heavy. It was heavier than most of the other things that he was used to wearing.

He put the belt around his waist and tightened it as he was shown and then adjusted the tunic.

Ryan really wished he had a mirror that he could look in to see how he looked. It felt good, It looked good when it wasn't on him, so he just actually assumed it was going to look good now. Ryan was adjusting his belt when he heard someone outside calling.

"Ryan are you ready?" Kanti said as she popped her head in through the flap.

"Yes I am." He said turning around so she could see him, and then asked, "How do I look?"

Kanti didn't say anything right away and Ryan noticed that she was just standing there staring at him.

"Do I not look OK?" Ryan asked.

Kanti nodded her head quickly and then smiled and said, "You look very handsome."

"Thank you." Ryan said, as he started to walk out of the tent following Kanti.

As they stepped out of the tent Ryan noticed that Cita was standing there waiting.

She turned and looked at Ryan, then a big smile crossed her face. "That looks so good on you Ryan."

"Thank you." said Ryan, "With all the hard work that Kanti had into making this. It is pretty."

Both the girls smiled and giggled, Cita looking at Ryan said, "I think you mean to say beautiful Ryan, not pretty."

Ryan just smiled sheepishly and said, "Yes the work on this is absolutely beautiful."

Kanti was pleased that Ryan was wearing the tunic and that he seemed to like it so much. She was also glad because all the work that she had put in it all those years ago was not going to waste.

Cita smiled watching Kanti looking at Ryan and then said, "Well, let's escort this young man to the festivities." She then hooked her arm around Ryan's arm and signaled Kanti to take the other side.

The trio walked across the field, and as they were approaching the meeting area, Ryan could hear drums along with chanting some. He looked up and saw people sitting around while other people were up dancing. As they got closer, he was amazed at all the colours on the outfits that people were wearing. He has seen something like this once in Arizona when he took his goddaughter to a Navajo celebration called a sing. That was planned, but this just seems more natural and spontaneous. Ryan noticed two men talking to a man with long black hair that hung down his back. They were pointing in the trio's direction. The man stood up and turned around and stared at Ryan approaching. As they got closer, Ryan took stock of the man. He was tall, just about Ryan's height, well built, very muscular, long, black hair hanging down almost to his waist, and dark piercing eyes.

Ryan also noticed something as he started walking towards him. He walked with an arrogant swagger. Something Ryan hadn't seen in any of the people that he met so far. Ryan decided he wasn't going to like this man but wasn't too sure why. As he got closer. The two women broke off from Ryan and stood on either side of him.

The man called as he approached, "I see you have a strange new friend." The man was looking very smug, as he came to a stop.

Ryan smiled but said nothing.

"The man looked at Kanti again after giving Ryan a cursory up and down glance and asked her, "Are you not going to introduce me to your white-haired friend?"

"Yes." she said looking at Ryan, "How rude of me. Ryan this is Stakota, he lives in three sister's camp. Stakota, this is Ryan."

Ryan looked the man in the eyes, smiled and said, "Greeting. Stakota."

Stakota stared at Ryan for a while without saying anything, then put a small grin on his face and said, "Greetings white hair." He then smiled at his own little joke.

Ryan did not smile, but looked at Stakota and said, "It is not white hair. My name is Ryan."

The man stared at Ryan for a few moments, deciding that he wasn't going to give him any more of his time as he started to turn away. He noticed something that he had noticed before he turned around and looked at Ryan again, noticing what he was wearing. Stakota knew full well who he had received that tunic from because he had had his eye on it for many years, ever since she made it for Toltin and thought that he was going to get it once they were mated.

He looked at Kanti and snapped "You gave the stranger Toltin's dress tunic?"

Ryan wasn't too sure he liked the tone of the man's voice and was going to say something, but Cita jumped in saying "Yes, she did. It's not like Toltin would be using it anymore, and Ryan needed a ceremonial tunic. It really should be no concern of yours."

Stakota was visibly upset and was going to respond, but then decided he didn't want to do it in front of Kanti, so he graciously smiled instead and said, "Of course, you are right, it does not have nothing to do with me." and then turned and walked back to the group.

Ryan looked at the women and said, "I do not think that man likes me very much."

Kanti didn't say anything, but Cita spoke up. "Of course she does not like you. He has been running around telling everybody that Kanti is going to be his mate."

Ryan's eyebrows raised and he looked at Kantit and asked "Really?"

Kanti glared at Cita then turned to answer Ryan, "Yes, he has been saying that. The only problem is He has never discussed it with me to find out if I was interested. He just naturally assumed I would be because he is the great Stakota."

Ryan could tell that she was pissed and thought he would tease her just a little bit by looking at her and then asking, "So, not interested then?" Hitting her with his best smile.

She looked up at Ryan, shook her head and then started walking away. Ryan started to follow her Cita then passed Ryan to catch up.

Cita looked at Ryan and said, "Well I thought that was funny." and then carried on her way.

As Ryan approached the group Neudal and Ayana beckoned him to come over and sit with them so they could watch the dancing. Ryan went and sat next to them. Tisha came up and sat beside him.

"Where is Zeus?" Tisha asked.

"He is back at my tent feasting on a very large bone that Nila gave to him. He is going to be good for the next little while. I do not think we will be seeing him for a while." Ryan answered.

As he sat there watching the dancing, somebody handed him a cup, which he took and thanked them. He took a sip smiled, looked over at Neudal and said, "This is Anya's tea, right?"

"Yes, it is." Neudal answered.

Ryan leaned in and conspiratorially said to Neudal, "Her tea is my favorite."

He looked at Ryan and whispered, "Mine too."

Ayana heard what the men were talking about and smiled to herself. They watched the dancing for a while, and Ryan kept noticing out of the corner of his eye that Stakota was glaring at him. He didn't want to say anything or be rude but a young child sitting next to him noticed it and said to Ryan, "Stakota is really staring at you. Why?"

"I do not know." answered Ryan. "Maybe he just thinks I look funny. Remember, you are used to me, new people are not. That is why."

Ryan looked around noticing there were a lot of new faces, and he was getting his fair share of sideways glances from people. They would look quickly and then turn and look away. Ryan understood this, as he was basically a novelty to them. They had never seen it before, and they knew nothing about him. He just decided not to let it bother him and he was going to enjoy the day.

Ryan noticed Stakota get up and go sit next to Kanti and start talking to her.

For some reason that Ryan could not figure out, this really bothered him. Ryan watched them for a while trying not to stare. He was happy to see Kanti and Cita get up and go sit with Latona and Nila.

Ryan was also pleased to see that Stakota was not very happy about them leaving. They sat watching the dancers with Tisha sitting on Ryan's lap. After a while the dancing stopped, and everybody was sitting around talking.

Stakota, who was sitting ten or fifteen feet away from Ryan called over, "So white hair. Where did you come from?"

Ryan decided not to let this man get to him, so he smiled and said, "Far away."

"Why is your hair so short?" Stakota continued taunting.

Ryan thought about that for a moment wondering why he was asking about his hair being so short. It wasn't particularly short by his standards. He then looked around and for the first time noticing it was short by the standards of the men that were around him.

Ryan decided not to answer the question and just shrugged his shoulders.

"So, we have a man who comes from far away with his white skin and white hair!" Stakota said loudly. "Does he have any skills?"

That was when Latona decided to enter the conversation, "He has great hunting skills." He said looking at Stakota. "The other day when we were out hunting, he put two arrows into a large male elk before any of us could take a shot."

"I find that hard to believe." said Stakota, waving his hand dismissively.

"Are you calling me a liar Stakota?" Latona said glaring at Stakota.

"No, not a liar but I am sure you are exaggerating Latona. Stakota said smugly.

Tolbar then joined in saying, "He is not exaggerating. There were eight hunters there, all of which saw Ryan make the kill."

Latona wanted to push it but decided he would just let it go. Not wanting to rise to Stakota's taunts.

Mekome spoke up and said, "Plus, he has been teaching everyone new wrestling moves."

Stakota smirked then asked in a very condescending tone, "Wrestling moves?"

"Yes, Ryan is a great wrestler. Probably one of the best there ever was, and he has been teaching us." Said Mekome looking at Ryan.

"I find it hard to believe he could be the best that ever was, because you know I am." Stakota said glaring at Ryan.

Tolbar smiled, looking at Stakota and said, "You were, but maybe not anymore. I guess we will see at the wrestling competition tomorrow."

"Why wait for the competition? Stakota announced, clearly agitated. We could wrestle right now."

"I do not know if I want to wrestle right now." said Ryan thinking about damaging his new tunic.

"No!" Stakota shouted. "If you are the greatest wrestler of all time white hair, I must see this. Are you afraid of getting hurt?"

Ryan was really getting pissed off being called white hair by this asshole.

"Why not. If that's what you want let us go out to the grass and we will have a competition. If I win, you will no longer call me white hair. You can call me by my name, which is Ryan. Agreed?"

"I agree, but I will not have to worry about that white hair." Stakota said with a smug grin.

Ryan got up and started to walk out to the field. Almost everyone else got up and started walking with him to the field. Ryan started taking off the tunic as he got to a flat spot in the field. Ryan called over Kanti and she walked over to him. Ryan finished taking off the tunic and handed it to her.

"Would you please look after this for me? I do not want to wrestle in it and get it damaged." Ryan said.

Kanti smiled and nodded her head. Ryan handed it to her and as he turned around, he saw Stakota standing there frozen and wide eyed. He also heard a lot of people in the crowd starting to murmur. Ryan couldn't understand what was going on at first and then realized it was the tattoo. A lot of the people here had never seen it before. They may have heard about it but until they have seen it, it would be quite a surprise.

"What is that on your arm?" Stakota demanded.

Ryan had just about enough of this guy and said smiling, "It does not concern you Stakota. Ready when you are."

Stakota took his tunic off and started stretching. Ryan noticed that he had a muscular build, with six pack abs, muscular arms, and no fat anywhere.

He also noticed that tucked into his belt he had what at first Ryan thought was a hatchet, or an axe. But when he looked at it closer, he noticed an animal jawbone attached to a stick that gave the shape of an axe. It had leather wrapped around the handle, with decorative feathers hanging off it, and it looked like the leading edge had been sharpened. It would not be a good axe for cutting wood, but it would be a formattable weapon. What Ryan was wondering now was why was he keeping that on his belt and not taking it off.

"I have a feeling this is going to be dirty." Ryan thought to himself.

The crowd had closed in around the two men forming a natural rink. Stakota was strutting around the outside looking at the crowd puffing his chest and telling everybody what he was going to do to Ryan not once looking at Ryan. Ryan kept his eyes on Stakota and wondered when he was going to make his move.

Tolbar yelled, "Be careful Ryan, he can be tricky."

Ryan turned his head and smiled in Tolbar's direction, Stakota, seeing the opportunity swiftly moved in and with his right leg swept the feet out from underneath Ryan. Ryan hit the ground, surprised at how fast his opponent was. Ryan rolled over three times and jumped up quickly before Stakota could land on top of him. Stakota backed up, turned and faced the crowd and declared in a loud voice, "He can not be that good if he was taken down so easily. "Did you tell me he was teaching the men how to wrestle, or the women."

Ryan kept his composure, looked at Stakota smiled and asked, "Did we come here to talk like little girls, or wrestle."

Ryan could tell that his comment upset his opponent, as he turned quickly and glared at Ryan. Then without warning, Stakota charged. Ryan could see that he was going to try to tackle him and waited until he got close enough then dropped down, grabbed each of Stakota's arms, rolled onto his back, put his feet on Stakota' stomach as he rolled straightening his legs and flung him in the air as he continued to somersault and come back up on his feet. Stakota flew at least ten feet in the air before he came down hard on his back, knocking all the wind out of him. Ryan did not move in for the kill but stood there waiting for him to get air back into his lungs. Stakota slowly rolled over onto his hands and knees and got up. What Ryan did not notice is that while he was getting up, he grabbed a handful of grass and dirt in each hand. Stakota slowly walked towards Ryan and without warning threw the grass and dirt into his face. He then launched at Ryan hitting Ryan in the midsection, wrapping his arms around his waist, and started to lift him into the air. Ryan knew what was coming, his opponent was going to flip him over his head so that he landed on his back, and he would come down on top of him. On a wrestling mat this would hurt, but on the hard unforgiving ground it could be crippling. Ryan did not hesitate and took both of his hands opened wide and slapped them down on each side Stakota's head over his ears, stunning the man. Stakota dropped Ryan, and once Ryan hit the ground, he pivoted and hooked his right leg behind Stakota and pushed him back so that he fell over, and Ryan pinned him. Ryan got up and started walking towards Latona with a smile on his face.

Suddenly, he heard Mekome call out, "Ryan, watch out!"

As Ryan turned around, he saw the Stakota getting up what's that jawbone weapon.

"OK, so this shit is getting real." he said to himself.

He took two steps back and pivoted to face Stakota at an angle. Stakota came in getting ready to swing the hatchet towards Ryan's head. Ryan waited and once he had started this move Ryan stepped in and rather than blocking the axe, blocked Stakota's arm with his left arm, then took his right arm and swung his elbow into Stakota's jaw. Ryan saw the man's eyes roll back into his head, and he collapsed to the ground. On the way down Ryan took the axe from his hand and threw it across the field. He then turned and started to walk back towards Mekome and his family.

"Thanks for the warning." he said to the young boy as he put his arm on his shoulder.

"No problem." said Mekome, "He looked really mad."

Neudal leaned in and said to Ryan in a quiet voice, "I think you have an enemy now in Stakota."

"Unfortunately, I believe you are right." Ryan replied, turning and looking back into the centre of the makeshift ring. He noticed that the two men that Stakota was talking to as he walked up were now helping him off the ground. He had regained consciousness but was still a little groggy and they were helping him off to the side.

Ryan reached down and touched his ribs Realizing they were quite sore, Stakota charged into him pretty hard, and he was hoping that he had not cracked a rib.

Kanti came over, looked at Ryan and asked, "Are you OK? I can not believe he tried to attack you like that."

"Well, it could have been a lot worse." Ryan said to her looking at Mekome, "If I had not been warned."

"You're holding your side, are you sure you are not hurt?" Kanti asked, looking concerned.

"My ribs are a little sore, that is all." Ryan answered.

Before he could say anymore, he felt someone grab his arm and start pulling him away. He looked down to see Skyseeker.

"Hello Skyseeker." he said, "Where are we going?"

She said, "Come with me, I want to look at those ribs."

Ryan was hoping they were only bruised because he had cracked some ribs many years ago doing a stunt and remembered it hurt like hell for a long time. Skyseeker led Ryan to her tent and they both entered.

"Sit." she told him.

Ryan did as he was told and sat down watching Skyseeker take some cooking stones from a small fire that was burning in the hearth and place them into a basket filled with some water. She then put what looked to him like some powder into the water and then stirred it. She then reached into another small pouch and added a dash of something else, again stirring the mixture.

"I will let that steep for a while." she said to Ryan. "Now let me have a look at your ribs.

she poked and prodded for a little while asking him where it hurt and how much it hurt. Ryan answered the questions truthfully and when she was done her examination she said, "The good news is I do not think you have cracked or broken anything."

"That is good." said Ryan and then continued, "I had cracked a rib a long time ago and it took quite a while to heal."

Skyseeker just smiled at him and said, "You will probably feel a little bit of discomfort for a few days, but it will not be as bad as it was when you cracked your last rib."

She then sat across from Ryan looking him in the eyes and said, "It is getting near the time you and I will have to sit down and have a talk serious talk."

Ryan matched her stare back and just nodded his head.

Skyseeker added, "I do not think today is going to be the day, but possibly tomorrow or the next day if that is Ok with you?"

Ryan laughed a little and said to the old lady, "Is it really going to matter if it is OK with me or not?"

A huge smile lit up Skyseeker's face and he could see where Kanti got her smile from. "No, you are right it would not matter."

Ryan smiled and said, "When you feel this time to talk, you let me know and we will sit and talk."

Still smiling she got up, went to the cooking basket and scooped out a cup of liquid for him. "Drink this." she said.

Ryan took the cup and sipped at it. It had a strange taste to it, and he found it a little bitter.

"Not my favorite tasting tea." He said to Skyseeker.

"It is not tea." she said to him smiling, "It is Willow bark for your pain."

"Willow Bark," Ryan said surprised.

"Yes." said Skyseeker, "Willow bark tea and it's good for pain."

"OK." Said Ryan as he drank more of it.

"Drink it all before you go." said Skyseeker.

Ryan looked at her nodded his head and gulped down the tea'

She said, "It will take a little while, but you will notice the pain starting to subside."

She then gave him a small leather pouch and said, "If the pain comes back and you need to make a tea by using three pinches of this." She then demonstrated by taking some out between her finger and thumb. "Let it steep for a while before drinking it."

Ryan nodded his head and said, "Thank you Skyseeker for making me feel better."

The old woman just smiled and waved for him to go. Ryan got up, turned around and headed out of the tent. Ryan thought that he may go and lay down in his own tent for a while and as he was walking, he heard Latona call his name and start walking towards him. As he caught up, Ryan noticed that Latona had his tunic in his hand and realized that he had left it on the field when Skyseeker had pulled him away.

"I thought you might want this." Latona said as he walked up to Ryan handing him the tunic.

"I do." said Ryan, "I can not believe I left it there. I would have been very upset had something happened to this."

"Well, I saw Skyseeker dragging you away. Is everything OK?" He asked with genuine concern in his voice.

"Yes, it is, I just have some sore ribs, and I am going to go lay down for a little while. Skyseeker gave me some Willow bark and she says that will relieve the pain. So, I thought I would lay down for a while then when I am feeling better, and I will come back out and join the festivities." Ryan said.

"You had better, or we are going to come and find you. Just so you know Tisha is playing with the little wolf, so you do not have to worry about where he is." Latona said.

Ryan just smiled and said, "When the wolf gets tired, he knows where his bed is."

Latona smiles and headed back to the crowd and Ryan turned and headed back to his tent

When Ryan reached his tent, he climbed into his bedroll and tried to find a comfortable position where his rib did not hurt so much. He lay there for a few moments, thinking of the day's events and decided that he really did not like Stakota. Ryan was wondering why he took such a dislike to him, was he jealous of the attention he showed Kanti. "That is ridiculous." he thought, "She is not interested in me. I wish she was though." he mused.

The next thing Ryan knew he heard his name being called and he was gently being shaken. As he woke up and opened his eyes, he saw Cita bending over him, shaking him gently. At first, he was surprised and then looked past her and saw Kanti standing there.

"What is wrong?" he asked, sitting up.

"Nothing's wrong." She said, "We just came to make sure you were Ok."

"Yes, I'm fine." He said adding. "I must have just fallen asleep. Skyseeker gave me something to help the pain in my ribs and I came back, and I fell asleep."

Kanti smiled and said "I am willing to bet that grandmother put more in the tea than just willow bark."

"What do you mean?" Asked Ryan.

"She probably put something in there to help you rest because you did look a little worked up after that episode with Stakota." Kanti said, smiling at Ryan.

"Yes, that man did get under my skin a little bit." Ryan admitted. "I do not know what his problem is with me."

Cita smiled, looked at Ryan and said, "I do." as she turned and looked at Kanti.

"Well then, what is it?" He asked the two women.

"Well." said Cita, "Stakota has been telling everybody that will listen that he is going to be Kanti's mate."

Ryan looked over at Kanti asking. "You said that before. Is that true?"

Kanti saw a look of disappointment on Ryan's face and smiled a little before answering, "It is not true. Stakota wants to be my mate and thinks that he is going to be. But he has never asked me to be his mate."

"And if he did?" asked Ryan.

Kanti looked at Ryan and smiled and said, "I do not think he is the kind of man that I would want to have as a mate."

"Have you told him that?" asked Ryan.

"No, I have not told him that." She admitted.

"OK, so in his mind, he still thinks you are going to be his mate. No wonder the man does not like me." Ryan said.

"Why would he not like you for that?" Asked Cita.

Ryan started to turn a little red and quickly said, "No reason,"

Cita looked at Kanti with a big smile on her face, then turning towards Ryan said, "Well, you should put your tunic back on and we should get going. You have already missed the feast, but Nila and Ayana have saved food for you. Tolbar told us to come and get you, so you do not miss anymore.'

Kanti added. "There has been storytelling this afternoon and dancing. It has been a lot of fun and you missed it, sleepyhead.

"It seems I did." said Ryan as he smiled and put on his tunic. "Would you two pretty women please lead the way."

As they walked across the field, Ryan noticed there were several different fires in different locations. Cita and Kanti led Ryan to the fire pit that Ryan had been to many times.

As they were walking up to the fire pit, Cita said, "You are going to enjoy the meat, it was cooked in a ground oven, and it is so tender. It just falls apart."

Ryan said to her, "I'm looking forward to it. I'm really hungry."

As a trio we're walking up to the group Stakota was watching them approach and was not happy that Kanti had gone and got the white haired man. As they got close to the fire pit Kanti went and sat on the closest side with Nila and Latona and Ryan went around and sat with Ayana and Neudal. As Ryan was walking towards them, Ayana got up and walked over to a large log that had food laid out on it and brought a platter back for Ryan.

"We missed you at all the storytelling this afternoon." Neudal said to Ryan as his mate handed Ryan the plate of food.

Ryan smiled and said, "Thank you Ayana. This looks delicious." Then turning to Neudal he said, "Yes, Skyseeker gave me a drink to help with the pain I had and before I knew it, I was sleeping in my tent."

Neudal and Ayana just smiled at Ryan and said, "She must have felt that you needed it."

Ryan smiled to himself thinking, "I wonder if that old woman roofies a lot of people.

Ryan looked around and then asked, "Where is Zeus."

Ayana pointed out into the field, where there were a bunch of children running around chasing the little white wolf. They would stop, and then one of the children would throw a stick and the little wolf would run after it, pick up the stick, and then all the children would chase the little wolf. It would run away, and when the children got tired and stopped chasing it, the pup would turn around, come back and drop the stick down, sitting there waiting for them to throw it again.

Ryan laughed at the shenanigans and asked. "Have they been doing that all afternoon?"

Ayana smiled and said, "We are not going to have to worry about them sleeping tonight. They are going to be exhausted."

Ryan smiled and said, "I am glad he has been entertained all day, but I have kind of missed the little one."

"He started to head back to your tent at one point this afternoon, but then got distracted with more children that showed up to play with him. You are going to have one tired little wolf at the end of the day." Neudal said watching the children playing.

Across the fire pit Stakota sat there watching Ryan noticing that he kept glancing over towards Kanti, and then when Ryan wasn't looking Kanti was glancing in his direction. This did not make him happy at all. The more he noticed, the madder he got. After the embarrassment of being put down in front of everybody he felt this was just more of an attack on his manhood. The longer they sat there the more Stakota descended into a foul mood.

Tisha and the little wolf came running back into the area. As they passed the man Stakota reached out, grabbed the little pup by the scruff of the neck and held him up.

He stood up to make sure he was seen and said in a loud voice, "This little one would make a good hood, or perhaps a good pair of mitts. Why are you letting it just run around the camp?

The little wolf was squirming and trying to get down so Stakota shook the wolf a few times and added, "It would be better off being skinned." looking around defiantly at everyone.

Tisha screamed out, "Let go of Zeus!"

Stakota just looked at her and shook the wolf one more time causing the little wolf to cry out. Tisha ran up and hit Stakota hard in the side of his leg with the stick. Stakota was shocked. He dropped the little wolf and backhanded Tisha. The little girl flew back about four feet hitting the ground on her back and started crying. The little wolf ran to the girl, turned around and started growling at this big thing in front of him that just hurt his little friend. Tisha was laying there crying, when Stakota took a step forward looking like he was going to kick the little pup.

When Tisha saw this, she threw the stick at Stakota, hitting him in the chest. Stakota backed up about three paces becoming enraged. He let out a bellow and started moving towards the little girl. Kanti looked over at Ryan in time to notice him leaping for one side of the fire pit, through the fire, to the other side, landing squarely between the little girl and the crazed man.

Stakota was surprised and stopped instantly staring at Ryan. The look on Ryan's face was that of a mad man, he didn't say a word, but he took three quick steps to put himself nose to nose With Stakota for a few moments. He didn't say anything. He just looked the man square in the eyes. Stakota felt very uncomfortable and wasn't too sure what to do after being put down so quickly and hard earlier in the day.

Ryan then moved his face even closer to Stakota and said in a cold hard tone, "You hit Tisha, or my wolf again, you die!"

There was an audible gasp from all the people around him. Unbeknownst to Ryan, in the culture where everybody must get along and are interdependent on everyone else, one never made a verbal threat of death or harm to anybody unless possibly as a joke. This was frowned upon because if you did not like somebody, or the way somebody was doing something, you either stayed away from that person or you ignored it. Ryan continued to stare down Stakota at this point having no idea what he was going to do. Ryan did realize that he really had given Stakota no way out now that he had said his peace, but now Stakota must save face.

Suddenly, Ryan got a big smile on his face and in a loud voice said, "OK!... Good!" Nodded his head and slapped Stakota on the shoulder.

Everybody around visibly relaxed as Ryan turned around, walked over and picked up Tisha and walked her around the other side of the fire pit to her mother and father, with the little wolf following right behind.

As he leaned down and handed Tisha over to Ayana, she took her crying daughter and whispered, "Thank you Ryan"

. Ryan didn't answer just nodded his head and sat down next to Neudal looked at Tisha and asked, "Are you alright butterfly?"

Tisha just smiled and nodded her head.

Stakota went and sat down with the two men that Ryan had noticed him talking to earlier and had helped him after the wrestling.

Once he had sat down one of the men said, "It is a good thing that you did not decide to take him down."

"That was rude. The other man said, "He is lucky that you are such a patient man."

Stakota just nodded his head and said nothing. For the rest of the evening, he continued to watch both Ryan and Kanti, noticing the glances back-and-forth. Stakota finally decided to go over and talk to Kanti who was sitting with Cita, so he got up and walked over to the two women and sat down next to her.

Stakota looked at her, smiled and said, "I was wondering if you wanted to go for a walk later tonight?"

Kanti just stared at him for a while and then shook her head and said, "No, I do not think so."

"Why not? Is it because of your white haired friend?" He asked.

"No, he has nothing to do with it." She answered and then continued. "I just watched you hit a child."

"That child hit me with a stick." said Stakota trying to defend his actions.

"Regardless, she is just a child, and you hit her, knocking her to the ground and then you were going to attack her again." Kanti said, looking at him.

Stakota stuttered for a moment and then said, "I was not going to attack her again. I was just going to come in and teach her a lesson."

"Oh really? What kind of lesson would that have been?" She asked, "A slap across the face?"

"You can not let children disrespect you!" explained Stakota to Kanti, still trying to defend himself.

"You should not hit a child!" said Cita glaring at the man. She then continued. "I do not think I need to sit with you anymore." She then got up and started to walk away.

Kanti looked at Stakota, then called to Cita, "Wait for me. I am going to come with you."

Kanti got up and started following her friend to the other side of the fire pit. Stakota watched the women as he walked away, then got up, walked over, and sat with his two friends.

Ryan spent the rest of the evening with Ayana, Neudal and Tisha, spending a lot of time comforting the little girl and making sure that she was Ok. As everyone talked, Tisha climbed onto Ryan's lap and closed her eyes, and he started to rock back-and-forth trying to get her to sleep. She seemed fine, except for a nasty bruise that was starting to show on her cheek. Every time Ryan looked at it, he got more upset.

"I wish I had head butted that prick in the face." He thought to himself, but then thought that it probably worked out better in the long run.

Cita and Kanti were talking with Latona and Nila and Kanti kept glancing over and watching Ryan.

Her mother noticed this and commented. "Ryan sure is good with children isn't he."

Kanti was watching Ryan rock Tisha to sleep, turned and looked at her mother smiling and said, "Yes, he is. I can not believe Stakota struck her."

"It surprised me as well." says said Latona shaking his head. "I expected more from him than that."

"She is just a little girl, of course she can be a handful, but that is still no excuse to hit her like that. If he could hit a child that easily, he could just as easily hit his mate." Said Nila looking at Kanti.

"Do you really think so?" asked Kanti.

"Yes, I do." said Nila shaking her head.

"Well, I am not going to have to worry about finding out." Kanti said, glancing over at Stakota sitting with his friends. "I have lost all interest in that man."

"That may be a good thing." said Latona looking at his daughter, and then glancing over at his mate.

"Well, it's getting late, and we should turn in." said Cita.

"I will walk back with you." Kanti said as the two women got up and started to walk away.

Ryan noticed the two women getting up and leaving, wishing that they were coming over to talk with him. or at least one would come over and talk to him.

As he watched Kanti walk away, he thought to himself, "Admit it, Ryan. You are definitely smitten with that young woman."

Ayana said something to Ryan which he did not catch as she said in such a quiet voice. He turned, looked at her and said, "Sorry, I missed that."

She just smiled and said, "Tisha is fast asleep. Maybe you should give her to me, and I can take her back and put her to bed."

"Would you like me to carry her back? Ryan asked.

"No, thank you though. I have been carrying her for a long time and I know I will only be able to do it for a little while more, so I will carry her."

Ryan handed the sleeping little girl over to her mother and watched them walk away.

Ryan looked at Neudal and said, "I think I'm going to turn in as well."

Neudal glanced over at Stakota sitting with his friends then said to Ryan, "After you leave, I do not think I am going to enjoy the company." Neudal then smiled, put his hand on Ryan's shoulder and continued, "Maybe it would be good to put some separation between the two of you at least for tonight."

Both men got up and walked off into the night heading back to their respective tents.

On the walk back to his tent Ryan noticed his ribs were starting to bother him again.

"That Willow bark really did the trick." He thought, "I think I will make some more up when I get back to my tent so that I will be able to sleep through the night."

When he got back to the tent, the little wolf ran inside, jumped onto his bed, circled three times, then curled up to go to sleep.

"I imagine you will be tired." He said to Zeus. "All that excitement and running around you had, you're probably going to sleep for the next three days."

Ryan started a small fire and put a few cooking stones in it. He knew he didn't have to have a big fire as he only had to heat a few stones because he was making such a small batch of tea. Once he felt the stones were hot enough, he poured some water into a cooking basket and then placed one stone in and let it warm the water and shortly after that, he then placed the other stone in with a sizzle. He threw a third stone in just to make sure the water was hot. Once he felt it was hot enough. He scooped out a cup of water and then following Skyseeker's instructions put three pinches of the powder into the water, stirred it and then let it sit to steep. Ryan sat there staring into the small fire thinking about how his life has changed in such a short period of time and how for some reason he seemed to be accepting it and not having a total mental breakdown. The more Ryan thought about it, the more he thought it was these people that were making the transition easy for him. They were helpful, they were friendly, they were always there to help. What Ryan didn't realize is that they were thinking the same about him. He was always there to help if he saw somebody that needed some help, he was the first person to step in and offer that help. If he wasn't too sure what they were doing, he would sit back and watch for a little while until he gained some insight into what tasks they were doing and figured out the best way he could offer to help.

Ryan felt that the Willow bark had steeped long enough and drank it down. The taste was not any better this time than it was with the last one that sky seeker had given him however, if it worked as well, he'd suffer through the taste.

Suddenly, a commercial came to him that he had seen back in Arizona. "It tastes awful, but it works." He couldn't remember the product it was for, but that part of the staying stuck in his mind and was definitely true with Willow bark. Ryan climbed in his bed and lay there for a few moments. The dog moved to get into a better position and then both him and Ryan fell asleep.

Chapter 6

Ryan was dreaming that dream again that all men loved, the one where he was being pleasured by a beautiful woman. Ryan suddenly realized this dream seemed a little different and started to come to the conclusion it wasn't a dream. Somebody was fondling him underneath the covers. Ryan laid very still and opened his eyes and looked at the fire hearth noticing the fire had gone out. He must have been asleep for a while. He could barely make out the shape of somebody kneeling beside him. He decided to lay very quiet and see what happened. His body betrayed him though as he became hard, and the fondling turned to stroking.

"Whoever this is, she knows what she's doing." Ryan thought to himself.

Ryan laid there enjoying it, trying not to move, when suddenly he felt a warm pair of lips on his member, involuntarily bringing a moan from Ryan. He heard a little giggle and then his mystery lover kiss the tip and straddle him, slowly impaling herself on him. She then started a slow, rhythmic movement which Ryan soon matched. Ryan noticed that his new lover was going a lot slower and taking it a lot easier.

"Was this someone new or had one of the others returned." he thought.

The woman on top of Ryan slowly and lightly raked her nails down Ryan's chest, a sensation that Ryan found quite stimulating and enjoyed immensely. She leaned over Ryan and her hair tumbled down onto his chest, stimulating him even further. Ryan leaned up and took one of her nipples in his mouth, gently starting to suck, causing her to gasp and move faster. Ryan laid back down and move his hands up her body and started fondling her breasts and gently played with her nipples. Ryan noticed that her breast were firm and full, similar to the woman that visited the first night.

"I wonder if this could be the same woman." he thought to himself. As they continued to make love to each other. Ryan found that thoughts of Kanti were playing across his mind. He tried to block them out but found he could not, and then just decided to go with it. The woman on top started to speed up and Ryan could hear her starting to moan. Ryan was ready to climax himself, but was holding off, hoping that they could do it together. As the rocking came harder and her desire became more apparent, Ryan was not too sure how long he could hold off. Finally, she started moaning loudly, and Ryan could hold off no longer and they both exploded in pleasure together.

The woman collapsed and laid across Ryan's chest still breathing heavily. Ryan enjoyed the feeling of her heaving breasts on his chest and started stroking her back. He was starting to feel a little bit guilty fantasizing about Kanti while making love to this woman. He decided that he was going to say something to this woman but wasn't sure how she was going to take it.

As the woman sat up. Ryan reached out grabbing her waist, not wanting her to pull away and leave quickly like before.

Ryan looked up into the darkness and said, "Thank you. You are great. But I do not know if we can do this anymore."

He felt the woman on top of him stiffen and heard a very soft, "Why?"

"I have strong feelings for someone else in the camp, and I do not think it is right making love to you while I am thinking of her." Ryan answered already feeling guilty.

A soft "Oh." came from the woman still straddling him, then in a whisper she asked, "Who?"

Ryan was not going to answer her, but then decided it would probably be for the best If he did. Looking up into the darkness, he said, "Kanti".

There was no reaction from the woman still straddling him. Suddenly, Ryan realized what he had done and quickly added, "Please do not tell anyone, because I do not think she feels the same way about me."

The woman just quietly said, "OK" and then laid back down across Ryan's chest.

Ryan put his arms around the woman and rubbed her lightly on the back. The woman twisted her head, moved up and slowly started nuzzling Ryan's neck. Ryan found that he really enjoyed this, then realized that it somehow felt familiar.

Ryan put his arms on the woman's shoulder and pushed her up. He blurted out, "Kanti?"

He heard a giggle and then the woman said, "It's a good thing you were not standing up, or I would have had to put you on your butt again." She then leaned down and kissed Ryan on the mouth.

Ryan kissed her back not believing this was happening. He then asked, "Was it you that came to me last time?"

"I have been here once before a few days ago." She admitted.

Ryan was confused and asked, "But why?"

"When you first came to the camp, I thought you looked handsome, and you looked like you would be fun for a little role in the bedroll. As you now know I lost my mate many years ago. I have not been with a man for quite a while, so I thought it would be fun to sneak in and have my way with you." Kanti answered.

"But you only came the once?" Ryan asked.

"Yes, I only came the once. I did come again, but you had someone else with you that had the same idea that I did." Kanti said.

"And who was that?" Ryan asked, "Do you know?"

"I do know, but I did not know at the time." She answered.

"Are you going to tell me?" Ryan asked.

"I really should not." Said Kanti, but the more she thought about it the more she thought why not. "It was Cita."

"Cita!" Ryan said in surprise.

"Yes, I was coming to meet you when I heard you and someone in there. I did not know who it was, so I left. It was a day or two later that Cita told me that she had snuck in and had her way with you. I tried not to show any emotion when she told me, but she has been a friend of mine for many years and picked up right away that something was wrong. she asked, but I would not tell her.

Finally, she wore me down and I explained to her that I had been to visit you the night before and was going back again when I heard her in there. I told her not to worry about it because I had no claim on you, but her being my friend, she said that she was not going to visit you anymore. Then after the way I saw you were so good with Tisha and the way you kept looking at me when you did not think I was watching you. I thought tonight might be a good night to come visit. But I did not want it to be as quick as it was the first time." Then she added, "Do not let Cita know. She would be embarrassed."

Ryan held her to him and kissed her again. Kanti quickly sat up and was starting to get off Ryan when he reached out, grabbed her waist and blurted out a little louder than he expected. "No, do not go."

Kanti bent down, kissed him on the forehead and said, "I am not leaving. I'm just getting off you. I must be getting heavy on you now."

Ryan reached out to pull her down on top of him again saying, "You are not heavy at all, and you can stay there as long as you like."

Kanti giggled and then said, "That is a wonderful offer. I may just take you up on it."

The two laid together and talked for a while, and then made love one more time before they fell asleep.

Ryan awoke to a sound that was unfamiliar to him. He laid there for a moment trying to figure out what it was. Kanti stirred, then rolled over looking at Ryan and said, "It is raining."

"Of course." Said Ryan, "That is what I am hearing, the rain on the tent."

Kanti smiled and said, "Yes, I love that sound."

Ryan then noticed that he was getting splashed by droplets of water. "I am getting wet." He said, looking up and pointing to the smoke hole.

Kanti looked up smiling saying, "Yes, the main smoke flap is open and it is allowing a lot of rainwater to come in. You are going to need to go out and close it."

Ryan looked at her and asked, "How do I do that?"

She laughed, smacked him on the chest and jumped out of bed fully naked, and ran out the tent. Ryan was looking up when he saw the flap get pulled back across the smoke hole, leaving only a small opening at the top and allowing less rainwater to enter the tent.

The tent flap opened, and Kanti came running in soaking wet exclaiming, "It is really raining out there!"

She then looked at Ryan, smiled, and ran over towards the bedroll.

"No!" said Ryan, "Stay away, you are wet."

Kanti ran back to the bedroll and jumped in on top of Ryan and started rubbing herself all over him.

"You are so wet." he called out.

"I Know," She said laughing, "So next time, you go out and close the flap. Now it is up to you to get me dry.

A grin came over Ryan's face as he pulled Kanti over onto her back slowly started sliding down her body saying, "Do not worry, I will make sure I get you nice and dry."

When they were finished, they laid facing the wall of the tent spooning, with Ryan's back to the door. Ryan gently kissed her shoulder and the back of her neck.

"Let us give it a rest." she said teasingly.

"I do not think so." said Ryan as you reached out and grabbed her buttocks.

Suddenly, the tent flap opened, and somebody came into the tent. Ryan rolled over to face the door and was now laying on his side. He looked up and saw Latona coming in with his head down, trying to shake water out of his hair and clothing.

"I am sorry for bursting in unannounced." he said, "But it is raining so hard out there. I needed to get into someplace dry. Because it is raining so hard Nila was worried that you were going to be bored and wanted to know if you would come over for an afternoon meal and a visit." He said finally standing upright and looking at Ryan who was laying on his side watching him.

He then noticed that behind Ryan it looked like a young woman was laying there. Latona could not make out who it was but smiled at Ryan and said, "OK. I see you are not bored."

Ryan sheepishly smiled and before he could say anything Kanti popped her head up onto Ryan's shoulder and with a big smile on her face said, "Good morning father."

Latona just stood there for a moment looking stunned.

Ryan began to feel awkward and said, "I am sorry Latona."

A big smile came over Latona's face and he said, "There is nothing here that needs an apology, Ryan. As a matter of fact, I think I should be thanking you."

"Thanking me?" asked Ryan confused.

"Yes." Latona said staring at his daughter. "I have not seen my daughter smile like that in many seasons. I thought she might have forgotten how. So, it's nice to see the smile back."

Ryan felt a lot better as Latona's statement took a lot of the awkwardness out of it for him.

"I will go and tell Nila that you are not bored, and that you have found a way to amuse yourself during this bad rainstorm." Latona said looking at the two of them.

Ryan smiled and said, "Thank you, and thank Nila for the invitation."

"Oh no, the invitation has now been extended." said Latona. "You will be coming for evening meal because both Nila and I insist." He then looked at Kanti and said. "You as well daughter.

They both looked at each other and then back at Latona and said, "We will be there."

Well, I am going to get back to Nila." and with that, he smiled, waved and went out the tent.

Ryan and Kanti looked at each other and then burst out laughing. She said, "The look on his face was so funny."

"It was good, you could tell he was surprised." said Ryan, then started nuzzling her neck.

Latona was walking across the field heading back to his lodge when Stakota came running up to him.

"Latona!" he called out. Latona stopped and waited for him to catch up.

"Have you seen Kanti?" He asked. "I have not been able to find her today."

Latona resisted the urge to turn and look back at Ryan's tent, looking straight at Stakota instead answering, "No, I have not seen her today. She could be off with Cita or one of the other women. You know how it is when we have visitors, everybody wants to visit, and it is hard to track someone down."

Stakota just nodded his head and said, "Thank you Latona." and headed off,

Latona watched the man walk away and thought to himself, "My daughter has made a much better choice with Ryan."

He continued walking back to his lodge trying to decide whether he should tell Nila or not. Of course, he would, he could not keep something like this from his mate. He did decide that he was going to wait till just before dinner and then spring it on her.

With the weather being so bad Ryan and Kanti decided to spend the afternoon in the tent. Ryan started a fire and made some tea. He had some dried meat that Ayana had given him, so that's what they had for their afternoon meal. The little wolf got up and went racing outside to relieve itself, then came running back in shortly after finishing his business, not liking the rain.

Ryan laughed at the little pup, thinking it was incredibly funny until it decided to climb up on the bed getting them both wet.

Late in the afternoon Kanti said, "I am getting quite hungry now, it may be a good time to go over to my mothers for our evening meal."

Ryan agreed, so they cleaned up, got dressed and headed towards her parents' lodge.

"I'm really glad Ryan found something to do on such a miserable day." Nila said to her mate. "I will admit I was a little surprised because most people are just staying indoors today because the weather is so bad."

Latona was just sitting there smiling up at his mate. When she noticed his smirk she asked, "What are you so pleased about?"

Latona's smile got even bigger, and he said, "I know I should have told you earlier, but I wanted to keep it a surprise until Ryan and Kanti came over for evening meal."

Nila looked a little concerned as she asked, "What should you have told me earlier? What surprise?"

Latona's smile broadened and he said, "I should have told you the reason that Ryan was not bored and did not want to come over for afternoon meal."

Nila looked at her mate and then asked, "Ok, so then tell me now why Ryan was not bored and could not make it."

"He was with a young woman. She had spent the night with him." Latona said still smiling.

"Good for Ryan." Nila said, then asked. Do you know who it was?"

"Yes, I do, and I was really quite surprised." Answered Latona, dragging it out to tease his mate.

"Was it Cita?" Nila asked. "I think she likes him."

Latona could not keep it to himself any longer and blurted out, "It was Kanti. They were together last night and still together this morning when I was there."

A look of surprise came over Nila's face and excitedly she asked, "No? Really?"

"Yes, I was so surprised this morning when I went to visit. I stepped through the tent unannounced because I was so wet and I was shaking off all the rainwater, then when I looked up, I saw Ryan laying on his side facing me. That is when I noticed there was a young lady laying beside him, but I could not see her because Ryan was blocking my view. Suddenly our daughter's head popped up and she said hello to me."

Nila looked stunned and couldn't say anything quite yet, so Latona continued, "Her beautiful smile is back. I saw it and it melted my heart."

Nila put her hand to her chest and looked like she was going to cry. "I am so happy for them." She said.

Latona nodded his head and said, "She looked happier than I have seen her in a long time."

Nila's eyes were starting to water when they heard Ryan and Kanti starting to come down the log steps.

Latona went to put his arm around his mate and said, "Do not let them see you crying, they may mistake tears of joy for tears of sadness."

She looked up, smiled, wiping her eyes as Ryan and Kanti came down the log.

When they got to the bottom Ryan lifted his tunic and presented the little pup.

Looking at Nila and Latona said, "I hope you do not mind, he wanted to come but did not want to walk in the rain. He is such a little baby."

"That's OK." said Nila. "I have a bone over here for him. I think he will enjoy it."

Zeus ran over to Nila as he was starting to associate her with a source of great food.

"Is it still raining hard?" Nila asked.

"Yes, it is." Answered Ryan.

"It looks like this may be setting in for a couple of days." added Nila as she handed a bone with a good chunk of meat on it to the little pup. Zeus quickly took it and ran over to his place, laid down and started chewing on it. Nila turned, walked over to her daughter and gave her a big hug.

"What is that for?" asked Kanti.

"Just because I love my daughter." Nila said as she pushed her back and then turned around and started walking to the cooking baskets. "Would you like tea?" She asked over her shoulder.

"Yes please." said Ryan.

"Thank you, mother,". Kanti added.

Ryan handed his cup to Nila and Kanti went and got her cup from the shelf.

"So." asked Nila shrewdly, as she was getting the tea. "What has been going on?"

Ryan smiled, looked at Kanti who was also smiling, then they both looked over at Latona, who just shrugged his shoulders.

"Mother, I am sure father has told you what is going on." Kanti said.

Nila turned around with cups of tea and handed them to the young couple saying. "Yes, he told me, but I want to hear it from you."

"Wow, that is direct." said Ryan. He then looked at Kanti, continuing, "I will let you do it."

Kanti smiled, looking at her mother as she sat down. Ryan walked over, sat next to her and put his arm around her. A gesture that Nila found quite touching.

"Well." Kanti started, "We both knew we liked each other, I think Ryan is a good man."

"And I think your daughter is a beautiful woman." Ryan interrupted.

Kanti looked at Ryan, started to blush a little, then turned back and looked at her mother. "It has been a while, and I have been thinking about it for a number of days, and it is all new right now." She said.

"Are you happy?" Asked Nila.

"Yes, I am. Very happy." Kanti said, looking at Ryan.

Latona looked at Ryan rather seriously and asked, "And you Ryan, are you happy?"

Ryan looked at Latona, then Nila, finally turning and gazing into Kanti's eyes, pulling her close to him. Looking back at Latona he said, "I have never been happier in my life."

This brought a large smile to both Nila and Latona. "That is all we need to hear." Latona said smiling.

A slight frown came over Nila's face, which Kanti caught and asked, "What is wrong mother?"

"There is nothing wrong with this Kanti. I am just worried that Stakota is going to make trouble."

Ryan said, "He can make all the trouble he wants. He has no claim on Kanti, nor will he ever have."

Latona just nodded his head and said, "That is good." Then looking at his daughter continued, "I thought about this earlier, and you made a better choice. After what I saw Stakota do the other night, I do not trust the man." He then looked at Ryan and said, "You should not trust him either."

Ryan nodded his head and replied, "I do not trust him. The man is arrogant, and a bully."

"He is also very sneaky." added Latona. "I have heard stories, but nothing can ever be proven. Be careful Ryan."

"I will be careful Latona, do not worry." and then looking at Nila said, "Nila, I will look after your daughter."

Nila smiled, got up and said, "I have no doubt that you will Ryan" then turned and walked over and picked up a platter of food and brought it back to the group.

They enjoyed their evening meal, and then afterwards sat around the fire drinking tea and talking.

Kanti got up and walked to the centre log and looked up and then came back to the group and said, "It looks like the rain is slowing down, I think Ryan and I should get back to our tent before it starts up again."

Nila smiled at Kanti's reference to "their" tent and said, "That is probably a good idea."

Kanti and Ryan said their goodbyes, picked up the little wolf who was not happy about leaving his bone, until Kanti picked it up showing the little wolf that it was coming with them as well. Once Ryan got Zeus tucked into his tunic, they headed up the log stairs to the field.

"You were right." said Ryan, "The rain has let up a bit." He then looked to the west and saw the dark clouds and added, "But I think the sky is about to open up again."

The two held hands as they walked across the field.

Nila smiled looking up at Ryan and said, "My mother seemed very happy that you and I were together."

Ryan smiled, looked down at her and agreed, "I know I saw that as well. It is always nice when the parents give their blessing, even though they did not say it."

"They did that." Said Kanti. "Both my mother and father were smiling, laughing and joking with us. I know my mother and father well enough that if they were not happy with you and I being together I would have picked up on it."

"That's good to know." said Ryan.

The two of them continued to cross the field holding hands and when they reached their tent, Ryan held back the flap for Kanti, and they both entered.

What they did not know was that just across the field at the tree line Stakota was watching them and had been watching them since they left Latona's lodge and started walking across the field, then entering the tent. His anger had grown to a complete and absolute hate for Ryan. As he stared at the tent, he said to himself, "How can she be with such a man? I will need to make sure that he disappears so he will no longer be in her life. Kanti needs to be with me, not that hideous man. Yes, he needs to go." With that he turned and walked away.

Ryan woke the next morning to the sound of the rain falling onto the tent. He laid there for a while listening to it and then he felt Kanti start to stir next to him.

She rolled over looking at him and said, "It looks like we are in for another day of rain."

"I have an idea." Said Ryan smiling at her. "Why don't we just stay in bed all day."

Kanti looked at him and said, "That would be a great idea, but I would like to get a few things of mine from the women's tent and bring them over here."

"We do not need to do that today, Do we?" Ryan asked.

"I would like to do it today if we could." she said.

"I guess we could. If you want to." Ryan said, a little disappointed.

Kanti looked up at him smiling and said. "You know it does not mean we have to get out of bed right away." She then started to run her hand down his chest over his stomach moving it lower, then looked up at him with a sly grin and added, "We could stay in bed a little longer."

Ryan looked at her and said, "I like that idea." Then leaned in to kiss her.

In the early afternoon after they had a midday meal, the two of them headed towards the woman's tent. As they were walking across the field, Ryan looked at Kanti and asked, "Why is it called the women's tent?"

Kanti looked at him and answered, "It is because the single women without mates preferred to share a tent together."

"Why?" asked Ryan.

"In the evenings we can talk, and it gives us company. We also weave, make cooking baskets, and go foraging together. In the winter we do not always get the chance, so in the summer we like to visit and socialize."

"Who are you sharing a tent with?" Ryan asked.

"Well, I'm sharing it with Cita who you know, as well as Kaya and Shinta. I am not too sure if you know or not." Kanti answered.

"I have met them, but I do not know them well." Ryan said.

When they got to the tent, only Cita was there.

"You are sitting in the tent by yourself." Kanti said.

"Well, my best friend ran off and met a man." she said with a smile. Then looking at Ryan said, "Hello Ryan."

Ryan smiled and acknowledged the greeting with, "Good afternoon, Cita. How are you today?"

"I am well. I am just sitting here weaving some mats." Cita said, smiling at Ryan.

"Would you like some help?" Kanti asked.

"No, I am just doing it past the time since the weather is not so nice. What brings you by?"

"I came to pick up a few items to take back to our tent." Conti said.

"Your tent?" Cita said, raising her eyebrows and smiling.

Kanti blushed a little looking at Ryan then back at Cita.

Ryan said, "Yes, our tent. "Hopefully Kanti will be staying with me full time."

"That is great!" said Cita with a big smile." I thought it would only be a matter of time with you two, the way you were giving goofy eyes at each other when either of you were looking."

"We were not." said Kanti.

"Yes, you were." said Cita," Everybody in the camp noticed it."

"Or maybe it was just you are very observant." Said Ryan grinning at her.

"It could be." Cita said. "As well as being so pretty, I am also quite observant."

Kanti began rolling up a few woven mats and putting some of her clothing into baskets.

Cita looked at her and said, "There is some dried meat and some greens in those baskets over there. I was going to be going and getting some fresh ones today, so why don't you take those, and I can refill the baskets."

"Are you sure?" asked Kanti.

"Absolutely." Cita said, "It will give me something to do today as well."

Ryan looked at Cita and said, "If you are looking for something to do, why don't you come by and visit us for an evening meal tonight."

"That would be wonderful. I will be there." Cita said

Ryan helped Kanti pick up their bundles and then started out of the tent.

Kanti turned around and said, "Then we will see you tonight for evening meal."

"Absolutely." Said Cita with a smile and then gave Kanti a little wink.

Kanti giggled as she turned around and headed out to catch up with Ryan.

As they walked across the field, Ryan said. "I probably should have thought that out. What are we going to serve for an evening meal?"

"You still have elk meat from the hunt that we can go get from the cool storage." Kanti answered.

"Oh." said Ryan, "Really?"

"Yes." said Kanti. "No one goes hungry. Everyone hunts and gathers, and the food is shared equally. However, you get the hide of the animal that you killed, and if you would like any favourite portions that you would like such as the liver, heart, or anything like that, you can claim that as well."

"Well, I would just be happy with some meat right now." Ryan said.

"Let's go back to the tent, drop these off and we can go get something for evening meal." Kanti suggested.

"OK." said Ryan, and the two headed back to the tent

"Hello!" Cita called out as she entered the tent. I hope I am not too early?"

"No, you are right on time." Ryan answered.

"I hope it was Ok, Kedman came to visit with me, and I invited him to join me. Is that alright?" Cita asked sounding a little nervous.

"That is fine." said Ryan, "Kanti has cooked enough for eight people."

Cita looked relieved, saying, "Thank you."

"So, when is he coming?" asked Kanti smiling at her friend.

Before Cita could answer the tent flap parted, and a young man came in shaking the water off his clothes.

The young man looked to be a little older than Cita and stood just under six feet Ryan estimated. He had an angular face, long black hair in two braids and looked in good shape. Ryan suddenly recognised this man as one of the men that he taught wrestling that day.

The young man looked at Ryan and said, "Hello Ryan. You probably do not remember me, but my name is Kedman."

"Welcome Kedman. I do remember you. You and your friend were at wrestling that day and picked up the lesson very quickly. I was quite impressed." Ryan said smiling at the young man.

The young man beamed with pride, thankful that Cita heard Ryans compliment. He then turned to Kanti and said, "Thank you for having me for an evening meal Kanti. It is very gracious of you."

"So." Said Kanti looking over at Cita as he put cooking stones into her tea basket. You were visiting Cita today, just a friendly visit?"

"Yes." answered Kedman, "I was out on a hunting trip and got a grouse and thought Cita might want the feathers."

"Well, that was very thoughtful of you." Kanti said smiling at Cita, who she could tell wanted her to shut up.

Kanti decided that she would tease Cita later and then asked. "Tea you two?"

Cita and Kedman both took out their cups and handed them to Kanti.

As Kanti was getting the tea, Kedman asked, "Will you be teaching more wrestling any time soon Ryan?"

"A few people have been asking me so we will see what happens when the weather gets better." Ryan answered. "It was a lot of fun, so I look forward to doing it again soon.

"I know there are several of us that are looking forward to practising again. We learned so much from you last time, and we are all sure that you have a lot more to teach us." Kedman said eagerly.

"I am glad you feel that way." said Ryan. "I know there are some in the camp that do not."

Kedman just nodded his head and said, "I assume you are talking about Stakota?"

Ryan noticed that he said Stakota's name with a bit of loathsomeness in his voice. "You do not like Stakota I take it?" He asked the young man.

"He has never been one of my favourite people." said Kedman, "I find him to be a bully, and after hearing about him hitting that young girl the other night, I really have no use for the man. What type of man strikes a small child?"

"My thoughts as well." said Ryan.

"OK enough talk about Stakota. He is not worth our time." said Cita with a smile, sipping her tea and looking at Kedman.

They sat around and had a nice visit and shortly Kanti showed up with a platter of cut meat and cooked greens.

"It smells delicious," said Kedman.

"Thank you." said Kanti.

"It looks like I may have gotten a good cook." said Ryan.

Smiling Kanti reached out and gave him a punch on the arm saying. "I am more than just a cook you know."

Ryan put his arm around her smiling and coyly said. "Oh, I am fully aware of that."

Cita started to chuckle and asked. "Do you think we can make it through dinner before you two try to hit the bed rolls."

Kanti's face went red, and she looked at Cita saying, "Quit teasing, or did you want me to start telling stories?"

Cita just looked at her friend and answered, "No, I am good thank you."

Over the evening meal Kanti started to notice that her friend was awfully quiet and being very demure. She was laughing at all Kedman's jokes, which she had to admit were funny, and sat there playing with her hair and staring at him. Ryan had also noticed this and wondered if he looked like that when he was around Kanti. That brought a smile to his face.

Kanti noticed the look and asked, "What are you smiling about?"

Ryan just put a finger to his lip and then said, "I will tell you later."

As the evening wore down, it was very apparent to both Ryan and Kanti, that Cita was smitten with this young man.

As they were saying good night, Kanti hugged her friend and whispered in her ear, "Do not worry I will not come to the tent too early in the morning, just in case you have somebody that spends the night."

As she pulled back, she saw that her friend's face was turning red, but also noticed that she had a very big smile on her face.

After they left Ryan looked at Kanti and said, "Was it just me, or did that seem to look like she had found her one and only."

"I have never seen her like that." Kanti said. "I am so happy for her, if this is what she wants, then it is good."

"Do you know Kedman well?" Ryan asked

"I know him through other people, and I have never heard anyone say a bad word about him. I hear he is a hard worker, always helpful, and a very good hunter, which is good because that would mean he would be a good provider for Cita." Kanti answered

"Is being a good hunter important to women?" Ryan asked.

 "Of course it is." Kanti said. "If a man does not hunt, how is he going to get food for his family?" Then looking at Ryan and smiling added, "But I have nothing to worry about. From what I hear, I am with one of the best hunters the men have ever seen, or am I with one of the luckiest hunters that anyone has ever seen?" She asked jokingly.

"Let's just say it may be a bit of both." Ryan said chuckling.

 "That sounds good. Let me put this away then we can have some tea and then go to bed. Said Kanti starting to rinse out the cups.

 "Or we could just go to bed." said Ryan.

"We will get there soon enough, just let me clean up and have some tea." Kanti said.

Ryan pretended to pout, which only made Kanti chuckle. "You must learn to be patient young man." she said to him.

Ryan walked over behind her and patted her buttocks, and then started to help her clean up.

"OK, let's have an early night." she suggested smiling up at him.

"Sounds good to me." Ryan said talking Kanti in his arms.

Chapter 7

Nila heard her mate coming down into the lodge and she asked, "How was Tolbar today?"

"Him and his mate are well. Like everyone they are waiting for the rain to stop. The good news is it seems to be letting up now. It is not raining nearly as hard as it was this morning." Latona answered back.

"That is good news. I imagine people are getting tired of being stuck inside." Nila said.

"I am sure you are right." Latona said walking up to his mate. He noticed that she was packing a bag with different items. "What are you doing?" He asked.

"Well. I just thought I would put some dry meat and a few other things together for Kanti and Ryan, then walk them over this afternoon." Nila said in a casual tone.

"Oh." Said Latona, "You know that Kanti and Ryan got some elk the other day. So, I am pretty sure they are going to be Ok for food."

"You can never have too much food." Nila said, looking at her mate, who just stood there smiling at her.

"Are you sure it's that you want to give them food, or do you want to go over there and be nosy?" Latona asked smiling at his mate.

"I am not snooping." said with a smile. Then continued, "When a mother does it. It's called being concerned."

"Oh, is that what it's called." Latona said with a smile coming up behind his wife, "Then maybe I should come and be concerned as well."

She turned and looked at her mate and said, "You are just as curious to find out as I am."

"Maybe so." he said bending down and kissing her on the cheek, "But I am not allowed to show it."

"Oh, that's right." she said, "Men are not supposed to show curiosity, or vulnerability."

"That is correct." he said, "But I may walk you over there just to make sure that you get there safely."

"Of course, I hope you do. I might get attacked by a ravaging herd of mountain sheep or gophers. It is such a long way between here and their tent." Nila said smiling at her mate.

"I know." Latona said, "That is why it would be helpful to have a big brave man like me around."

Nila just shook her head and continued packing. After a while, she asked, "Are you serious about coming because I think I am going to go leave now."

"Yes, I will definitely come with you." Latona said.

As the two left and were walking across the field, They looked up at Rocano and Skyseeker walking towards them. Once they caught up with the couple Rocano said to Latona, "Chica from three sisters is having a meeting with some of the other men about a possible buffalo hunt and wanted to know if you would like to attend."

Latona looked at his mate and said, "It looks like you will have to be curious for the both of us."

She smiled and said, "Do not worry I will. I will see you when you have finished." She then asked Skyseeker, "Would like to come with her to visit with Kanti and Ryan."

"I would love too." Said Skyseeker." I need to talk to Ryan anyway."

As the two continued walking, Nila asked her mother, "Have you heard about Kanti and Ryan?"

Skyseeker looked at her daughter and answered, "Yes, I heard the other day that they are, how should we say it, seeing each other."

"How do you feel about it?" Nila asked her mother, looking for a reaction on her face.

"I will let you know once I have seen whether Kanti is happy or not." Skyseeker said.

"She is very happy." said Nila, "I think you will be surprised."

"I hope so." The grandmother said. "It has been a long time."

When they got to the tent Nila scratched on the outside and called out to Kanti. Kanti pulled back the flap to let in her mother, and then a big smile came over her face as she noticed her grandmother with her.

"Please come in." she said to both the women.

As they entered the tent, Nila was surprised to see young Tisha sitting on a mat playing with the wolf. As she looked around Nila noticed it had changed quite a bit since last time she had been here, it was starting to look more like a lodge. There were four mats around the fire pit, there was wood piled up in the back for use, as well as food baskets and cooking baskets. Nila thought that this place looked like it was now being lived in.

Skyseeker walked over to the little girl and asked, "Hello Tisha, how are you today?"

"Good." Tisha answered.

Skyseeker reached out and lifted the little girl's face and turned it towards her. She had a purplish bruise under her left eye, and on her left cheek. Skyseeker didn't say anything, just looked at Nila and Kanti and then over at Ryan. She could tell that Ryan was not very happy about the marks on the child.

"That is a nasty Bruise." She said to Tisha

"Yes, it hurts a little, but it is not too bad now." The little girl said to the older woman.

"That is good." said Skyseeker. "You're a brave girl."

Tisha just smiled and continued stroking Zeus.

"Where is your brother?" Nila asked the little girl.

"At home. Mekome has been making a bow for Tolbar for when everybody goes hunting, Tolbar said he really liked the bow that Mekome had made for Ryan, and he would like to have one himself." She answered.

"It is really a good bow." Ryan said, "Your brother does very good work."

Tisha just smiled and continued, "Well, Tolbar came over and asked Mekome if he would make him a bow, and he would trade it for some arrowheads that he had made."

"Mekome would be very happy that Tollbar asked him such a favour." said Nila.

"Oh, he was." said Tisha excitedly, "He has been working on it for two days now and putting in a lot of time to make sure it is just right. Everybody has been so busy being inside with all the rain I did not get to see Zeus, so I wanted to come over and play with him and Ryan and Kanti said that that would be OK, and I could come for a visit. We have had tea and everything.

Mila looked up at her daughter, smiled and said, "Speaking of tea?"

"I will make some mother. Would you like some grandmother?" Kanti asked.

"Yes please." the old woman said, then turning to Ryan asked, "Will you be available tomorrow morning?"

"For what?" Ryan asked.

The old woman just looked at him, smiled and said, "For a visit."

"A visit?" Ryan asked suspiciously.

"Yes, after your morning meal I will come and get you and we will have…" She hesitated for a moment and then continued, "A visit."

Ryan still suspicious, smiled and asked, "So now this is the time for the question, is it?"

She just looked at that and said, "You know the answer to that Ryan." And then turned and asked Kanti, "Could you put some dry berries in the tea?"

Nila watched her daughter go about preparing the tea, then watched Ryan playing with Tisha and the little Wolf.

It was not hard for her to imagine this as one big happy family and hoped that this would come true for her daughter and Ryan. Nila looked over at her mother who was also watching the scene before them.

Smiling, her mother looked over and caught her daughter glancing at her and said, "You were right, this is good for her."

Kanti turned around and asked, "Did you say something grandmother?"

"No, my child. I was just talking to your mother." The old woman said smiling at her granddaughter.

Remembering the package that she brought Nila said, "Oh, by the way, I brought a few things over for you and Ryan."

Kanti was a little surprised and asked, "What did you bring?"

"Well, I brought over some dried meat because you could never have too much of that, but I had already packed it when Latona told me that you had a good supply of elk meat here."

"Yes, we did, because we invited Cita and Kedman for an evening meal last night." Kanti said.

"That was nice." Said Skyseeker. "Are Cita and Kedman a couple?"

"No, I do not think so." Grandmother, "But I would not be surprised if it happened sometime soon."

"That would not be a bad match," Skyseeker nodded her head then looked over at her daughter and asked, "What else did you bring her?"

"Oh yes." Nila said, "I also brought you a couple of extra cups and some bowls for when you have guests, so you will always have cups for tea and bowls for soup or broth."

"I have my own cup." Tisha said holding it up.

"That is good. You should always have your own cup and bring it with you wherever you go, because you never know when you're going to get the offer of tea or something to drink." Skyseeker said to the little girl.

"I know, Ryan gave me tea today." Tisha said with a smile again holding up her cup.

Kanti took the cups and bowls as her mother pulled them out of the bag and went and placed them on a shelf that her and Ryan had built the other day.

Nila looked around and said. "You have decorated quite nicely."

"Thank you. it was just a few things that I had at the woman's tent that we brought over. We need to get a few more things, but we will work on that over the next week or so." Said Kanti smiling at her mother.

Nila just smiled and nodded. Kanti came over with two cups of tea for Skyseeker, and her mother, handing them to them.

"Here you go." she said to her mother, then looking at grandmother said, "I put some dried blueberry in there. It should help the taste."

"I always did like tea with berries in it." The old woman said. Ayana makes a very nice tea, and I am sure that's what she puts berries in it as well."

They all sat around and talking for a while, when Kanti asked her mother, Tisha and her grandmother if they would like to stay for evening meal.

Tisha said, "Thank you but I must get back or my mother will be worrying about me, because I did not tell her where I was going. She then got up scratched the wolf stomach and said, "Goodbye." Then skipped out of the tent.

"She is quite something," Ryan said.

"Yes, she is." Nila said, "And that is a very nasty bruise she has on her face."

"I would like to put that same bruise on Stakota's face." Ryan said not looking pleased.

Skyseeker looked over at Ryan smiled and said, "Ryan, you were new with us and probably do not know so I will explain it to you. We all must live in harmony and live in peace. We do not threaten one another with any form of harm, and we do not threaten anybody with death. I was not there the other night, but I heard what happened. We also do not tolerate abuse of children but threatening to kill Stakota openly like that was not something that should have been done. You did get around it by turning it into a joke, and that lightened everybody's spirit. But you cannot openly threaten a member of the people, you are going to have to learn to control that impulse."

Ryan said, "You cannot be Ok with what he did to Tisha."

The old lady stared at Ryan then slightly raised his voice, "No Ryan, I do not condone it.! However, there were better ways to express your displeasure, other than threatening to kill him."

Ryan lowered his head and softly said, "Yes, I know. Once the words left my mouth, I knew I should not have said it, but there was no way to take it back."

"That is true." Skyseeker agreed, "But you did make a joke out of it lighten the mood and it worked well in your favor. Do not worry you will learn the ways of our people Ryan." She then looked over at her granddaughter and continued, "You will have people that love you and are willing to help you. You must listen and be willing to learn."

"I will." Ryan said looking at Kanti.

Skyseeker smiled and then said to Ryan, "There is a small part of me that wishes you had actually smashed him in the face."

Nila was surprised and said, "Mother, you can not say things like that."

"Why not? Asked Skyseeker, "We are all family, and I am just stating my opinion. However, Ryan, we are glad that you did not, because that would have put us into another situation that I think no one here is prepared to deal with at this time. It would have been frowned upon and there would have needed to be a council meeting. So, moving forward, just be wary of Stakota, I do not trust him, and I believe you should not trust him either."

"I do not trust him." said Ryan, "As I told Kedman last night, I think he is a bully, and quite possibly a coward."

"Well, you have made an enemy of him, so just be careful. He is very sneaky and would not trust Tanak or Demat either." Skyseeker said.

"Who are they?" asked Ryan.

"Those are his two closest friends, or should I say hangers on. They are always around telling him how great he is, and how wonderful everything he does is." Skyseeker answered.

"Oh, I remember seeing them." Said Ryan. Then turned to Kanti smiling added, "Do not worry everyone. I will behave myself and be a very good boy."

Kanti came over, handed him tea, and then kissed him on the cheek. "That's good to hear." she said, then turning to her mother and grandmother asked, "Would you like to stay for evening meal."

"I would love to." said Nila, "But I am going to get back and prepare something for your father. He has gone to a meeting, and he may not get back until late, so I like there to be food there for him when he gets home."

"How about you, grandmother?" Kanti asked.

"No." said Skyseeker. "I must go as well. I have some things to prepare tomorrow for mine and Ryan's journey tomorrow."

"Journey?" Asked Ryan, "I thought I was just going to be answering some questions."

"You are." Said Skyseeker with a smile, "Do not worry. I do not mean a physical journey, I mean a spiritual journey."

Kanti snapped her head around looking at her grandmother asking, "You are taking Ryan on a spirit journey tomorrow?"

"Yes, child I am." answered the old woman. "You know very well my dear I have a number of questions that need to be answered, and I will take the journey with Ryan first, and then I will have better idea of what questions to ask." she said still locking eyes with her granddaughter.

Ryan noticed that Kanti looked rather concerned and asked her, "Is there something I should know about?"

Kanti broke eye contact with Skyseeker turned, looked at Ryan with a nervous smile and said, "No, everything will be fine."

Kanti looked back at her grandmother and asked, "May I come along as well?"

Skyseeker just shook her head and said, "No my child, not this time. I think Ryan and I will travel alone."

With that Skyseeker smiled, thanked Ryan and Kanti for the tea, stood up and started to open the tent.

When she got there, she turned around and said to Ryan, "I will come and get you tomorrow after morning meal."

Ryan just nodded his head and said, "OK. I will see you then."

After Skyseeker left Kanti and Ryan visited a while longer with Nila until she announced that she had to get back to her lodge, she excused herself, got up and before she left Kanti came over and gave her a big hug thanking her for the gifts that she brought earlier that day.

"I am glad you could make it mother, even if it was just to be nosy." Kanti said smiling at her mother.

"Your father said the same thing." said Nila with a smile, "And I'll tell you what I told him. When you are a mother it is not being nosy, it is being concerned."

Kanti reached out, hugged her mother again then said, "Well, thank you for being concerned."

Nila smiled and left. Once Nila had left, Ryan looked at Kanti and said, "You seem a little nervous with Skyseeker's talk of us going on a spirit journey."

"I was not nervous just surprised." She said.

"Why?" asked Ryan, "Have you ever been on a spirit journey?"

"No, I have not. That is why I was surprised. My grandmother is teaching me about healing and the medicines, but she has not started to teach about the spirit and the spirit world." she said.

"Skyseeker is teaching you?' Ryan asked.

"Yes, the elders of our people always pass on their knowledge on to the young to keep traditions and customs alive. Skyseeker is getting older and if she should die, a wealth of knowledge will die with her. She said that I have a natural ability to learn healing, so she is taking it upon herself to train me." Kanti said.

"Wow, that is great." Said Ryan.

"Yes, there is a lot to learn, and hopefully I will be able to pass it on to one of my children someday." Kanti said smiling.

Ryan walked over and put his arm around her and gave her a kiss on the lips, looking into her eyes he said, "We could practice tonight you know."

Kanti was not quite sure what he was talking about. Ryan said nothing but kept looking in her eyes.

Suddenly she started to smile, getting   his little joke. "You are right." she said, "There is no harm in practicing."

The next morning Ryan woke up early as he had a bit of a restless night because he couldn't get the phrase "spirit journey" out of his mind. He got out of bed, trying not to disturb Kanti and started a small fire to heat the rocks to make some tea. Ryan had a little dried meat thinking that was all he was going to have this morning, and he would sit there and wait for Skyseeker to come and call for him. Once the tea was made Ryan sat there sipping on his cup when he noticed Kanti starting to stir. She reached over to where Ryan should be and feeling that he wasn't there she sat up quickly noticing him sitting by a small fire drinking tea.

"You're up early this morning." she said.

"Yes, I had a bit of a restless night last night." He said.

She pretended to pout and said, "That is too bad. I tried so hard to tire you out last night."

Ryan smiled looking at her and said, "You did a good job. I just woke up early this morning and could not get back to sleep. Would you like some tea?"

Kanti smiled nodding her head, she threw back the covers. Ryan gazed at her naked body as she got out of bed and stretched, she then went and put a loose wrap around her waist and sat down across from him. He poured her a cup of tea and started to hand it to her, he spilled some because he was not watching what he was doing but gazing at her exposed breasts.

She caught the cup and said, "Be careful, You almost spilled it on me."

Ryan smiled and said, "What can I say, your beauty distracted me."

"My breasts distracted you." She said laughing.

"Same thing." Ryan said laughing as well.

They heard a scratch on the outside of the tent then Skyseeker asked, "Ryan, are you awake?"

"Yes, I am Skyseeker. Would you like to come in for some tea?" Ryan answered.

"No Thank you. I think we should get going." Skyseeker answered.

"I will be out in a moment." Ryan replied. Then finishing his tea, he leaned over and gave Kanti a kiss saying," I will see you when we are done."

Kanti smiled but he noticed a concerned look on her face. "Do not worry, I will be fine. Skyseeker will keep me safe."

He then got up and walked outside and greeted Skyseeker.

Ryan walked with Skyseeker towards her tent, but as they got closer Ryan noticed the Skyseeker was starting to veer off and head up towards the tree line. They walked for a while following the tree line, when Skyseeker turned and started following a path that Ryan hadn't noticed until just now. They walked in amongst the trees for a while and Ryan thought about asking Skyseeker where they were going, but thought better of it, figuring he would just find out where he was going when they got there. After a while of following the trail, it opened into a clearing that Ryan never knew was there. Looking into the centre of the clearing Ryan saw a dirt mound covered in pine branches. It looked like one of the large lodges that were on the main field by the river, but this one was smaller.

It had a smoke hole in the top and Ryan noticed that smoke was coming out of that hole. As they walked around it instead of going climbing up the top and going down the center, he noticed that there was a ramp cut into the Earth leading down into the pit house as an entrance. As they started down the ramp Ryan saw that at the end there was a large buffalo hide covering the entrance, acting as a door. They moved the hide aside and entered. As he walked inside Ryan took a moment to let his eyes get accustomed to the dim light. He looked around noticing that the inside construction was like Latona's Lodge, but this one was much smaller, and it was not as high. It looked like it was about Seven feet high in the centre coming down to about five feet around the edges. There was a circular fire pit in the middle, with four logs placed around the fire pit, setback about five or six feet. Draped over each of these logs was a fur that was laid out in front of the log as well. Ryan noticed that off to the side were two elderly men, one that Ryan had seen with Skyseeker before, and the other one Ryan had never met.

"Are these men coming with us?" Ryan asked Skyseeker.

"No." she said, looking at the two men. "They are here to make sure we can find our way back."

Ryan wasn't too sure if he liked the sound of that but was not going to start asking more questions as he figured he was going to find out what was going on shortly. Ryan noticed that with the fire going in the center of the lodge It was quite warm inside.

Skyseeker looked at Ryan and said, "I suggest that you take your shirt off. You will find it will be more comfortable."

She then led him over to one of the logs, beckoning him to sit down with his back to the log and his feet stretched out in front of him.

"It is actually quite comfortable." Ryan thought, "These furs are very thick. I wish I knew what they were."

Skyseeker, then walked over to one of the men who handed her two cups filled with liquid. She then brought one of the cups over to Ryan and handed it to him saying, "Drink this."

"If I asked you what is in it, would you tell me?" Ryan asked.

Skyseeker smiled and said, "It is just Some herbs, moss and some mushrooms."

Ryan smelt it and then took a sip. He found that he did not like the taste that much and wrinkled his nose.

"I suggest that you just drink it down quickly. That will help you fight the taste." The old woman said.

Ryan took her advice and swallowed the drink down in two quick gulps. Skyseeker took the cup from him and then walked across to the other side of the fire. She sat up against the log, also taking off her top. Ryan noticed that she had symbols painted on the upper portion of her body, but didn't want to stare at her because he thought it would probably be impolite. One of the old men came over and handed what looked like a handful of grass to Skyseeker. She thanked the man who went back and sat down next to the other man across from Ryan and her. Skyseeker took the handful of grass and put the tip of it in the fire, it ignited and started to burn. She blew it out, moving it in front of her letting the grass smoke filling the room with a gray haze.

Ryan was expecting to start choking because of the amount of smoke that was in the lodge, however he found the smoke to smell quite sweet. "Just sit back and relax." Skyseeker told Ryan.

Ryan wasn't too sure what was going on but decided to take her advice and just lean back against the log and watch the fire. The two men reached beside each other and picked up two small drums, slowly and lightly beating on them while chanting in a very low tone. Ryan was concentrating on the fire and listening to the drums when he started to feel a little strange. "It must be the drink that I was given," he thought and just decided to relax and see what happened as he was staring at the fire through the smoky haze that seemed to be getting thicker. He noticed that the haze was starting to vibrate, and as he was looking across at Skyseeker, it seemed as if he was looking at her through some sort of heat haze that you might see in the desert. Then he noticed that the smoke seemed to be closing in from the sides and suddenly he could see nothing in front of him but a gray wall of smoke. Ryan wasn't too sure how long he was looking at the gray wall, but he started to hear voices. He listened and thought that they sounded familiar. He continued with his eyes open, looking straight ahead and suddenly the mist started to clear and he found himself back at the job fair in Arizona at his college.

"What the hell is going on?" Ryan thought to himself as he looked around. Bill was there, and Jack was there as well.

"So, son, what do you say? You think you would like to be a cowboy?" Bill asked.

Ryan just stood there looking at Bill and Jack, who were looking back at him expectantly for an answer.

Ryan smiled and then asked, "Why the hell would I want to be a cowboy?"

Because cowboys get laid more than dishwashers." Bill answered.

"Isn't that the truth." Jack added.

Ryan just smiled and said, "I would love to come and work for you."

Suddenly, the smoke came in and the gray wall came back. Then the mist cleared again, and he was sitting at a table with Bev and Ron Hartwell in front of him, with Bev going on about how skinny he was, and how we needed to eat more.

Ron looked at his wife and said, "Bev, leave the poor boy alone."

Mrs. Hartwell smiled, put a piece of pie in front of Ryan looking at her husband and said, "I will leave him alone as soon as he gains a little more weight."

Ryan smiled and said, Mrs. Hartwell, I weigh more than I did last time I was here. I keep telling you I'm not losing weight."

Bev just smiled, waved her hand and said, "Well, I can't see it."

Ryan looked around the table thinking it was great to be back at the ranch again when he suddenly noticed that sitting at the end of the table was Skyseeker, not saying anything just sitting there watching him. The mist came over him again and this time when it cleared Ryan was sitting on his horse riding out on the ranch with Bill in front of him and Terry off to the side. Ryan looked around feeling the sun on his body and the wind in his hair, as well, he could smell the smells of the Ranch.

"Timing has a lot to do with the outcome of a Rain dance." Bill was saying.

"Do you think you're ever going to get tired of those cowboy sayings young fella." Terry said.

"I don't think Bill is going to let us get tired." Said Ryan with a smile.

As they kept on riding Ryan was so happy. It was so great to be with his friends again, especially Bill, but how can he be with Bill? Bill died. They rode for a while and as they rounded a bend in the trail Ryan looked up and sitting on a rock watching them approach was Skyseeker

Ryan quickly looked back at Terry and asked, "Terry, do you see anybody sitting on that rock over there?"

Bill turned around and asked, "Are you on drugs kid? There's nobody sitting on that rock."

Ryan just smiled to himself and enjoyed the ride for a few moments more before the mist came over them again. The next time the mist cleared, he was out on the field sitting on Zeus trying to save Jerry from the bear. As before, Zeus managed to run the bear off and Jerry scrambled to safety. As Bill came riding up to him, Ryan looked past him at Skyseeker standing with the camera crew watching him. The next thing he knew. Ryan was sitting in the tattoo parlour getting the large bear tattoo with Ross, Jerry, Terry, Jack and Bill standing around him. Ryan looked at his friends and looked at the tattoo artist and then thought to himself, "I remember this well."

As he looked out the window of the shop Ryan saw Skyseeker standing there staring In, nodding her head.

As the mist came in again, Ryan wondered where he would wind up next, but was not happy, as when the mist cleared, he was at Bill's funeral.

Ryan hoped that this would be a quick visit, but unfortunately, the whole funeral seemed to play out from the eulogy to the reading of Bill's letter. Ryan felt his heart sinking again just as it had on that fateful day of Bill's funeral. The haze started to come in and much to Ryan's relief, he was at Trudy and Deborah's wedding. It was a great time bringing a smile to his face. Next, he was transported to Jack and Cindy's wedding with laughing and dancing. Ryan wished he could stay but felt the mist coming. He then found himself at Terry and Samantha's wedding dancing with Trudy and Deborah. Then it was Jack and Cindy's wedding with Ryan smiling thinking about all his friends and how much they had meant to him.

When the mist cleared again, he was sitting on the couch with Trudy on one side, Deborah on the other and little Nina his goddaughter, sitting on his lap giggling as he tickled her.

"You really do spoil her you know." said Deborah.

"Of course I do." Ryan said, "It's my job, isn't it?"

"Yes, it is." Said Nina smiling up at her Godfather, then asked, "When are we going to the park?"

Ryan smiled, bouncing her on his knee a few times and asked, "When would you like to go to the park butterfly?"

"Now." she demanded.

"Well OK, I guess we can go now, then." Ryan said.

Trudy looked at him and said, "She has you wrapped around her little finger."

Ryan looked at Deborah, then at Trudy and said, "No she doesn't."

Nina looked up at Ryan smiling and said, "Yes, I do. Let's go."

Ryan started laughing as he put her down and stood up. Nina reached up and grabbed his hand and they started walking towards the door. Ryan looked up and saw Skyseeker standing in the kitchen doorway smiling and nodding her head. Ryan nodded back at her and then turned and started walking with the little girl out the door. As Ryan opened the front door stepping through, the scene around him changed and he was now on an airplane. Ryan was in the aisle seat and seemed to remember that this might have been the flight to Los Angeles. When he looked next to him across the aisle, he saw sky seeker, sitting at a window seat with her eyes wide, looking all around in terror. The haze came in and quickly enveloped them again, and when it cleared, he was standing in front of a window, feeling wet and cold. He was covered in some sort of gel. Ryan looked around and saw a man standing there with a propane torch and realized that he was on a movie set preparing to do a stunt. Ryan remembered this stunt and prepared to get ready as the man came up with the torch and set him on fire. He stood there for a moment, waiting for the director to scream action. As soon as he heard it, he took four steps and dove through the window. He knew that he was two stories up, and that there was an airbag outside.

He made the turn in mid air and landed into the airbag on his back with his feet spread apart. As the airbag started to deflate, he could feel and see the safety crew jumping in with the fire extinguishers going. He was out in no time and the director called, "Cut."

As Ryan stood up everybody was cheering, laughing, and giving him high-fives. When he looked over there was Skyseeker standing there just shaking her head. Ryan was trying to figure where they were going to go next but was not prepared for where it took him. He seemed to be in three or four places at once. When things came clear, he was climbing over the waterfall at Johnston Canyon. Ryan started the descent just like he did the first time repelling down, then climbing up and then climbing down again. He looked up into the sky and noticed that it was still the strange colours and the flashing, was still there as it was the first time. When Ryan looked down onto the lower observation deck, he saw Skyseeker looking up at him, then looking up at the sky in wonder. When he got to the position where he started to feel the tingling sensation, he cut the rope just like he did before, and as before there was a large flash, but this time he didn't hit the water. The mist started to come in again, this time the mist didn't clear, and Ryan felt like he was suspended in nothingness.

Not knowing which way to go, or which way was up or down. Ryan started to hear drums and chanting in the distance, the more he listened and concentrated on them, the louder and the closer they seemed to get. They started to slide away from him, so Ryan concentrated even more, and the sound got louder and closer. Ryan continued to concentrate on the sounds of the drums and the chanting through the mist. Suddenly the mist started to clear, and Ryan found himself lying on a fur with his back up against the log staring at a fire. Ryan sat there for a while, trying to get his bearings.

Ryan tried to get up, but a wave of nausea came over him and he quickly sat back down. He looked across the fire at Skyseeker and saw that she was just staring at him.

The two men got up and walked over and started to talk to Skyseeker. She shook her head, made a motion and the two men left, leaving just her and Ryan in the lodge. Ryan was trying to process all that he had seen in his spirit journey but could not comprehend what had happened to him.

He sat there for quite a while deep in his thoughts when he heard Skyseeker say, "We need to talk Ryan."

Ryan looked up and saw that Skyseeker was standing next to him. Ryan looked up at her smiled and asked, "I guess you have a few questions now?"

Skyseeker sat down next to Ryan saying nothing for a few moments then turned to face him and said, "I think I have more than a few questions Ryan. The first being it is not where you are from, I should be asking, it is when you are from? Is that correct?"

Ryan smiled at her and said, "Yes that is a question you should ask."

"I saw things that I could never have imagined." She said to Ryan, shaking her head and looking down. She then looked up at him and said, "You could fly."

Ryan smiled and said, "Yes, not me, but we had something called a plane that we could get in and fly from one area to the other in no time at all."

"Do you know how far ahead you came from?" she asked.

Ryan just shook his head and said, "It is many, many, many, lifetimes. So many that neither I, nor you could comprehend."

"The changes." she said, "There were so many people, big lodges, and why did they set you on fire?" She asked, looking at him.'

Ryan smiled realizing how strange it all must have seemed to her. "That was my job back then. I did a lot of things that would be hard for me to explain now to you in this time."

She then looked at him and he could tell a thought had just popped into her head. "So that is why you do not know how to live like the people." she said to Ryan. "It is because you are not from this time."

"That is right." said Ryan.

Skyseeker continued, "I have been watching you ever since you arrived here, and I could not understand why you could not do simple tasks such as starting a fire or other things. I noticed that when you would come upon a group of people doing a task, you would sit and watch them for a while until you have the task figured out, then you would go over and offer to help. That way the people that you were offering to help thought that you knew how to do it. Well, all the time when in fact, you were just learning it right then". She smiled at him and then asked, "Am I correct?"

Ryan smiled at her and said, "You are very observant, and you were also correct. There are a lot of things that I know that are totally useless to me now, but with the help of people like Mekome, Tolbar, Latona, Mila, and a lot of other people, I have slowly been learning."

"Well, we will have to speed up your teachings.? Skyseeker said.

"How can you do that without letting people know where I am from."

"I do not think it would be a good idea to tell anyone where you are from at this time. All they need to know is that you come from far away and that is it." She said.

"What about Kanti?" Ryan asked.

Skyseeker pondered this for a few moments and then said, "I think we will tell her in time, but not right now."

"I do not like to keep things from her." Ryan said.

"That is good." said Skyseeker," But you are not going to be keeping this from her, you are just going to…" She thought about it for a moment then continued, "Delay telling her for a while.

"OK." said Ryan, "You know best."

"Let's hope so." Skyseeker said. "We shall see. I still have a number of questions that you and I are going to have to go over, but I think we will need our heads to clear a little. I do have a question for you now."

"Sure." said Ryan, "What is it?"

"In our vision, there were two ladies, and there was a little girl that you were bouncing on your knee. You seemed fond of her."

"I am." said Ryan, "That is my goddaughter, and the two women were her parents."

Two women can have a baby in the future?" Skyseeker asked in surprise.

"No." said Ryan laughing, "She was adopted."

"Oh." said Skyseeker, then asked, "What is adopted?"

Ryan smiled, thought about it for a moment, and then answered, "Sometimes a man and a woman who are mated cannot have a child, or two men, or two women that are mated cannot have children, and there are people out there that have children that do not want them, so the people that do want them can adopt them, and make them their own children."

"Oh." said Skyseeker, nodding her head, "So with the people if a mother and father have an accident and are killed, then the child may go live with a relative and be raised as their own child."

"It is similar." said Ryan, nodding his head.

"I can see why you get along with Tisha so well. She reminds you of your goddaughter, doesn't she?"

Ryan just smiled at how perceptive Skyseeker was. "Yes, she does Remind me of my goddaughter, and maybe that is why I spoil her a little bit."

"A little bit!" said Skyseeker with a big smile on her face. "Well, we need to get dressed and go get some food. I don't know about you, but I'm incredibly hungry."

"I am very thirsty as well." Said Ryan.

Skyseeker started to walk over to get the water, when she stopped, turned looking at Ryan and asked, "you are learning our language quicker than I have ever seen any visitor. Is this something that they can do in your time?

"No, I am just very good at learning new languages. I have been for some time." Ryan answered.

Skyseeker nodded her head then reached over and grabbed a water bag and filled two cups with water.

"Here this will have to do for now." She said as she handed him the cup.

Ryan took the cup saying, "Thank you. This will be fine."

After they drank the water and got dressed, they left the lodge. As soon as he got outside. Ryan looked up and noticed that it was a lot later than he thought it should be. It felt like he hadn't been in the lodge for an hour, but looking at where the sun was in the sky, it looked like it was late afternoon. "We were in there for quite a while." Ryan thought.

"It did not seem like it, but it's been the better part of the morning and most of the afternoon." Said Skyseeker as they started to walk back to the camp. Once they broke from the tree line and got to the field Skyseeker said goodbye to Ryan and started to head towards her tent, leaving Ryan to continue towards his. As Ryan started to cross the field, he heard his name called. Turning he saw Stakota striding towards him looking angry.

"I really do not feel like dealing with this asshole." Ryan thought to himself but stopped and waited for him to catch up.

"What kind of man are you?" He asked Ryan.

Ryan looked a little surprised and asked, "What are you talking about?"

"How could you let Kanti go off gathering by herself?" Stakota asked.

"I did not allow her to do anything." Ryan replied. "I have been with Skyseeker all morning and into the afternoon."

"Oh, then you do not know?" Stakota said, looking surprised.

"Do not know what?" asked Ryan,

"That she decided to go gathering by herself up on the north trail. People should not go into the woods by themselves." Stakota told him.

"I don't know why she would do that." Ryan said.

"Well, I just heard from some of the hunters the big brother bear may be in the area." Stakota said, looking concerned.

Ryan's face went white, and he looked around quickly. "Which way did she go?" He asked Stakota.

Stakota pointed to the north end of the field and said, "At the end of the field, just slightly to the west is a trail leading north, it's a straight trail with no branches on it. That is the trail that she took, but that was a while ago. She could have gone a fair distance by now."

Fear gripped Ryan as he said, "Thank you for telling me, Stakota."

Then he started to jog across the field. He wanted to run full out as quickly as he could to get to her but knew that he would not be able to keep up that pace, so he fell into the rhythm of a quick jog and headed across the field.

As Stakota watched Ryan run across the field, a smile came over his face. "That is it. You run right there." to himself. "I have a surprise waiting for you."

Stakota was not happy when he saw Kanti and Ryan walking back from Latona's lodge the other night holding hands, and he became enraged when he found out that the two of them were together.

"You need to disappear white hair." he thought, "This is going to make it happen."

He turned and slowly started walking across the field as he passed Ryan's tent, the flap opened and Kanti stuck her head out, looking around.

"Good afternoon." Stakota said to Kanti.

She looked up in surprise and said, "Oh, hello Stakota, I did not see you there. Did you happen to see Ryan anywhere?"

Stakota made a show looking one way and then the other, then back at Kanti saying, "No, I have not seen him today at all."

"Oh." Kanti said looking down, a little disappointed. Before Stakota could say anything else, Kanti said, "Thank you." then duck back into the tent.

Stakota stood there a while, staring at the tent, thinking how much he was going to enjoy being with her once Ryan was no longer around.

Chapter 8

Ryan continued jogging down the path For quite a while, figuring he must be coming up close to having traveled a mile. He would slow down occasionally, to a brisk walk and look around. He noticed that the forest is quite thick but from time to time he would come out into a small clearing. He would then stop, look around and call out Kanti's name, hoping that she would answer. There was always nothing but silence and once he found the trail on the other side he would carry on.

Further down the trail Demat said, "I do not think we should be doing this."

Tanak Replied, "Do not worry about it. It will be quick, and it will be easy."

"I have never killed anyone before." Said Demat.

"Neither have I." said Tanak, "But Stakota's plan is simple, as Ryan comes running down the path we will step out and hit him with our clubs until he is dead, then drag his body further into the woods and let the animals finish him."

"I do not know." said Demat, "The man has done nothing to me, and now we are supposed to kill him."

"You are not turning into a scared woman, are you?" Tanak asked, "Because if you do not help, I will make sure to let Stakota know that it was all me."

"No, I am going to help." said Demat, "I am just not comfortable with it, that is all."

Just then both men heard Ryan calling Kanti's name far off in the distance.

"He is still a way away, but he should be here soon. Let's get into our positions." Tanak said.

Both men split up with each going to one side of the trail and hiding behind a tree. The area that they had picked for the ambush was quite thick with overgrown trees, a mixture of fir, and some birch. They stood there waiting for Ryan to arrive.

As Ryan quickly continued down the trail, his increasing anxiety and fear kept him moving. What if something happened to Kanti? "Let her be OK, let her be OK." He kept saying to himself as he carried on.

Up ahead Tanak and Demat heard him approaching. Tanak signaled across and Demat nodded his head in acknowledgement. As Ryan kept jogging up the trail, he noticed he was getting into a thicker portion of the forest, and he needed to pay more attention to his footing on the trail, so he slowed down. In doing so Demat miscalculated Ryans distance and stepped out six feet in front of Ryan holding a club. Ryan stopped looking at this man that appeared out of nowhere noticing that he had a club in his hand. Demat was surprised at how far Ryan was away, so he screamed and charged him. As Demat brought his club down, Ryan took two quick steps back causing Demat to miss. When Demat's arm reached his lower arc, Ryan stepped in and with an open palm, smashing the man in the face, breaking his nose.

The man dropped the cub, and Ryan quickly picked it up and tossed it farther into the woods. Ryan then noticed another man holding a club jump out onto the trail in front of him, behind his first attacker. Ryan quickly grabbed the man in front of him, spun him around, and put his arm around his neck, propping him up between himself, and the new attacker. Tanak didn't know what to do, he couldn't attack Ryan without hurting his friend who is now bleeding profusely from his nose. Ryan started pushing Demat towards Tanak and quickened his pace as he got close, he released his hold on the man and shoved him as hard as he could into his new attacker. Both men tumbled to the ground. Ryan then looked around and decided to step off the trail. Moving off to the side and into the dense forests, Ryan knew That this would stop them from being able to swing their clubs from side to side and they would now have to swing straight down to avoid hitting trees, giving him a slight advantage. As he moved amongst the trees, he heard the two men talking to themselves and Ryan suddenly remembered who they were. He thought to himself, "These are friends of Stakota. This whole thing was a set up. I bet Kanti didn't even come down this trail." Ryan started to become angry and looked through the growth for his adversaries as they came off the trail to hunt him down.

"OK Ryan." he thought, "These two are not out for a tea party. They either want to hurt you badly or kill you." Ryan settled on the latter and decided that this is not a time for finesse, he needed to end this quickly. Ryan moved deeper into the forest, keeping his eyes on his attackers as best he could, as they moved in and out of the trees.

When Ryan got to a particular cluster of trees he started to circle around, the two men did what Ryan had hoped they would do, and split up with one coming around one way, and the other going the other man coming the other way. Ryan smiled to himself and waited for a few moments before he made his move. He decided to go after the one that still had a club and if need be, he could deal with the one whose nose he broke earlier, after. He quickly moved his way around the trees as quietly as he could. Tanak was watching his footing, not noticing Ryans approach until it was too late. When he noticed him, he swung the cub at Ryan's head, but did it sideways instead of up and down, allowing the club to hit several branches stopping its momentum, and allowing Ryan to step in and kick the man between the legs. Tanak let out a grunt, and Ryan stepped in, took the club away from him, threw it further in the forest, then spun the man around, stood him up and ran him into a tree face first, then flung him back on his back. The man curled into a fetal position and started vomiting. Ryan then turned his attention to the other man. As Ryan moved his way around the grove of trees, it became apparent that Demat had heard what was going on and stepped further into the forest to avoid Ryan.

Ryan looked around but could not see the man. He slowly backed his way deeper into the forest and then crouched down listening for any sign of the attackers. He crouched there for quite a while and heard nothing. He heard them talking earlier but now it was quiet. Ryan made a slow circle around to where he left Demat, but there was no one there. Ryan stood still for a long time concluding that the men had left.

Ryan shook his head and started walking back towards the camp thinking about what he was going to do to Stakota when he got there.

Stakota was hanging around at the end of the trail trying not to look conspicuous waiting for his two friends to come back and tell him that the job was done. He heard someone coming and when he looked up, he saw both men, however they looked bloody and battered.

As they came up to Stakota he turned on The men asking, "What happened. Is it done?"

Both men shook their heads and explained what happened. Stakota started to become enraged, and his face started getting red. The two men backed up, knowing they were about to face his wrath. Suddenly a smile crossed his face, and both men looked at each other and then at Stakota.

"Don't worry, my friends, I have just come up with another idea that will work just as well." Said Stakota. Then explained his idea to the two men, who also smiled and nodded their agreement. The three of them quickly headed across the field to find Latona and some other men.

By the time Ryan had walked back to the end of the trail, he was furious. He could not believe that Stakota would try to have him killed. It made no sense, or maybe it did. He thought, "I knew he was sneaky and untrustworthy, but now I know how far he will go."

As he walked up into the field, he looked up and saw a large group of people standing there, and when they noticed him, they all turned and stared. "I wonder what's going on there?" Ryan thought to himself.

As he walked up to the group of people. Latona came and met him asking, "Is it true Ryan? Did you beat these men?"

Ryan was surprised at the question but answered, "Yes, I did. They were trying to kill me."

"I Told you he would say that." Tanak said glaring at Ryan. "We were not trying to kill you. We just made a bad joke, and you decided to beat us."

"What are you talking about?" Ryan said, looking at the Man, "You attacked me in the woods."

"We did no such thing." said Demat, "We know we should not have made that crude joke about you and Kanti."

Ryan was puzzled and couldn't figure out what was going on and asked, "What crude joke?"

Latona said, "These men claim that as you were walking across the field, they made a crude joke that they should not have made, about what they would like to do to Kanti and asked you if you would mind. They then say that you became enraged and started yelling at them, so they decided to just go for a walk up the trail, then you followed them in and attacked them."

"I did not." said Ryan objecting in a loud voice. "That's not what happened."

"Oh." Said Stakota with a smirk, "You are going to claim these men just attacked you for no reason? Why would you even go up that path if not to attack them."

When Ryan realized what was happening, he looked at Stakota and said, "I went up that path because you told me that Kanti had gone up there on a gathering trip by herself and that big brother bear was in the area, so I went looking for her, as you knew I would."

Stakota put on his best surprised face and looked around at everyone gathered around saying, "Ryan, I have not seen you since the night of the fire pit when you threatened to kill me." emphasizing the word "kill."

At that moment, Ryan wished he had killed him.

Stakota went on. "I saw Kanti at her tent, and she was looking for you. She asked me if I had seen you. I would not I have not told her that I had seen you, but I did not."

Ryan looked at Latona and Tollbar who were standing together and said, "Latona you must believe me, I did not attack these men. I went out looking for Kanti because of the story I was told by Stakota, and then these two men were lying in wait for me. I think they were going to try to kill me and leave me in the forest."

Ryan looked over and saw Skyseeker standing there, looking stoic and not saying anything.

"Well Latona." Demanded Stakota, "You know what happens now, he needs to be banished."

Latona did not say anything and suddenly Kanti came running up and threw her arms around Ryan. "Are you OK?" she asked.

"Yes, I am. Do not believe what you are hearing right now." Ryan pleaded.

Kanti looked straight at Stakota and said, "I would not believe anything these men say about you, Ryan."

"You might need to change your mind on that." Said Stakota still smirking, "Your man is about to be banished."

"I never said he was to be banished1" said Latona glaring at Stakota.

"But that is what is required." Said Stakota glaring back.

"We shall see." Latona said. "We will need a talking circle. I will call one for tomorrow morning, and a decision will be made then.

"Well, that decision had better be banishment." Said Stakota, "This man," he said waving his hand Ryan "Can not go around beating innocent people."

"As I said Stakota, we shall see tomorrow." Replied Latona still glaring at the man.

Kanti was still hugging Ryan when Skyseeker walked over to the couple. As she stood there.

Ryan looked at her and said to Skyseeker, "I did not do this, Stakota told me that Kanti had gone on a walk by herself, and that big brother bear was in the area, so I went down the trail to help her."

"As he knew you would." Skyseeker said.

Ryan was a little surprised at the comment but continued, "When I got down the trail, those two men came out of hiding and tried to club me to death."

"It is fortunate that you are such a good fighter." Said Skyseeker with no tone or emotion in her voice.

Ryan looked at her and said, "Skyseeker. I promised you I did not do what they are saying, I was only defending myself."

Skyseeker looked at him, smiled and nodded her head and said to Ryan, "I believe you, but we have three people that say you attacked them, and want justice. We will see what happens tomorrow with the talking circle, but I have a few ideas."

Ryan had a nervous smile and leaned down and kissed Kanti on the cheek. "I'm sorry." he said to her "I am such a fool to have trusted him."

"She just looked at him and said, "You were worried about me, and that may have blinded you a little."

Ryan smiled down at Kanti and said, "Try a whole lot."

The two of them started walking back to the tent.

Once there Kanti said, "Let's have a meal and get you cleaned up."

Ryan and Kanti sat drinking tea when Ryan asked her, "What is banished? It was a word I had not heard anyone say before."

Kanti looked at him thinking about how to explain for a moment, then said, "It means sent away."

"Sent away?" Ryan asked, looking concerned.

"Yes, if you are banished you are sent away, and you have no people. You become a person with no people. That means that no one can take you in, give you shelter or assistance." Kanti said.

"No one?" Ryan asked.

"Well, what normally happens is the person will travel or go on a long journey and wind up staying with people that have no knowledge of who they are. But they always live in fear that somebody else on a journey they recognize them and tell the people they are with about their indiscretion, and they will then be banished from them as well and have to continue traveling." Kanti said

"Well, that does not sound good." said Ryan.

"It is not. I can not imagine what it would be like to travel and not have any people of your own." Said Kanti.

"Well, I hope that does not happen tomorrow." Said Ryan.

Kanti thought about it for a moment then looked at Ryan and said. "If it does, I am coming with you."

Ryan looked at her and was a little shocked. "You can not come with me Kanti, you have family here. You have your mother, your father, Skyseeker."

"I know." she said quietly, "But I do not want to be here if you are not here."

He leaned over and kissed her on the cheek and said, "I will tell you what, let us not worry about that until tomorrow."

"Tell me the whole story Ryan." Kanti said, looking up at him.

Ryan proceeded to tell the whole story from running into Stakota, him running trying to find her down the trail, to being jumped by Demat and Tanak. "They wanted to kill me and leave me in the forest for the animals. I am convinced of that. That way it would just appear that I had disappeared. That way Stakota thought that you would come running to him."

"That will never happen now." Kanti said, "After all the things that that man has done, I do not want to be near him. I can not believe he would go this far."

"Well, he really wants to be with you." Ryan said to her smiling, "And truthfully, I can not blame him." He playfully snuggled up to her, and she pushed him away saying, "Stop that, this is serious."

"I know it." said Ryan, I am just trying to lighten the mood."

They sat quietly for a moment, and she looked at him and asked, "How did your journey go Today?"

The question caught him off guard and he answered, "It was interesting."

"Can you talk about it?" She asked.

"Not right now." Ryan said, "Your grandmother wants to talk to me a little bit more and ask me some more questions. She said once that is done, I can tell you."

Kanti smiled at that and said, "OK, I can wait."

The little wolf climbed on Ryans lap looking for attention, so Ryan started scratching him behind his ears. Zeus curled up on his lap and enjoyed the attention.

Later that night as they were laying in bed, Ryan was trying not to think about the next day and realized he had forgotten to ask Kanti what a talking circle was. He rolled over facing her and was going to ask her but realized by her shallow breathing that she was asleep. He laid there for a while longer thinking about it, and then he himself joined her.

In the morning Kanti was up first and was in the process of making some tea and was carving up some elk when Ryan woke up.

Kanti looked over at him smiling and said, "The tea will be ready shortly."

Ryan just laid there on his side watching Kanti prepare the morning meal and the tea. He also noticed there was a bowl off to the side.
"What is that for? Ryan asked.

"I think maybe we should scrape your face before we go to the talking circle this morning," she said.

Ryan smiled and said, "Shave."

She looked at him and repeated the word back as a question, "Shave?"

"That's what it means to scrape your face. Where I come from, you shave."

"Oh." Kanti said, "I like that word. Then you need a shave." she smiled, hoping that she got it right.

Ryan rubbed his whiskers and said, "Yes, I do, and hopefully you are going to do it for me, so I don't cut my face up like I did last time.

Kanti just smiled and said, "We could look after that after the morning meal."

When Ryan had eaten and was on a second tea he noticed Kanti had a bowl with some flowers in it, which she was adding hot water to and grinding up making a soap foam. She then splashed warm water on his face and then rubbed on the foam. After working it into an area, he grabbed the special piece of flint Skytal gave them and started shaving his whiskers. "I hope Stalnay brings some of this flint back when he comes back." she said to Ryan as she continued working.

Ryan had never heard that name before and asked, "Who is Stalnay?"

Kanti stopped and looked at him saying, "That is right, you would not know him would you. He is my brother."

"Your brother!" Ryan exclaimed, "I did not know you had a brother."

"Well, he had gone on a journey down south and he left as soon as the snow started melting. Hopefully he will be back before it falls again." she said.

"I look forward to meeting him." Ryan said with a smile.

"I think he will like you." she said then continued. "He did not like Stakota. I should have listened to him, but I did not."

"So, is there a lot of this flint in the area that he was going to?" asked Ryan.

"No, it is still further south, but there is a lot more people coming up to the Buffalo jump that he is going too, so a lot of trading will be going on. Hopefully, he can come back with some. Now quit moving around or I am going to cut you."

Ryan watched her as she went back to shaving him and again tried to suppress a chuckle as he noticed again that when she was concentrating, her tongue stuck outside of her mouth just a little bit.

When she was finished, she said with a smile as she splashed water onto his face, "There you go, now you are all clean with no face hair."

"Well hopefully they can see what a good-looking man I am and will let me stay." Ryan said while smiling at her.

"It worked for me." She said smiling back, "But I don't know about the rest of the people."

Ryan looked at her and the smile left his face as he asked, "How many people do you think will be there?

Kanti thought about it for a moment, then looked at him and said, "There should be everybody from the camp, and they will be in the centre, other people will be on the outside."

Ryan wasn't too sure what that meant, but just nodded his head like he understood. A short time later, they heard Latona calling from outside the tent.

Kanti went out and talked to her father for a few moments and then came back in.

"They are ready for us." She said. Then added, "Where you go, I go."

Ryan stepped out of the tent and greeted Latona, "Good morning, Latona."

Latona smiled and nodded his head. The three walked across the field, and as Ryan looked in the distance, he saw a large group of people Sitting on the ground. As he got closer, he could see that there were two rings of people. There was an inner ring, which seemed to have everybody that was a member of this camp in it, and then an outer ring, which had a lot of people that he was not familiar with. He saw standing off to the side, Tanak, Demat as well as the Stakota. As they got closer. Stakota broke off from the group and went and sat with the people in the outside circle. Ryan was led over and stood about ten feet away from Tanak and Demat. Latona then went through the outer ring of the first people into the centre ring and sat down.

Skyseeker stood up and walked to the centre of the rings scanning the assembled group of people, then addressed those in the center ring, "We are here today to decide on Ryan's fate."

She then signaled to Stakota, who walked to the centre of the circle, stood there, and told the story of how Ryan followed Tanak and Demat into the woods and beat them senseless for a small joke that they told about Kanti. He embellished a few things, then told the crowd that the only reason that he was telling the story was that his friends were beaten too badly.

He then finished by raising his voice saying that Ryan should be banished.

Skyseeker stood up, glaring at him and said, "That is enough! the decision of what we will do will be made by us, not by you.!"

A red flush came over Stakota's face as he went and sat down.

She then stood there, looking at the crowd and said, "I will speak for Ryan." with that. She continued by relaying the story that Ryan had told her how he was tricked to go into the woods, looking for Kanti and was jumped by Tanak and Demat, and was only defending himself. She agreed that he did in fact, beat them, but only while trying to take their weapons away from them, preventing himself from getting killed.

When she had finished, she said. "We will now have a show of hands for Tanak's version. Of the story."

She looked around and counted the raised hands. There were not many.

She then asked, "Now, Ryan's version?"

There were far more hands raised for Ryans version of events then there were for Stakota's tale. Skyseeker noticed the Stakota was staring around nervously at the raised hands in Ryans favor. Unfortunately, because there were some people that did believe Stakota the matter could not be dropped even though far more people believed what Ryan had to say.

"We seem to be at a slight impasse." Skyseeker said, taking in the crowd. There was a murmur amongst the people when Latona stood up and walked to the center of the circle.

"I have known Ryan since he arrived, and I believe him to be an honourable man." Latona started.

"Then you think we are liars?" Stakota interrupted, standing up and glaring at Latona defiantly."

"I did not say that." Latona said, looking at him. "And you may want to let me finish before you interrupt me as I am in the centre of the circle and the one allowed to speak."

Stakota looked around and realized that he had spoken out of turn and quickly sat down.

Latona continued, "My heart feels that we should believe Ryan however, since everyone is not in total agreement, I think we must test."

Skyseeker looked at Ryan, thought about it for a moment and nodded her head," Yes, Latona that is a good idea. We will conduct a test, but should Ryan pass the test, I would also then put to everyone here that he is considered a permanent member of the people of the valley."

There was a loud murmur among the people in the outer circle however, the people in the inner circle were all nodding their heads in agreement.

"Then it is done. Tonight, we shall allow Ryan to meditate, and he will be tested first thing in the morning." Skyseeker said addressing the crowd.

Ryan didn't know if that was a good thing or a bad thing, but everybody seemed to think it was a great idea.

"What kind of test am I going to have to take?" he asked himself.

He looked over at Kanti sitting next to her mother, she was smiling, but it was a nervous smile.

He looked over at Skyseeker, who in a loud and commanding voice said, "All those in favour of the test?"

Ryan watched as everyone in the center circle, and most of the people in the outer circle raise their hands.

"It is done!" Skyseeker said and then turned and walked out of the circle.

Latona came over, putting his arm on Ryan's shoulder and said, "Well that is good, at least for now, there is no punishment."

"For now?" Ryan asked.

"Yes, you will be tested tomorrow morning." Latona said smiling.

"And how does that work? Ryan asked.

Latona smiled and said, "Do not worry, we will talk about it later." Then he walked over to join his mate.

Ryan stood there for a while looking around, not too sure what to do as everybody started to disperse and go on their separate ways. He looks around, trying to find Kanti and then noticed her in an animated conversation with Skyseeker. He was too far away to hear what they were talking about, but it looked like a very intense conversation. Kanti was nodding her head up and down, and then Skyseeker was shaking her head from side to side and moving her hands around, trying to make a point.

Ryan decided that he did not want to interrupt that conversation, so we turned and started to head back to his tent. As he was crossing the field he heard his name called and looked up to see Tisha running towards him with a little pup chasing behind her.

Ryan stopped and waited for the little girl to catch up and she looked up excitedly Asking, "So what happened? Mother wouldn't let me come. She told me to go and get Zeus so he would not show up and distract everybody. So, I have been playing with him out in the field, we have been having a lot of fun."

Ryan couldn't help but look at the little girl, so full of enthusiasm and smiled saying, "Well Tisha, I do not know what happened."

"They are not going to send you away, are they?" She asked, looking quite upset.

"No, I have to do some test tomorrow." He explained to the little girl.

like that explained everything she said, "Then that is OK then. You are not going away today?" she asked.

"No, I am not." He said.

"Good, then come play with me and Zeus." She said smiling.

Ryan just laughed as the little girl took his hand and started to lead him away.

"OK, what would you like to do?" He asked the little girl.

"I do not know." She said. Then, looking like she was really trying to think of something, she said, "Let's go find Mekome."

"Why should we find Mekome?" Ryan asked.

"He was going to come down and listen at the talking circle and then he was going to go get some of his friends and shoot at targets." The little girl said.

Ryan thought to himself that could probably be a very good distraction. "OK let's go find him.' He said.

As they started walking Ryan looked at the little girl and asked, "So what is a talking circle?   "

The little girl turned around and looked up at him. She was surprised and asked, "You do not know?"

Ryan quickly replied, "Well, it is different for different people in different areas."

Tisha smiled saying, "Oh, Ok. If people have something they need to talk about that they feel is important, they go to a talking circle. Whoever stands up in the centre of the talking circle is the one that is supposed to be the one talking. If you want to talk then you must wait for the person in the center to finish, and then you can go to the center and talk. If you do not wait, then you are very rude."" Ryan shook his head, starting to comprehend, "."OK." Said Ryan, "But there were two rings."

"Yes, sometimes there can be as many as three rings. It depends on how many people there are. The first ring is the people that the talk is about those are the people that can cont., contibl…" She hesitated not being able to remember the word her mother used.

"Contribute." Ryan suggested

"Yes, that is the word." she said smiling then continued," Those people can contribute to the conversation. The outer ring or ring are usually just people that are there to listen and do not have anything to say or are not involved."

Ryan thought about that for a moment and then nodded his head. "OK, good to know."

Tisha looked up at him asking, "Is that the same as where you come from?"

Ryan smiled, nodded his head and answered, "Yes. They are almost the same."

The girls seemed satisfied with that answer, and they continued walking to the practice area. When they got to the field where the boys usually practice there was no one there.

The little girl looked disappointed and said, "I guess they decided not to do it after all."

Ryan smiled as he looked over the little girl's head and said, "No, I think they are going to do it, because here they come now."

She turned around and yelled, "Yay, are you going to see if they will let me shoot too?"

Ryan just smiled looking at the little girl and said "Why not ask Mekome yourself? I am sure he would let you."

"I don't know if he would or not." She said putting on a little pout.

"Oh, I am pretty sure he will." Ryan said smiling at the little girl, "But sometimes boys forget things and do not offer all the time. Sometime you have to ask them."

"Oh." she said, "OK, I will." She said, and they waited for the boys to come.

"Hello Ryan." Mekome said as he walked up.

"Hi Mekome." Ryan said, "I hear you young men are going to be doing some target practice today." Then looking at Tisha he asked, "Can we join you?"

"Yes, that would be fun." He said, "I think we have an extra bow."

"I could go and get mine." Ryan said.

"I think we have an extra one for you to use, if you would like, and while we are practicing, maybe you could tell us about the arrow in the ground."

Ryan was confused for a second and then understood what Mekome was asking. "Yes, I can definitely do that." He said.

Once the targets were set up, they all stood around getting ready to start practicing. The boys all started to get their arrows together while started stringing up their bows. Ryan noticed that Tisha was still standing there and had not asked her brother if she could join in.

Ryan leaned over towards Mekome and in a quiet voice said, "You know, your sister would really like to join in. She is just too shy to ask you. You know you let her last time you practiced, and she was quite good."

"I know she was. I was surprised." Mekome said.

"Well then maybe it would be nice if you invited her to join the practice." Ryan said, nodding at the young boy.

Mekome thought about it and said, "You are right, I should ask her." he then walked over to his little sister and handed her a bow that was obviously too big for her. "You can practice with us if you would like Tisha." he said to his sister.

A huge smile came across the young girl's face. "Really. Yes, please. I want too." she said excitedly.

"Good." he said, "Then come and join us."

The little girl told Zeus to stay, and surprisingly, the young pup sat down, looked at her, and then laid down with his paws outstretched in front of him, watching them.

As the boys were lining up getting ready to shoot at targets Mekome asked, "We heard that she stuck an arrow in the ground on the elk hunt, Why?" He asked.

"Yes, I did." He said to the young boys. "The reason I did that was if you were carrying your arrows in your quiver on your back, a second arrow is harder to get at if you need to take a second shot. If you place one or two arrows in the ground in front of you, they are within easy reach should your first arrow miss. you could quickly pick another arrow up, load it into your bow and then fire it then shoot it. then if that one hits, and you need a third one. you have another one sitting there."

All the boys just nodded their heads.

"Maybe that is something you would like to practice today. I have seen you all shoot at the targets, and you are all pretty good at hitting them." Ryan suggested.

All the boys nodded their heads in agreement and the first boy walked up, he put two arrows in the ground in front of him, and then one arrow in his bow. He fired off the arrow in his bow then quickly grabbed the second arrow out of the ground and let it fly, followed by the third. They were surprised at how fast they could fire off three arrows. So, for the rest of the afternoon the boys practised rapid firing three or four and even five arrows. Tisha got in on the fun with the help of her brother and even some of her brother's friends. Like the last practice, they took their time to help her, and to teach her how to do certain things. Ryan could tell the little girl was having a great time being included in this activity with her big brother.

As he watched Mekome's friends giving her pointers he said to Mekome, "You know your sister adores you and wants to copy everything that you do."

Mekome smiled saying, "I know she wants to do everything I do. I do not think she adores me."

"Oh, she does." said Ryan with a smile, "And one thing you must remember is, she is your sister, and she is family, and family is very, very strong. She is part of you, and she has your blood in her as well."

Mekome thought about that for a moment and just smiled at Ryan, so Ryan continued, "You need to take care of your sister because you are almost like her guardian to her, and you will always be her big brother."

Mekome nodded his head in understanding and then walked over to also help give your sister some tips.

Ryan could see that the little wolf was getting fussy and didn't want him running onto the practice field.

So, he said to the boys, "I have to go now, and I am taking Zeus with me, I do not want him getting in the way of your practicing."

All the boys nodded their heads and waved at him as he walked back to the tent. When Ryan walked into the tent, he was surprised to see Kanti sitting there drinking some tea.

"Oh, there you are." he said with a big smile on his face.

She turned around, looked at him and said, "I saw you practising with the boys, and I did not want to come and interrupt. You seemed to be having a good time."

"I did." Ryan said, "I looked around after the talking circle and you were gone."

"Yes," she replied.

"I was going to come over and talk to you, but you and Skyseeker were in what looked like a very serious conversation."

"We were." she said, and then looking at him continued, "I told Skyseeker that if you were to get banished, I would be coming with you."

Ryan sat down beside her reaching for her hand and said, "Kanti, you can not leave your family to come with me. If I am banished like you said, I will be a person with no people. You have people, you have family, it would not be right."

"I told Skyseeker that that is what you told me, and she seemed surprised, but I am adamant about this Ryan." Kanti said firmly.

"Well, let us deal with it when we must deal with it. Right now, I am not going anywhere until after the test, whatever that is." Ryan then looked at Kanti asking, "What is this test that Skyseeker mentioned?"

Kanti shook her head answering, "I do not know."

Ryan was a little surprised and asked, "You do not know?"

Kanti shook her head and said, "That is because it could be different things at different times. It could be a physical test, It could be a mental test, or it could be a test for the spirit. It is up to Skyseeker to choose."

"Oh, So if I pass the test, I get to stay, and if I fail, I have to leave, is that right?" Ryan asked.

"Yes." Kanti answered, "It is how hard Skyseeker makes the test."

"Well, that is good to know." Ryan said.

Kanti looked into Ryans eyes and said, "You know Skyseeker thinks Stakota, Demat and Tanak are lying, but she cannot prove it."

"That makes me feel better." Said Ryan.

"What makes you feel better?" asked Kanti.

"That Skyseeker believes that I did not attack those men." Ryan answered

"Because you told her you would not, and that you would be, as you said, a good boy." Kanti said smiling

Ryan chuckled a little and said, "Yes I did say that."

Kanti looked surprised as she just remembered something and then asked, "Ryan would you like some tea?"

"Yes, I would." said Ryan, then asked, "Do we have any of that elk meat left? I am a little hungry."

"Yes, we do". She said as she handed him a cup. She then went and got some meat and then handed him some flat pieces of what Ryan took to be bread.

"Where did this come from?" Ryan asked.

"Mother made it and brought it over just before you showed up." Kanti said.

Ryan tasted it, deciding it was delicious. As Ryan ate, they talked for a while about how he was tricked into going down that trail. Kanti was a little surprised that she was pleased that he would take such a risk just for her thinking that she could possibly be in danger. After a while, there was a scratch on the flap and Skyseeker stuck her head through the tent opening.

"Hello grandmother." said Kanti.

"Skyseeker, would you like some tea?" Ryan asked the elderly woman.

She looked at Ryan and said, "I will have a quick cup, because we must go and prepare for the test."

"So soon?" Ryan asked, looking at her.

"Yes Ryan, it's best if we get this over with." She said as she sat down while Kanti handed her a cup of tea.

Ryan looked at Sand said, "Skyseeker, I did not break my word. I did not attack those men. I defended myself, that is all."

Skyseeker smiled and said, "Yes, Ryan, I believe you. Unfortunately, I cannot say the same for Stakota and his two friends. Them, I do not believe."

Skyseeker sat sipping in her tea, when the little wolf came over to get some attention. The old woman reached down and started scratching Zeus behind the ear, she then looked up at Ryan and said, "Kanti told me that if you get banished, she is coming with you."

Ryan started to protest but Skyseeker held her hand up and continued. "She also told me that you told her not to, because she has family, friends here and it would not be fair for her to suffer your punishment." Skyseeker then stared directly at Ryan and added, "That tells me so much about the kind of man that you are Ryan."

Ryan looked a little confused and asked, "How so?"

Skyseeker smiled and answered, "Well, a selfish man would want someone to come with him so he did not have to be alone, regardless of what it would do to that person. A caring man would first think of that person and worry more about them, than he would about himself, which is what you have done. Whether my granddaughter goes with you, or not, that is up to her, but I hope it does not come to that." She continued scratching the little wolf who was enjoying it immensely.

"Have you decided on the test Yet, grandmother?" Kanti Asked.

"Yes, I have, and just so you know Ryan will not be coming back to the tent tonight, He will be sleeping in a small travelling tent in the field." Skyseeker said smiling.

"Will the test be hard?' Kanti asked.

"You shall see." she said, "But I am sure Ryan will pass our little test, as it is the fairest for this situation."

Ryan was curious to find out what this test was going to be but knew that if Skyseeker wouldn't tell Kant, she wouldn't tell him.

"It must be something really good." Ryan thought to himself as he sat there drinking tea with Skyseeker.

After a while, Skyseeker stood up and announced, "It is time to go."

With that, Kanti put out the small fire while Ryan finished his tea, and they headed out of the tent starting across the field. They had not gone too far when Ryan heard a little yip and turned around seeing Zeus, he smiled and waved, calling the pup.

The three of them started walking across the field with the little pup following behind them.

Ryan remembered Skyseeker mentioning a small tent and was looking around to see if he could see it but saw nothing in the camp field. The trio walked down to the river following Skyseeker. She then turned west along the river, following it for what seems to be about a mile to Ryan. They came to a clearing where Ryan saw several people sitting around a large campfire. As Ryan got closer, he noticed that to the south of the campfire towards the river there was a platform covered with a deer hide with some items on it. On the other side of the campfire, about twenty paces away was a small tent. When they walked up to the fire, Ryan noticed it was Ayana and several other people that he knew. They all greeted Ryan and told him to join them around the fire. Ryan sat down and Ayana came over and offered him some tea which Ryan accepted eagerly.

"Here you go." she said to Ryan. Then smiled and added softly, "I know you like my tea the best."

Ryan smiled, winked at her and said in a low voice, "Yes, I do. But do not tell Kanti."

Nila brought over a platter with meat and greens on it for Ryan to help himself. Ryan looked around at all the other people eating and drinking tea and chatting away and thought to himself, "This seems more like an evening meal than anything else."

Kanti came over and sat down beside him as the little pups wiggled his way between the two of them and laid down. Ryan handed the little wolf a piece of meat which he immediately started chewing.

The group chatted and talked for a while and Ryan looked around noticing that Stakota, Demat, and Tanak, were nowhere in sight.

"I wonder where those assholes are?" Ryan thought to himself.

Latona, Tolbar, Corna, and Skytal, started talking and telling stories of past hunting trips, with their successes and failures, as well as all the funny things that happened along the way. Before long Ryan noticed that it was starting to get dark. He then looked up in time to watch Stakota, Tanak, and Demat come strolling into the clearing. Ryan watched Stakota walking up to the group with that arrogant swagger and wished to himself that he had tried to participate in the ambush, so that he could've taken a piece out of him as well.

When Stakota reached the group of people he asked in a loud voice, "Are we getting ready to start the test soon?"

Skyseeker locked eyes with Stakota and answered just as loudly, "We will be ready to start the test, when I say we are ready to start the test, not you."

The two continued to stare at each other until Stakota broke his gaze and turned away. Skyseeker was thinking to herself that it was about time that they should get started but was now going to hold off just to keep Stakota waiting.

She turned and asked Latona if he had any more hunting stories. Latona smiled nodding his head and continued regaling the crowd with them.

When Latona was finished and Skyseeker felt that Stakota was properly agitated, she stood up and announced, "It is getting late, we shall now start the test. Ryan, please stand."

Ryan stood up looked around, then walked over to Skyseeker. They started walking towards the raised platform on the side opposite the tent. When she got there, Ryan noticed there were two stones sitting on the table as well as two pieces of white bark. Skyseeker reached down and turned over the first piece of bark, and Ryan noticed that it had a black dot on it. She then turned the other piece of bark over and Ryan noticed that that one had an X marked on it.

Skyseeker looked at Ryan and said, "I will mix these two pieces of bark up and place the rocks on them to hold them down. They will sit here all night while you are in the tent meditating and, in the morning, we shall all gather here, and you will be called out of the tent and to pick one of these pieces of bark up. If you should pick up the X, then you failed the test and you will be banished. However, pick the dot and that proves what you said to be true, and you will get to stay." She then turned to the crowd adding, "Everyone can wish Ryan a good evening, and you will have to leave. Daryo is going to stay and watch the entrance to Ryan's tent to make sure he does not leave."

Ryan looked at Skyseeker and asked, "Who is Daryo?"

She pointed to the elderly man standing off to the side. Ryan recognised him as the one that he had seen with Skyseeker several times. He smiled to himself, happy that he now knew the man's name after seeing him so many times. When Skyseeker and Ryan turn to look back at the platform, they noticed Stakota standing there examining both pieces of bark in his hand.

Skyseeker watched him for a while then asked, "You seemed very curious about the bark Stakota."

Stakota put the pieces of bark down quickly turning towards Skyseeker looking like a small child that had just been caught doing something wrong and said, "I was just looking at them."

"Skyseeker smiled and said, "Well, now you have seen them, so you can join the rest of the group in saying good evening to Ryan, and then head back to camp."

Stakota looked at Ryan, smirked, then turned and walked away, followed by his two friends. Ryan was about to say something to Skyseeker when Kanti came up and put her arms around his waist.

As she stood beside him, Ryan leaned down and gave her a kiss saying, "I guess I will see you tomorrow morning."

She smiled at Ryan and said, "We will be here."

Kanti stood beside Ryan while most of the other people came up to say goodbye to him, and then slowly started heading off to the main camp.

Skyseeker remained and once everybody had left said to Ryan, "You will have to stay in the tent for the entire evening. If you need to go out to relieve yourself in the middle of the night Daryo will be there, and he will come with you to make sure that you do not go anywhere near the platform."

"All right." said Ryan and started to head to the tent. Ryan heard a little Yip and turned around to see the wolf standing there wagging his tail.

"Would it be Ok if Zeus comes with me? I would like him to spend the night so that way I will have some company." He asked Skyseeker.

She thought about it for a moment, not being able to come up with any objection to it and said, "Of course the little one could join you."

Ryan signaled the pup, and he came bounding up beside him following him to the opening of the tent. Ryan studied the small tent noting that it was quite small and made for only one, maybe two people. It was not very high, and it looked like it was just a hide laid over a frame, staked down on the four corners with a slit in the end away from the fire as an opening. Ryan climbed inside and saw that there was a bed roll and a covering as a bed. He laid on the bed and the little wolf curled up beside him.

"I can't believe the test is picking a piece of bark. I was expecting so much more but nothing quite this simple. Well, at least I have a fifty, fifty chance of picking the right one." He thought to himself.

Ryan tried not to keep thinking about tomorrow, and all the excitement of the day, as well as all the food he ate, Ryan fell asleep quickly. Ryan was awakened by the low growl of the little pup beside him. Ryan woke up, starting to stroke the wolf trying to get it to quiet down, but it continued his very low soft growl. Ryan heard another noise coming from directly out front of the opening of the little tent. Ryan listened to it for a while and realized it was snoring.

"Daryo must have fallen asleep." he said to the little wolf who just kept staring at the back of the tent growling.

Ryan was wondering what the little pup was growling at, so he went to the back of the tent managing to lift it up the edge and thought to himself, "This is not the most secure thing in the world. I could sneak out of here in a heartbeat, especially with Daryo snoring away at the front of the tent."

He lifted the hide a couple of inches, waiting for his eyes to adjust to the light of the fire. He was down low and couldn't get a very good view, but he saw somebody had snuck into camp and was now standing in front of the raised platform. Ryan watched as they lifted one piece of bark and then put it back, then lifted the other piece of bark, they crumpled it up in their fist and threw it onto the fire. He then noticed the person take a piece of bark out of the small pouch they were carrying and lay it down beside the other piece that was there and put the stones back on it.

 Ryan could not understand what was going on at first then suddenly realized, somebody had removed the bark with the circle, and replaced it with an X. Now there were two X's, so no matter which one I pick tomorrow it is going to be an X. Ryan still couldn't see who it was but had a very good idea that it was Stakota. Ryan had to hold back the little wolf as he wanted to go out and give the intruder a good barking too.

"No, stay here with me." Ryan said quietly pulling the pup back in, then letting the bottom of the tent drop back down again.

"This is great Ryan, no matter which one I pick it's going to be an X." Ryan thought about it for a while and could see no way out of this other than tomorrow he would say that he saw somebody coming in and putting an X down. As much as he would love to say it was Stakota, He could not. "I wish I had got a clear look at him so I could have said for sure." He thought. "I will have to take the test again and that will make it fair. Unless Stakota tried to say that I snuck out and changed it myself. That's also a possibility because I don't trust that man."

 Ryan could not get back to sleep. He lay there awake trying to come up with a solution to his current problem. He could tell it was getting close to morning as he saw the light starting to creep through the tent. Daryo was not snoring anymore, and he could hear him moving around outside.

 After a while, Ryan heard more people starting to show up but just laid there thinking, saying to the little wolf, "Well Zeus, looks like it's about time." He started scratching the little wolf behind his ears then continued, "No, I don't know what I'm going to do. I'm going to have to expose it somehow, I just don't know how."

 After a while he heard Skyseeker's voice outside the tent asking, "Ryan are you awake?"

 Ryan answered, "Yes, I'm awake."

 "Then you must come out and make your choice." She said.

 Ryan looked at the little pup and opened the flap of the tent, then signaled for the pup to run out which he did. Ryan followed Zeus out, then turned and started to walk towards the platform. There was a large crowd, and he noticed that somebody had stoked the fire back up again and felt the warmth of it as he walked by. Ryan stopped for a moment, thinking about something in the back of his brain that was just sitting there, but not coming to the forefront. As he took a few more steps towards the platform an idea came to him. A big smile crossed Ryan's face as he thought, "That's it. It's so simple, it's going to work."

He then continued walking to the front of the platform, waiting for Skyseeker to come up and stand beside him. He turned around and looked at the crowd, seeing Latona Nila, as well as all his new friends including Kanti standing there trying to smile, but looking nervous. Ryan flashed her a big smile and waved at her, then gave her a little wink which seemed to alleviate some of the concern that she had but not totally alleviating it.

He then turned and looked at Skyseeker asking, "When do you want me to make my pick?"

Skyseeker noticed the smile on his face and the cockiness in the way he asked a question and couldn't help a smile. She nodded her head and answered, "Anytime Ryan." She then stepped back watching to see what the man would do.

Ryan looked at both pieces of bark sitting on the table sitting on the platform. He put his hand above one, then above the other, and then moved his hand back-and-forth for a while, and then put hand up to his chin to look as if he was pondering which choice to make. Ryan suddenly reached out, grabbed a piece of bark, picked it up and pulled it close to his body moving it up to look at. Ryan held it in the palm of his hand smiling, suddenly yelling at the top of his lungs, "Yes! Yes! I did it. I picked the right one." Ryan started hopping around the fire continuing to yell, "Yes! Yes! Yes!"

Ryan then quickly crunched the bark in his fist and threw it into the fire, the dry barked caught quickly and burned before anyone could react.

"No!" yelled Stakota. "He can not do that."

Skyseeker turned and looked at Stakota asking, "Why not?"

"Because we will not know if he picked the X one or not." Stakota answered.

Ryan turned and smiled at him and said, "Of course we will Stakota. I just threw the dot in the fire so that means the one last remaining piece of bark will be the X on it."

Skyseeker turned and looked at Ryan with a mischievous grin on her face then back at Stakota and said "Yes, let us check if he is right."

"No, he will not be right." Stakota started to protest, then stopped realizing that he almost gave himself away.

Skyseeker glared suspiciously at Stakota and asked, "Why would that not be right? Do you think there was something tricky going on Stakota?" Not breaking her gaze.

Stakota quickly stuttered, "No. no, You are right, that is a way to tell."

Skyseeker smiled and winked at Ryan then said, "I am glad you agree."

"She Knows!" Ryan thought to himself, then walked over to the platform and flipped over the remaining piece of bark to show an X.

"Well, it looks like Ryan picked the right bark." She said to everyone there.

Kanti came running up and jumped into Ryans arms, giving him a long kiss. Other people started crowding around, congratulating him and patting him on the back, saying they knew he was innocent all along.

Cita wrapped her arms around him crying and said, "I am so happy for you and Kanti."

Kedman patted Ryan on the back saying, "I am glad you will get to stay my friend."

Suddenly Latona was at his side, grasping his arm, saying, "I knew you would pass the test, but now if you can excuse me, I need to go get something ready for this afternoon."

Ryan was a little surprised but just smiled and said, "OK, thank you for believing in me."

Latona looked him in the eyes and said, "I never doubted you for a moment Ryan." then turned and started walking back towards the main camp, along with several of the other members of the group. Ryan stood there for a while with people coming up, congratulating him and giving his best wishes and then heading into camp. When almost everybody had gone Ryan noticed that Stakota and his two friends were standing there glaring at him, Ryan just turned his back to them and ignored them as he put his arm around Kanti.

Skyseeker who was standing next to the couple said, "Well, I am very tired so I guess we should get back to camp."

Ryan looked at her questioningly asking, "So, that is it?"

Sky seeker smiled and answered, "You passed. I knew you would."

Ryan noticed Demat and Tanak had gone, leaving Stakota standing by himself staring at him.

Ryan looked at Skyseeker and Kanti and said, "I will be right back." Then strode over to Stakota with a huge smile on his face. Ryan wanted to make sure that anybody watching would see that Ryan was approaching in a jovial mood with no bad intentions. However, Stakota saw Ryan coming and became uneasy very fast.

"What do you want?" Stakota said as Ryan got close.

Ryan, still with a smile on his face and simply said, "I just came to say nice try."

"Nice try?" asked Stakota, not quite understanding.

Ryan still with a smile on his face explained, "Nice try. You tried to get me banished and you failed. But then again, I expect nothing less from someone like you."

Stakota knew he had been insulted and looked at Ryan's face, realizing what he was doing. He was trying to get him mad so that he would attack him, and everybody could say that it was Stakota's fault. So, he was not going to take the bait. "You can just go now Ryan." He said, trying to sound intimidating.

Ryan continued to smile, nodding his head and said, "Oh, I will Stakota." Ryan then turned looking at Kanti then back. "I am going to go pleasure Kanti a few times." Then remembering an insult that he heard decided to put a little malice in his voice and added, "While I am doing that, maybe you should go picking berries with the young girls."

Stakota's face became red as the anger grew inside of him.

"Well, like I said, I'm going to go have fun with Kanti, maybe you should go somewhere and have fun with yourself." Ryan said.

Ryan turned around, and walked back to Kanti, put his arm around her and started to walk away. He let his hand drop down to buttocks and he gave it a good squeeze. Stakota saw this and became enraged but decided to just turn and walk away.

Kanti looked up at Ryan and said, "You did that just to make Stakota mad didn't you?"

"I did not." Said Ryan. "I did that because I like your butt." "However, if it pisses that asshole off, that's a bonus." he thought to himself.

The trio started walking back towards the field with a little wolf following behind when Skyseeker looked over at Ryan and asked, "So, Ryan have you always been this cunning?"

Ryan turned to look at Skyseeker, not understanding the question and said, "I do not know what you are talking about."

"Oh really." Said Skyseeker with a grin, "The picking of the correct bark was only a task, it was not the test."

"It wasn't." Asked Ryan.

"No, it was not." Said Skyseeker, "It would be a silly test as there would be no way to find out any truths within it. It would just be by chance."

Ryan smiled looking at the old woman and then said, "I thought it seemed too simple."

"The true test was to see what happens before the actual task." She said, still grinning.

"I do not understand grandmother." Kanti said.

"Well, it is very simple. Would Ryan sneak out of the tent while Daryo was asleep and snoring to peek and see which bark had the X and which bark at the Dot. Or would somebody else sneak into the camp and try to do something tricky. That was the true test and Ryan, being an honest man that was telling the truth, never even thought of sneaking out the tent to have a look to see which one he would pick in the morning." The old woman said to her granddaughter.

"But how did you know somebody had come into the camp and changed the bark?" Ryan asked Skyseeker.

"Did what? Kanti asked in surprise.

"Zeus." Ryan said reaching down and picking up the little wolf and petting it. Ryan continued, "He started growling which woke me up, so I lifted the back end of the tent, and I saw somebody in the camp. I could not see who it was because they were on the other side of the fire and had their back to me. I then saw them take a piece of Bark off the platform and throw it in the fire. Then I watched them take another piece of bark out of their pouch and exchange it. I did not understand it at first, but the more I thought about it the more I understood that there were now two X's, and it did not matter which one I picked I was going to pick an X."

Kanti couldn't believe what she was hearing and asked, "You did not see who it was?

"No." Answered Ryan, "But I am pretty sure it was Stakota."

"It was." Skyseeker said to the couple, "Is that when you came up with your clever plan?"

"No." Ryan answered, "I was going to expose the fact that somebody had come into the camp and did something with them at night. Flip both pieces of bark exposing both X's, and then we would have to do it again. But as I was coming out of the tent walking towards the fire it struck me, if I destroyed one of them, the one that was left being an X would mean that the one I threw into the fire people would then assume it was the dot."

Skyseeker started to laugh then said to Ryan, "I am so glad you did what you did because you saved me a lot of trouble."

"What do you mean a lot of trouble?" Ryan asked.

"Well," Skyseeker said, "We knew that Stakota had switched the bark. We saw him doing it and we were going to expose it. When you had flipped over one of the pieces of bark, we were going to come and turn the other one over, announcing that Daryo and myself both had seen Stakota make the switch. Once that happened Stakota would have been the one going up for banishment. Which would have been a lot more trouble than you could imagine."

"How is that?" asked Ryan.

"I do not know if you are aware of this, but Stakota is the leader of the three sisters' camp's son. He has quite a bit of status and banishing his son would have brought trouble back to our camp and would have caused problems with our close relationship that we currently have with them. So, your solution proved you were innocent, but did not prove that he was guilty. However, we now know what kind of man he is."

"Yes, we do." said Kanti shaking her head.

"Well, I am glad it is over." Said Ryan, putting his arm back around Kanti's waist.

"That is the problem Ryan, I do not believe that it is over. I believe that Stakota's ego is badly bruised and he will try to do something about it." Skyseeker said shaking her head.

"I agree with you." said Ryan, "But I do not think he is going to do anything right away. He is going to have to lick his wound and try to come up with something else. I do not consider him a smart man, but I also do not trust him."

"That is good." Skyseeker said, "Just be very aware." She added.

"I will." acknowledged Ryan. Then looking down at the wolf said, "I have my wolf to protect me."

The little wolf found a butterfly and was chasing it around the field. Kanti looked at Zeus frolicking with the little insect, then looked back at Ryan saying, "Maybe he will get better."

"Maybe." said Ryan with a smile, and the group continued back into the camp.

As they got back to the tent, the little pup started to yip and run around. Ryan looked at Kanti as she started into the tent and said, "It looks like Zeus wants to play a little bit. I will chase him around and come in shortly."

Kanti smiled and said, "I will be waiting. "With that she disappeared inside the tent. Ryan chased the little pup around and then let the little pup chase him around for a while.

Chapter 10

Once they had both had enough Ryan and entered the tent and was surprised to see Kanti laying naked on her side, looking at him.

"That looks good." Said Ryan with a smile on his face.

"You were not here last night, so now you have to make it up to me." She said brazenly.

Ryan started to take off his clothes, just smiled at her and said, "OK."

Once he had undressed, he laid down next to her and lightly gently rolled over onto her back. He ran his hand down the side to her leg down her legs, and then started bringing them back up in between her legs. He started kissing her neck and worked his way down to her breasts. When his hands reached her mound, she let out a moan. Ryan sucked on her nipples for a while gently moving his hands between her legs, then started kissing her neck, her throat, and then her lips.

As they lay there later, both content and relaxed she was tracing her finger along the bear tattoo on Ryan's left arm.

She looked up at him and in a quiet voice asked, "Are you going to leave."

Ryan was surprised by the question. He looked at her and answered, "Of course not. Why would you ask that?"

"Well." she started, "I do not know where you came from, and I do not know if you are going back. So, I thought I had better ask."

Ryan leaned down and kissed her on the lips and said, "I am going nowhere." Then thinking about it for a moment and then added, "However, if I ever do, I want you to come with me."

She seemed happy with that answer and snuggled up close to him. "Good." she said, "Because I do not want you to leave."

Ryan laid there thinking about that for a moment, it seems like he had been here forever, but it had only been for a short time and for some reason it was feeling very natural, when it should feel very scary.

Just then the flap flew open, and Tisha came running in followed by the little wolf.

"Hi, Ryan." she said in an excited voice. She then noticed that both Ryan and Kanti were in bed.

"Oh." she said, then turned around quickly. "I am sorry, you two."

Both Ryan and Kanti started to laugh and said, "It is OK Tisha. We were just laying here talking."

"Are you sure?" she asked, still not turning around.

"Yes, we are sure." said Ryan.

"Good." Said the little girl turning around with a big smile on her face. "OK then." she said.

"What can we do for you?" asked Kanti.

"Oh yes." she said, "Latona wanted me to come and get you."

"Come and get us for what?" Ryan asked.

"There is a talking circle in the field and Latona wants you both there, that is all I know." She answered bending down and petting Zeus.

"OK." said Ryan, "You play with Zeus and let us get dressed and we will meet you outside, and then you can take us. OK?"

"OK." She said, then ran out of the tent with the little wolf chasing after her.

Once they both got dressed, they left the tent and called Tisha who was out in the field chasing a little wolf around.

Tisha came running up and said, "OK, it's this way." and they started walking down towards the river.

When Ryan looked up, he could see the circle Wasn't that far away from the tent, and then he got closer. He noticed that it seemed to be everybody from the camp. Ryan also noticed that there was only the one ring which looked like it had everybody from the valley camp in it. As they approached, people started waving at them. Latona asked all to sit and instructed Ryan to walk to the centre next to Skyseeker. He then asked Tisha if she would hold onto the wolf, so it was not running around and getting in everyone's way. She happily accepted this responsibility and ran over and picked up the little wolf who snuggled into her and looked around at all the people. Ryan walked up and stood next to the Skyseeker in the centre of the circle looking around at all the people surrounding him.

Ryan turned to Skyseeker and asked, "What is going on?"

She just smiled at Ryan and said, "You shall see." She then raised her hands, and everyone in the circle quieted down. When it was silent, she began, "All of you here know Ryan, he has only been with us for a very short while yet, I am sure he has helped most of the people in this circle in one way or another." Ryan noticed a lot of people were nodding and looking at each other in agreement."

Skyseeker continued, "Latona has put forward, and I agree that we should welcome Ryan into the camp of the people of the valley permanently."

Many people were nodding their heads in agreement and commenting back-and-forth.

Skyseeker let it go on for a few moments then raised her hands again saying in a loud voice, "Latona, Tolbar, and Skytal have all offered to host Ryan if need be."

Ryan wasn't too sure what's going on, but just decided to keep quiet and listen.

Skyseeker asked, "May I have a show of hands. All of those who are opposed to Ryan becoming one of the people of the valley raise your hand."

Ryan looked out, looked around and with all the people sitting in the circle, not one person raised their hand.

He then looked over at Skyseeker who was smiling and asked, "Is that good?"

"That is very good." She replied in a quiet voice. Then in a louder voice she asked, "All those who wish to welcome Ryan to the people of the valley. Please raise your hands."

Everyone in the circle raised their hands high, smiling in Ryan's direction.

Skyseeker then turned smiling at Ryan and said, "Well Ryan you are now a member of the people of the valley, you are no longer an outsider, but one of us."

The full impact of what Skyseeker had just said was slowly starting to sink into Ryan and he was starting to find himself being overwhelmed with emotions. "How could these people who barely knew him take him in like this? If the roles were reversed, he was almost certain that his kind would not be so accepting and willing to take that person in." He thought.

Ryan looked over at Kanti and saw that she was crying. She looked up at him, smiled, and wiped away the tears from her eyes.

Latona stood up, walked into the centre of the circle, put his arm on Ryan's shoulder and said in a loud voice, "Welcome home Ryan!"

Everyone in the circle started to cheer.

Kanti got up and rushed towards Ryan wrapping her arms around him. "I am so happy." she said.

Ryan could understand it because he was happy as well. He looked at Latona and asked, "Skyseeker said that you were willing to sponsor me. What does that mean?"

Latona smiled and answered, "You have no lodge of your own, you are currently staying in what we call a guest tent. What that means is that we will have to make sure that you get a lodge of your own, or in the winter share our lodge with us."

"You would be willing to do that?" Ryan asked.

"Of course, Nila and I would." Was Latona's answer, still smiling at the man.

Ryan just shook his head in disbelief, still trying to comprehend what was happening. Skyseeker came over gently putting her arm through Ryan's arm and started to lead him away.

Kanti started to follow as well, but Skyseeker raised her hand indicating to Kanti that she was not supposed to follow as her grandmother wanted some private time with Ryan.

When they had walked a short distance from the crowd and nobody could overhear their conversation she stopped, turned to face Ryan and said, "You are now one of us, but you and I have a lot to discuss." She said looking at Ryan.

"I imagine we do." said Ryan smiling at her.

"I have so many questions that I need to ask you, but I must ask them in a sequence that makes sense to me. She said to Ryan.

Ryan just looked at the old woman smiled at her and said, Whenever you are ready to ask the questions, I am ready to tell you the truth."

The old woman smiled at that and said, "I expect nothing less Ryan."

"When can I tell Kanti?" he asked.

"Once we have had our discussion, we can figure out how and what to tell her." she answered. "We will need to tell her together to help her understand."

"I do not want to lie or keep anything from her." Ryan said, looking at the old woman.

"I am not asking you to." she said, "However we can not just blurt something like this out."

Ryan thought about it for a few moments and then concluded. "Skyseeker was right. How crazy would it sound to just come out and say, "Hi, I'm from the future. They sure wouldn't want to keep me around after that." He thought to himself.

"OK." said Ryan, "You and I shall talk. I will answer your questions and then you let me know when we can tell her."

"That sounds fair." said Skyseeker. She smiled then patted him on the arm and continued, "You now have a home, Ryan. You have people that will care for you and that will look after you, as well as you look after them."

Skyseeker looked over at her granddaughter, she smiled and then looked back at Ryan saying, "And you have someone who really cares for you, and I hope you care for her the same way."

Ryan smiled at the old woman and said, "When you and I are having our talks, and after you have asked me all the questions that you want, I may have a question for you."

Skyseeker seems surprised and curious, "What would that be?" she asked Ryan.

"How someone makes someone else they mate." He said with a smile.

A broad smile came across her face, "When you are ready to ask me that question, I will be more than happy to answer it." Skyseeker said, then added. "So, I guess for now, this can stay between you and me, until you are ready. Now go to your mate to be."

Ryan smiled at the old woman's comment and surprised her by leaning in and giving her a quick kiss on the cheek. "I will do that."

Ryan then turned and walked away. Skyseeker blushed and was thankful there was no one around to see it. She watched Ryan walk up to Kanti, put his arms around waist and pull her into him. "I do not think she could do any better. That man really cares for her." She thought to herself.

"So." she said to Ryan, "Now that you count as a member of the people, what would you like to do first?"

Ryan gave her a sly smile and said, "Well since somebody made me all hot and sweaty earlier today, I think I would like to go for a swim."

Kanti smiled and looked up at him and said, "That sounds like a great idea. Let's go up the river a little way so we can have some privacy."

"I like that idea even better." Ryan said as they turned and headed towards the river.

The two walked down to the river and then up towards the clearing where Ryan had spent the night. About halfway there the couple found a nice spot where they could get down into the river that was secluded, and people walking by wouldn't be able to see them. They climbed down the bank, stripped off their clothes and jumped into the water. Ryan was starting to get used to how cold the water was, and it didn't seem to bother him as much. They splashed around like two small children without a care in the world. Ryan took her in his arms and carried her out of the water up onto the bank. They laid down on the grass for a while and let the sun dry their skin.

"Well, that was refreshing." he said to her.

"Yes, it was." She agreed smiling and then continued, "Mother has invited people over tonight for an evening meal to celebrate you becoming one of the people. We should get going soon."

Ryan thought about it for a moment and leaned over and kissed on the neck. She playfully smacked him and said, "No, we have got to get going, it would be rude to show up late."

"OK." Ryan said, "But then you owe me."

Kanti smiled and said, "Maybe tonight."

Ryan nodded his head and said, "OK, you are right we should get going, but I think I want to go in for one more swim."

Ryan went down to the edge of the river where he knew it was deep and dove in. He was swimming on his back for a while, thinking about how lucky he was, no pressures, no major commitments, and the love of a beautiful woman. He still could not understand why he was not more agitated with the situation, and why he was so at peace and willing to accept it. "Well, I guess it's just going to be one big adventure." He thought to himself as he rolled over onto his stomach and dove down deep into the river. As he neared the bottom of the river, he let out a burst of air and then started to follow the bubbles to the surface.

About the Author

Tom J. Corbett was born and raised in Vancouver British Columbia, where he spent his childhood and the start of his adult life. His father was a masterful storyteller and would tell stories from his time in the war or about building and working, logging camps up and down the coast of British Columbia. Tom moved to Alberta in 1981 where he met his wife Jennifer. Over the last 40+ years, he has travelled extensively through Western Canada with most of the travel being in Alberta and British Columbia. He inherited the love of storytelling from his father and is now starting to tell his own stories with the First White Man series. Arrival is the second book in the series.

Contact Author – t.jcorbett@yahoo.com

Coming Soon!

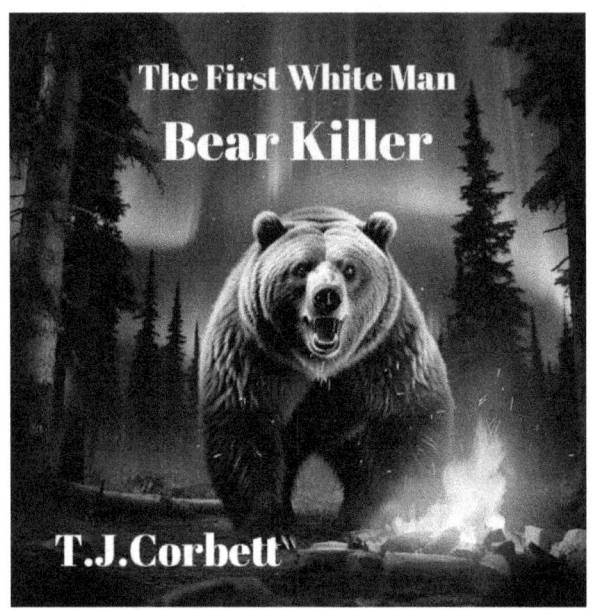

Book III
Bear Killer

www.ingramcontent.com/pod-product-compliance
Lightning Source LLC
Chambersburg PA
CBHW060358260626
47160CB00006B/2357